Anyone for Seconds?

Also by Laurie Graham

Anyone for Seconds?

Laurie Graham

Quercus

First published in Great Britain in 2018 by

Quercus Editions Ltd
Carmelite House
50 Victoria Embankment
London EC4Y 0DZ

An Hachette UK company

A CIP catalogue record for this book is available
from the British Library

HB ISBN 978 1 78429 796 1
TPB ISBN 978 1 78429 797 8

10 9 8 7 6 5 4 3 2 1

Typeset by Jouve (UK), Milton Keynes

Printed and bound in Great Britain by Clays Ltd, Elcograf S.p.A.

to the beady-eyed, green-winged tonybird

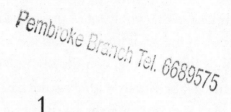
1

The postman came early. I was already up, kettle on, but next door's Maltese likes to make sure. It's *my* mail, dropping through *my* letterbox, but that little yapper won't let up till the whole damned street is awake.

I nearly didn't bother going to see what had landed on the mat. It's cold enough in this house without making any unnecessary detours into the permafrost zone. It's a strange thing, my front door. In the spring and autumn, when the weather's damp, it swells like one of those self-inflating dinghies. You can't budge it. If a fire should break out, Heaven forbid, it's the back door or perish. The rest of the year it rattles every time a car goes past. Daylight, wind, the smell of the mobile chipper. That door lets it all in. You'd think there'd be a couple of days a year when it'd be a perfect fit, but no. It's either a fire hazard or a rattling panel of very cheap wood. Also, it needs painting.

I only risked frostbite to pick up the post because I was sort of expecting, well, hoping for a letter from Tom. *Missing you. Let's give it another try.* Something like that. He could have phoned but a letter would be more his style. Besides, I don't

1

think he gets a whole lot of privacy since Simon and Tessa have been staying with him. He said it was just till their loft conversion is finished. I reckon they built York Minster quicker than their new bedroom with en-suite bathroom, but of course they didn't have Tessa managing the project.

Tessa is a perfect storm of everything you wouldn't want in a daughter-in-law: entitled, interfering, quick to take offence. There is no corner of Tom's life that she hasn't made her business. She could have had the place bugged. It wouldn't surprise me. You could get the locks changed and she'd crawl up a drainpipe. And thwart her at your peril. She does this Threatening Loom. Any act of subordination, such as not using the barbecue apron she got you for Christmas or shacking up with a lover and thereby threatening your son's inheritance expectations with a wrecking ball, you can bank on a full-throttle loom from Tessa.

It doesn't seem to bother Tom. He says she's not as bad as I make out and, anyway, she and Simon seem very happy and that's all that matters. But (a) how does he know Simon's happy? The man never opens his mouth. And (b) it isn't all that matters. If you move in with somebody while the builders take the roof off your house, you need to keep in mind that you're a guest, and guests do not throw out a perfectly good jar of juniper berries because of their own personal prejudices.

How Tom can prefer living with that pair to living with me I shall never understand. Okay, we had a few problems, a few housekeeping issues, shall we say? He kept hankering for the orthopaedic mattress that had cost him a packet, but mattresses can be moved. True, I've been a bit down too. I get narky when I'm not working, when there's not much money coming in.

Who wouldn't? I'm sixty-four years old. I should have my own TV show. I should have a car service picking me up, whisking me off to the studio. Not be sitting here with a flaking front door and two light bulbs out. I should be doing some of those celebrity gastronomy tours. Experience the Food of Puglia with Lizzie Partridge.

A passing Jack Russell was descanting with the Maltese. The letterbox was jammed open. Why can't the damned postman push the post right through so the flap closes? Hasn't he ever heard about domestic heat loss? Three envelopes. A final demand from ENERGAS. A Reward point statement from Budgens. Nothing from Tom. Just something from Global. Uh-oh.

Let me tell you, when magazine publishers go to the trouble of writing an actual letter, it's always bad news. If they move the furniture, ask you for an extra two hundred words, pay pro rata, or they decide it's time you got a new by-line photo, they pick up the phone. But when it's a case of Dear Lizzie they put it in a letter, knock on your door and run away.

These days, they'd probably prefer to send an email but I don't do email. It's a choice. It's not that I don't know how. I have an address and everything, but Tom took his computer when he moved out. Anyway, they say it's not good for you. They say staring at a screen can damage your eyes.

I called Louie. He sounded groggy. He said it was his normal middle-of-the-night voice. I hadn't realized Cornwall had moved to a different time zone.

I said, 'It's 8 o'clock.'

'I know,' he said. 'Did someone die?'

'I got a letter from Global.'

3

'They giving you the chop?'

'Probably.'

'Probably?'

'I haven't opened it yet.'

I heard Chas's voice, muffled.

Louie said, 'It's Lizzie. She needs emotional support while she opens an envelope.'

I told him not to be so patronizing. I just needed to hear a friendly voice.

'Well,' he said, 'the friendly voice department doesn't usually open till 10.30 but I can listen in sympathetic silence. Open the damned envelope. We both know what it says. Come along now. Rip off that Elastoplast.'

The first time I ever got one of those letters it was like Mike Tyson hit me in the midriff. It gets easier the next time it happens. No, it doesn't.

So my What's Cookin' column's got the heave-ho. New layout . . . with immediate effect . . . much-valued contributor . . . Now bugger off into obscurity, you pathetic, unwanted creature.

Louie said, 'How much were they paying?'

'Three hundred.'

'A week?'

'A week! A month.'

'Okay. Not a bank-breaker, then.'

All very well for him to say. I said, 'We haven't all been left property. We haven't all married money.'

'Cousin Ralph did not leave me "property". He left me a dismal little bungalow with rising damp. The Cheltenham place went to his sister. Like she needed it! And Chas and I aren't married. We have a civil partnership. Although if this Equal Love campaign gets anywhere, I think we might. Any excuse to wear a white suit.'

'The point is, you don't have to work.'

'But I do, sweet. I absolutely do. I don't want to be a kept man. How's Tom?'

'Still gone.'

'He'll be back. And the infant prodigy?'

He meant my grandson, Noah.

'Aced the Mensa test. Only wears a nappy at night. I'm surprised you didn't read about it in the papers.'

TWO-YEAR-OLD GENIUS POOS IN POTTY.

'Gosh. At this rate he'll overtake Chas.'

'So, are you working?'

'Nothing much until Whitley Bay. Rehearsals start in three weeks. *Cinderella*.'

'Ugly Sister?'

'Certainly not. I'm playing Buttons.'

'Buttons! Who did the casting? Buttons is supposed to be young.'

'Not necessarily. Buttons is a kindly, selfless character. He can be any age.'

'He has the hots for Cinderella. You're gay and fifty-five.'

'I am not fifty-five.'

'You can't be far off. Is Chas going with you?'

'He'll come up for Christmas. I only get Christmas Eve and Christmas Day off. Boxing Day, there's two performances. And he can't really leave the dogs for any longer than that.

Lucy's supposed to be dog-sitting and you know what she's like.'

Lucy is Chas's sister. She lives on pinot grigio and M&Ms and she seems to think dogs can do likewise.

Louie gets pantomimes since he became a National Treasure. He gets a lot of things. He turned on the Christmas lights in Barnstaple last year. Everybody loves him, yet if you were to ask them why he's famous they probably wouldn't remember that he used to be on *Midlands This Morning*. When he does panto the poster says something like 'Featuring TV Astrologer'. It doesn't say 'Disgraced TV Astrologer from a Long Time Ago'.

He said, 'Lizzie, don't be offended, but do you need some money?'

I told him I didn't. I mean, I'm not exactly destitute. You accept money from friends, it changes everything.

He said, 'What I want to know is, why aren't you and Tom Sullivan back together yet? Take your time. I can only accept your first answer.'

He always says that, ever since he hosted a season of *Spin to Win*.

'Because I'm a bad-tempered cow who's impossible to live with?'

'Correct answer! Lizzie Partridge, you have won the plasma TV and the state-of-the-art sound system. Will you come back next week and try for the car?'

'I will, Louie.'

'Great. Now bugger off, apply some lippy and get that dear man to the negotiating table.'

Everyone says I should get back with Tom. Like he's so damned perfect. Did you ever share a kitchen with somebody who insists on washing up while you're cooking? Put a spoon down for five seconds and it's in the sink getting rinsed before it goes in the dishwasher. Did you ever go on holiday with a person who has to get to the airport, like, a week before your flight? But everybody approves of Tom. Even Mum, and generally she doesn't approve of anybody. She said, 'He seems very steady.' Also, 'You're not getting any younger, Elizabeth.'

I waited till nine, till Tessa would have left for work. She's an estate agent. You'd think she'd just buy a bigger house instead of getting the slowest goddamned loft conversion on record. She must get first dibs, as soon as something comes on the market. I called Tom. No reply. He could have been out getting a paper, left his mobile at home. I tried him again a couple of times. Nine thirty I got his voicemail. So what's that all about? He sees my number, doesn't pick up, then he turns his phone off? Is he avoiding me?

I didn't leave a message straight off. I like to rehearse a bit first. I know I don't do good phone. Louie says I sound like a pit-bull bitch with PMT. I practised my 'warm and approachable' voice, made more tea, investigated the fridge. I keep buying too much food. I keep buying stuff I don't really fancy. For breakfast I had the stale end of a ginger cake soaked in evaporated milk. I have a thing about evaporated milk. It came on suddenly. I just had to have some. The same thing happened with pickled onions and pork pie. Tastes from my childhood. Tinned tomato soup. Am I going senile?

Tom called me. He sounded breathless. 'Running to get to the car before the traffic warden does. They only had three tills open in the supermarket.'

'I thought Tessa did the shopping.'

'She does. I was just picking a few things up for Sally. You okay? You sound tense.'

I did not sound tense. I'd been practising. And who the fuck was Sally? I told him about Global.

He said he was sorry. 'Not the first time it's happened, Lizzie, and it probably won't be the last. You'll bounce back. You always do.'

'Tessa and Simon still with you?'

'Yes. Actually, they've had a bit of a setback too. Their builder's gone into receivership, left them in the lurch. They'll be here a while yet.'

'Well, you know where I live. If you need a break.'

'Yes.'

'I have pigeon breasts.'

'Not the last time I looked.'

'Very funny. Okay. Well, I just thought I'd let you know. About Global.'

'Yep. Bad luck, that. Oh, buggeration. I got a ticket.'

I said, 'You'll have to put it on Sally's bill.'

But he'd gone.

I could have pan-fried the pigeon with sour cherries. Except I didn't have any sour cherries. I should have asked Tom. It would have given him a no-strings excuse to drop round. Chanterelles would work okay too. Even dried ones. I didn't have any of those either. Global owed me for last month, though. That'd cover ENERGAS.

I called Ellie.

'Can't talk. I'm running really late.'

'Are you working today?'

'Text me.'

My daughter, the multi-tasking career dragon in a black suit and trainers.

I called my mother. No reply, which was very odd. Tuesday mornings she does her ironing and she always answers the phone because, well, you never know. When you're eighty-nine your acquaintances are dropping like flies and she's a key link in the news alert chain. Pearl Minchin, peacefully, in her sleep. Pass it on.

It would take some extraordinary event to change my mum's routine, such as being summoned to Buckingham Palace to get a gong, or being slumped over the ironing board in the throes of one final mystery blackout, oblivious to the smell of scorching polyester.

Lunchtime, and I was still in my pyjamas, which was some kind of record. Two gherkins and a bit of blue cheese. Actually, more than a bit. Like, all of it. The phone rang. It could have been Tom, tempted by my pigeon breasts. It could have been Global, apologizing for an egregious clerical error and begging me to accept double pay as recompense, or it could have been Clint Eastwood, suggesting dinner. It was my mother.

'I called you earlier.'

'I know. I have Caller ID now. Philip did it for me. He said you can't be too careful these days.'

Ah, yes. My intrepid brother. Mr Belt-and-Braces.

I said, 'I think you probably can be too careful. Take Magellan.'

'Who?'

'Ferdinand Magellan. If he'd been too careful he wouldn't

have discovered wherever it was he discovered. So if you saw it was me why didn't you answer?'

'I was just on my way out. I was going to Nora Schofield's funeral. I didn't have time to chat.'

'I thought you didn't like Nora Schofield?'

'What's that got to do with anything?'

'I don't know. Seems a bit hypocritical, that's all. Unless you went just to make sure she really was dead.'

'There's no call to be facetious, Elizabeth.'

'Was it a nice funeral?'

'Not really. They had "Kumbaya".'

'Oh dear.'

'Yes.'

'You know, you should tell me what hymns you'd like. For when the time comes.'

'Don't you worry about that. Philip has a list.'

'How come you always tell Philip these things and not me? I'm the oldest.'

'Because I know that if I give him an important document he'll keep it somewhere safe. I've seen the way you live. Philip has never lost his passport.'

The low right hook. I should have seen that coming. My passport wasn't lost. It had slipped down the back of a drawer. And Philip doesn't need a passport because he never goes anywhere.

'They had a retiring collection. It was for Save the Rainforests. I didn't give.'

'What, not even a few brown coins? You old meanie.'

'It's not my business to save rainforests. I've never done them any harm.'

'I dunno, Mum. You used to write a lot of letters. All that Basildon Bond. You're probably personally responsible for the demise of at least one tree.'

'And, anyway, they never get the money. These charities. It all goes in somebody's pocket. Some higher-up.'

'Maybe. Although I don't think the people who live in endangered rainforests have pockets. I think they just wear loin-cloths. So how are you? Did you see Dr Gulati?'

'Yes. She doesn't know what to make of me.'

PENSIONER CONTINUES TO FLUMMOX MEDI-CAL EXPERTS.

'Nearly an hour, I waited. And there were people in the waiting room looked like they didn't have a thing wrong with them.'

'You don't know that. They could be seriously ill but holding up bravely.'

'If you're gravely ill you don't sit eating Hula Hoops and monopolizing the only copy of *Good Housekeeping*.'

'Was your blood pressure okay?'

'Yes. A bit low.'

'There you are, then. That can make you faint.'

'I don't faint. I have dizzy spells. And I'm sure Dr Gulati knows a lot more about it than you do. Anyway, I mustn't natter on. I expect you're busy.'

Not really, Mum. I just got fired so there's no point in pretending to work, and I live alone so there's no one else to notice the ring round the bathtub. No, not busy at all. I said, 'I'll call you in a day or two.'

'Don't worry about me,' she said. 'Philip often pops in of an afternoon.'

'Tell me one of the hymns you like.'

'What kind of a question is that?'

'A very reasonable one. You're eighty-nine years old. Are you going to live for ever? Tell me one that's on your list. If you don't tell me I might go behind Philip's back and order "Kumbaya".'

' "I Heard the Voice of Jesus Say".'

'There you go. That's a nice one. Very suitable for a funeral too. I Heard the Voice of Jesus Say, "Muriel Clarke, your time is up." '

'I suppose you think you're funny.'

Cheers, Mum. I'm pretty depressed, thank you for asking. I have no purpose in life. My two-year-old grandson has more in his diary than I do.

So, I was sitting on the kitchen table eating baked beans from the can when, out of the corner of my eye, I saw something move, along the floor, by the sink. I decided not to have seen it. It just seemed to me that no one gets fired, plus rejection by a lover, former lover, *and* an infestation of vermin all on the same day. It just doesn't happen.

But this damned voice in my head kept saying, 'You did see it. Yes, you did. Definitely. Get dressed. Go and buy mouse traps. Go and buy bait-boxes.'

I was in the shower, trying to think where I'd be able to buy a mouse trap, going through the town centre in my mind's eye. Cards. Coffee shop. Mobile phones. Scented candles. Pound shop. More cards. Sportswear. Newsagent. Another coffee place. Unisex hair.

And then I thought, Enough. I've had it. Let the mice take

over. Dry rot, wet rot, subsidence. Bring it on. I don't care. I don't particularly like this house.

When we bought it, Alec and I, it was what we could afford. It was okay. Only six miles from Brum, handy for the A38, but we planned to move on, move up in the world to somewhere a bit leafier. Harborne, maybe, or Edgbaston. Except, when it came to it and we could have afforded somewhere nicer, Alec moved on without me. I don't know why I'm still here. Reduced circumstances? Handy but not too handy for aged parent? Yes. Also lethargy. I should be living in a nifty apartment. Gas Street Basin or somewhere central. I should have enviable panoramic views and a Polish cleaner, but I kind of let things go.

People think I'm tough. Good old Lizzie Partridge. She always sees the funny side of life. Nothing ever gets Lizzie down. Well that's all they knew. I decided to disappear. Global and Tom and Ellie and Mum, they all needed a wakeup call.

I packed my little black wheelie bag. You don't want loads of luggage when you're running away. It draws attention to you. You get jammed in the stupid automatic gates and then people remember. Bad-tempered old bat in a pompom hat? Yeah, I seen her.

You can fit a surprising amount of stuff into a carry-on. But what do you actually need? How can you say when you don't know where you're going? Or for how long.

2

I thought I'd just get to the station and take the first train to wherever, but then on the bus into town I reconsidered. If I went somewhere small, I'd get recognized. I know you. You're on the telly. Used to be. But if I went somewhere big, to a proper city, somewhere where it's easier to remain anonymous, hotels cost more. Cities have snoop cameras everywhere too. HAVE YOU SEEN THIS WOMAN? B-and-Bs are cheaper but they find out all your business. They want to make small-talk over breakfast. Here on business? Staying long, are you? If Louie hadn't sold his inheritance I could have gone there, broken into Cousin Ralph's des res and hunkered down in Rustington-on-Sea. But he had, so I couldn't.

On the departure board my options were: London Euston, Manchester Piccadilly, Walsall, Liverpool Lime Street, Glasgow. A fine selection of hell-holes in which to hide and have a quiet meltdown while my loved ones appeal for my safe return.

There was also Reading. I'd never been to Reading. Shrewsbury. Been there, couldn't remember anything about it. Stansted Airport. Damnation. I could have bought a cheap ticket and flown off somewhere with CrapAir, only I hadn't thought to bring my passport. Aberystwyth? I knew that was in Wales. I just wasn't sure exactly where. I went into WHS to look for an atlas. The girl said, 'What's an atlas?'

I can now tell you that if Wales is a pig's head, Aberystwyth is kind of between the top of its snout and where its ears flop forward. It's seaside. I liked the idea of that. I could be a mysterious lone figure taking long walks, gazing sadly out to sea. Like Meryl Streep in *The French Lieutenant's Woman*. I bought an off-peak single and an egg mayo sandwich that tasted of nothing. They don't put any salt in them because Nanny says salt's bad for you and Nanny knows best. They could give you a little paper twist of salt, like you used to get in crisps packets, so you can be a grown-up and weigh up the risks for yourself. Shit, you have to die of something. It would be nice to eat a decent sandwich before you go.

I thought I'd buy a magazine but Nigella and Jamie were all over everything like a rash. Time was, I'd have had some of those magazine gigs. I can write. I know about food. But it's all changed. Nowadays, you're either big, like mega, with your own range of kitchenware, or you're history, invisible, a non-entity without so much as a lemon squeezer to your credit.

I didn't see that coming. I left it to my agent, Hegarty, to notice approaching career flop but I now know he wouldn't have noticed a bull elephant bearing down on him. Meetings were Hegarty's thing. It was agent-speak for lunch.

'Leave it with me, doll,' he'd say. 'As it happens I have a meeting on Thursday, could be useful.'

He'd had an interesting client list. Eclectic might be the word. Perhaps that was a sign that he was spreading himself desperately thin. There was a guy who got an Olympic silver for swimming or diving or something wet, years ago. He'd open galas and sportswear shops, stuff like that. There can't have been much in it for Hegarty. He also represented Kathy Mansour. Local girl with no notable talent marries Kuwaiti billionaire, divorces him and uses her bags of alimony moolah to make a series of futile bids for fame. Actress, singer, washed-up old glamour model. I imagine Hegarty did all right out of Kathy. She's Lady Something now, bringing a touch of real class to some noble pile. Then there was Sandie Mulholland. The one-dish wonder who stole my gig on *Midlands This Morning*.

Sandie was known mainly for her earrings and her African turbans. She was like a white woman who'd won an All-You-Can-Grab contest in the Kinshasa branch of Claire's Accessories. Diverse appeal. That's what they said. 'We need more diverse appeal.'

They didn't understand my viewers at all. My viewers didn't want Sandie Mulholland's goat curry. And that Judas Hegarty let it happen. Played off one client against another, the bastard. I didn't think he had it in him.

Hegarty's lunches went on till around three thirty by which time he'd be so rat-arsed he didn't know what he or anybody else had said. He'd do the sideways stagger back to his office, fall asleep at his desk, wake up around six, have a quick sharpener and tonic, make a few calls and then hold court in the Wellington until closing time. I should have fired him but he was the one who'd got me my slot on *Midlands This Morning* and I'd kept him for sentimental reasons, like a pair of useless satin wedding shoes.

I put the foodie magazines back on the shelf and picked out a

book instead. There wasn't a lot of choice. If you fancied picking up a copy of *Cold Comfort Farm* to see you through to
Aberystwyth, if you were thinking of getting round to *War
and Peace* at long last, you'd be out of luck. I bought *Unleash
Your Inner Giant* and the *Daily Mail*.

The girl said, 'Want your free bottle of water with that?'

'With what?'

'With your paper. You get a free bottle of water.'

'No, thank you.'

'No problem.'

'Why would it be?'

'Sorry?'

'Why would it be a problem that I don't want a free bottle of
water?'

'It isn't.'

Poor child. I shouldn't have picked on her like that. Her tiny
nightlight of a brain had a small stock of phrases. We're closed.
We haven't got none. No problem. It wasn't her fault that her
school had voided her into the employment toilet pan not
knowing what an atlas was. She'd probably tell all her friends
about me. The old nutter. No, she wouldn't. My existence, our
conversation, they didn't even register with her. All she was
thinking was, What will Lady Gaga wear next? And How
many minutes till I'm finished for the day?

I fell asleep after Telford. When I woke up I had dried dribble
in the corner of my mouth and the train was slowing down. I
asked the woman on the seat opposite where we were.

'Mack,' she said.

I didn't remember any Mack on the list of places before Aberystwyth. Then there was an announcement. 'We will shortly be arriving at MACKWYKWYKWYK. Please ensure you have all your personal items with you. Our next station stop, MACKWYKWYKWYK.'

Daffy Duck was now working as a train conductor. I recognized it when I saw the sign. Machynlleth.

She said, 'You going to Aber?'

'Aberystwyth, yes.'

'Got somebody at uni there?'

'No.'

'My youngest's at Lampeter. You got family in Aber?'

'No. Just going for a bit of sea air.'

'Oh, yes.'

I said, 'I wonder why they call them "station stops". They never used to. They used to say, "The next stop is . . ."'

'They bring new things in all the time,' she said. 'They're unmanned now, at Borth. They're making a museum in the old booking office. There's a machine for tickets, mind. Well, this is me.'

Dovey Junction. I was the only one left in the carriage, almost the only one left on the train. I was worried they'd notice me at the ticket barrier when I got to Aberystwyth.

MISSING TV COOK: FAMILY PRAISE ALERT RAIL STAFF.

I put my glasses on. Nobody ever recognizes me in my glasses.

It was dark. It was raining. If I had only thought to bring my passport I could have been landing at Palma, Majorca. Bad planning. In the past people have accused me of lacking spontaneity, of being too organized, writing too many lists. I name no names but at least I've never run out of petrol on the M15. I always have a lemon in the house. Almost always. It's only lately I've let things slide a bit, and see what happens? Act spontaneously and you end up soaked to the bone, six o'clock on a November evening, looking for a cheap place to stay in a town whose whereabouts you couldn't have hazarded, if asked over breakfast to pinpoint it on a map.

It was one of those chain hotels, the CheckInn. You could feel sorry for the staff, the blouses they make them wear. Did I have a booking? She was squinting at her computer screen like I'd just breezed in and demanded the Zsa Zsa Gabor Penthouse Suite.

I said, 'You're not telling me you're full?'

'We're pretty busy,' she said.

There was a soil management conference till Thursday, then something called Fursonality, starting on Friday evening. People dressed as furry animals.

I said, 'What do they do?'

'Various activities.'

'Do they arrive wearing their costumes?'

'I couldn't say. I've only been here since September.'

'They probably don't. It could be tricky if you got stopped for speeding. Or if you needed a pee.'

'How many nights did you want?'

'I don't know. A week. Maybe longer.'

She said I'd be asked to settle my bill at the end of a week and start a fresh tab. I took the only room they had. No sea view, and did I want the breakfast-included deal? £12 for a cup of tea and a kipper? I don't think so.

It wasn't really a no-sea-view room. It was a no-view-at-all room, unless you count a ventilation shaft. And would I please think of supporting the hotel's Glad To Be Green policy by using my towels for more than one day, because every little helps the environment? After due consideration, no, I bloody well would not. At home I wash my towels once a week and I don't dry them in a power-guzzling machine. I peg them on the washing line, just like I used to do with my daughter's nappies. So don't lecture me about the environment, Mr Glad To Be Green. I'll bet your kids' nappies go in a landfill. And one of the few pleasures of staying in a hotel that has psychedelic carpets and the faint smell of baked beans is the luxury of clean towels every day.

I turned my phone on. No messages, no missed calls. I turned it off again, dried my hair and went out for fish and chips. The rain had stopped so I went for a wander. It's not a big town, Aberystwyth. A couple of cinemas. A pier. How would I amuse myself? I was already thinking I'd have to move on after a day or two. I could rent a car and just keep rolling until concern for my health and whereabouts started to rob certain people of their sleep. How long would that take?

I'd spoken to them all that morning. Tom, Louie, Mum, Ellie. They probably wouldn't even think about me for at least a week. People lie dead for years, post piling up behind the door. Nobody misses them, not even the bank, until they start dripping through somebody's ceiling. This is a good argument for living in a flat on an upper floor. Your oozing corpse will be discovered a bit sooner.

Meanwhile, back in Northfield, I imagined all was quiet, except for the hum of traffic on the main road, the occasional yodel from next door's dog, and the rustle and patter of tiny rodent feet.

I shared the lift with two suits. One of them said that heavy overnight rain was forecast. His colleague observed that it was November so we shouldn't complain. I felt it was my turn to say something so I asked them if they were attending the soil conference. They were. I wonder how that happens to a man. They must have had their dreams. Going to be the next Rick Wakeman, or Syd Barrett. Then they wake up and find they've turned fifty and they're in soil management.

'Another full day tomorrow,' sighed one of them.

'Yep,' said the other. 'Looks like being a pretty full day.'

CONVERSATION EMERGENCY: PAGING OSCAR WILDE.

I was so damned tired I couldn't sleep. I kept the telly on, for company, Welsh with English subtitles, but I wasn't really watching. I was trying to guess who would be the first to miss me, and what they'd do about it. It wouldn't be Ellie, unless she wanted to contact me with some big breaking news about Noah, like they'd discovered he has perfect pitch, or he's in the top 20th percentile for building egg-box dinosaurs. And it wouldn't be Mum, unless, say, somebody died. She always lets me know about deaths, especially if it's somebody she didn't like.

In which case, when I failed to answer the phone she'd say something to Philip. I knew how that would go.

'I telephoned your sister but she's never at home.'

'Well, you know what she's like.'

'She might have gone on holiday. But I don't remember her saying anything.'

'Typical. Swanning off. She should have let me know. If anything happens to you, I need to know where she is.'

'Nothing's going to happen to me. I'm all right.'

'I know you are, Mum. It's just the principle of the thing. She's your daughter. She should be available.'

'Never mind. I've got you. And, anyway, I don't want to be any trouble. I've had my life.'

'Don't say that, Mum. You're never any trouble.'

Then there might be a bit of to-ing and fro-ing, Mum insisting she's a millstone hanging round the neck of the family, Philip swearing on a stack of Bibles that she's very low maintenance. Mum always wins those contests. You have to let her. She has few pleasures in life, but she does enjoy a good hair shirt.

My brother. It's hard to believe we sprang from the same loins.

Philip is younger than me. I remember the day he was born. Dad was waiting for me at the school gate, Lansdowne Road Infants'. First time ever, and the last, that Dad picked me up from school. He said there was a surprise waiting for me at home and I thought it might be a bike, or Aunty Phyllis, who was married to somebody called Osbaldo and lived in Argentina. She'd said in her last Christmas card that she might be visiting soon. I'd never met Aunty Phyllis but I really wanted to. Mum said she was flashy. I had no idea what that meant but I had a feeling I'd like it.

In fact Aunty Phyllis didn't come till later in the year but she didn't disappoint. She had bare legs and big clip-on earrings and she laughed a lot. After she'd gone you could still smell her perfume. Mum described it as 'cloying' and opened all the windows. But the surprise the day Dad fetched me from school was Philip. My baby brother. He was about the size of my Rosebud doll and the cardigan he was wearing was so big you couldn't see his hands.

In those days, when you were six you didn't notice that women were pregnant. Actually, the very concept of pregnancy was a closed book. When you were six you thought babies just materialized as per the Virgin Mary. Also, pregnant women wore bell tents. They could have had a three-ring circus going on under there. And Mum always had a sturdy build. We all did. It was inevitable, the amount of custard we consumed. So she probably didn't show much and my mind was on other things anyway. I was working on becoming more interesting.

My name, for instance, which I hated. I wasn't the only Clarke in the school and there were dozens of Elizabeths. At one point I decided to become Madeleine Michelle St Xupery and I wrote that in the front of all my Enid Blytons. So, what with one thing and another, it's no wonder Mum's growing belly escaped my notice.

Philip's arrival turned everything upside down, even when all he did was lie in his cot and look at the ceiling. As far as I know it was a completely normal birth, slotted in very efficiently while I was at school, but there were definite hints that he had barely made it. Mum got it into her head that Philip would always need special consideration from me because (a) I was his big sister, therefore I must shoulder more responsibilities and let him have my skipping rope or anything else he wanted even if I was playing with it and he was too young to skip. And (b) he had a bout of croup when he was three months old. Which can be nasty. My fantasy of holding him under water until he gave up the ghost was both cruel and infantile.

So, my brother became Philip the Helpless. Out of the same stable as Ethelred the Unready. He did okay, though. He got through school without drawing attention to himself, good or bad. Ditto the Electricity Board. He started work there the week after he finished school and there he stayed until they showed him the door a couple of years ago. Voluntary redundancy. They didn't need as many pen-pushers once they had computers to mess things up.

Personality-wise, a bit of a blank sheet, my brother. And then along came Yvonne. How they ever got together was a miracle. She must have made the first move, and the second. She was perfect for him. Perpetual motion in a miniskirt, capable, full of plans. Yvonne steered him up the aisle, steered him into fatherhood. She never asked much of him because she could do it all faster and better herself.

I was very fond of my sister-in-law. There was something irresistible about her advice and opinions. Your hair needs

layering. Why faff around all afternoon when you can get frozen Chicken Kievs in Iceland? You shouldn't wear orange. Ten
minutes with Yvonne was as bracing as running into the sea in
December. And then she got sick.

I don't know how much they'd told her. When I visited her
in the hospital she was raring to get home and sort out the inevitable consequences of her absence. She understood entropy.
Yes, she had cancer, but her main worry seemed to be that
Philip was using tea towels as floor cloths, and that he'd forget
to tape *Brookside* for her. Which, of course, he did.

They did some kind of operation and she seemed to get better. She even organized a night out to see the Hunkies when
they came to Birmingham on tour: Yvonne and her neighbours
and her friends from the slimming club. She was on great form
that night, wolf-whistling and carrying on. She had her photo
taken between two oiled hulks with cucumbers down the front
of their trunks. It's a nice memory of her.

After that everything went very bad, very fast, and Philip
was like a bunny rabbit caught in the headlights. I was with her
the day she died. She was in bed, very jaundiced, but she was
doing one of her Word Search puzzles and fretting about the
housework that wasn't getting done. Her last words to me were
'Just look at the state of those windows.' She hadn't been eating, but then she told Philip she really fancied a poached egg on
toast with plenty of salt and pepper.

Philip said, 'Is poached the same as fried?' so I told him to
bugger off and pick some daffodils to put on her tray while I
made the egg. He carried the tray upstairs. I could hear them
talking. I was still in the kitchen, writing a shopping list, when

he called down to me to bring him some paper towels. I'd thought eggs weren't the best thing for her. A drop of chicken soup might have been better. But, anyway, she'd eaten every morsel, sunk back against her pillows, and died. Just like that. Typical Yvonne. If there was something to be done – getting married, cleaning windows, dying – get on and do it.

So then Philip the Helpless became Philip the Totally Incapable. I went with him to the Co-op to arrange the funeral but I did all the talking, made all the decisions. It was like somebody had removed his battery. People rallied round. Little Maureen and Big Rita from along the street helped out with the kids. Casseroles appeared on the doorstep. We hadn't even got Yvonne's ashes back from the crem and everybody was saying he'd have to remarry. I couldn't see that happening. How can you meet women if you're slouched on the sofa with your eyes closed? He even allowed his cactuses to wither and that takes some doing.

I had a word with him.

I said, 'You did know Yvonne had cancer?'

'Yes.'

'You did know she was going to die?'

'They never said.'

'Did you ask?'

Silence.

I said, 'You've got to pick yourself up. You've got to do it for Kayleigh and Scott.'

Silence.

I said, 'If you want my advice you'll take those kids on a holiday. You can't sit here all summer maundering.'

He nodded. He said, 'What programme do you use when it says Dry Clean Only?'

The first year was tough. All the birthdays and anniversaries. And Christmas! Mum moved in with them for two weeks because, let's face it, cooking a turkey with all the trimmings is no job for a civilian. Muriel Clarke, the Field Marshal Montgomery of Christmas dinners.

Philip did book a holiday, though. Big Rita got in touch, to congratulate me after I'd made an exhibition of myself on live television. She said, 'Knockout, Lizzie. Good for you. Everybody's talking about it. And did you hear, your Philip's taking the kids to Disney?'

He bimbled along for a few years, learned how to use a can-opener. Then he met Wendy. He didn't go out looking for her. It was more a case of stumbling upon her at Little Maureen and Nev's silver wedding party. She was a widow, a bit older than Philip, a nail-technology instructor. It means she teaches girls how to give manicures. Whenever I'm with her I wish I could take a leaf out of the Queen's book and keep my gloves on.

Wendy took a shine to Philip. He's not bad-looking, actually. It's his personality that's like a sat-upon cushion. Next thing we knew, she'd moved in. Mum said she was after his money.

I said, 'He hasn't got any money. He's got a mortgage and two teenagers.'

'You know what I mean,' said Mum.

I did. It was Wendy's glamour she objected to. Of course, these things are relative. Wendy was no Elizabeth Taylor, but a woman may be judged by the extensive range of bubble-baths on her shelf. Also, Wendy didn't expose her nails to unnecessary risk. She got a cleaner in once a week. A cleaner! Mum declared that Yvonne must be turning in her grave. Turning in her urn. In death Yvonne had become my mother's ideal daughter-in-law.

Much as I miss Yvonne, I think Wendy has been good for Philip. She didn't hover, waiting for him to use the wrong cloth. He began to be more confident. And then becoming a grandfather really gave him a boost. It was like he suddenly woke up and realized he was the senior male in the tribe. That was when he became very attentive to Mum. Smoke alarms, Caller ID, chain on the front door. Philip Clarke, aged fifty-eight, hobbies: preventing stuff.

3

I went to a tearoom for breakfast. It was crowded, windows fogged up, Aber folk sitting in steaming raincoats. I did wonder whether I should go to different places, an anonymous woman, just passing through. Or was it better to become a regular and blend in? Not that there was a lot of choice. Café society wasn't a big feature of Aberystwyth.

Say you were on the run from the police: what would you do? Wear a wig? Some wigs attract attention. They shout WIG. It would have to be a very good wig.

Things you should always have at the ready for when you need to disappear and make people wish they'd treated you more considerately: wads of cash; a selection of top-quality wigs; a secret fully equipped hideaway, preferably somewhere that doesn't get forty inches of rain a year.

The third morning the woman said, 'Welsh cake, is it?'

So that was that. I'd become a regular, like it or not. Even if I went into Poundland and bought a red clown wig, they'd still remember I was Earl Grey tea, no milk, and a hot Welsh cake with butter.

There were no empty tables. A woman moved her bag off a

chair so I could sit down, didn't even break off talking to her companion. Sisters, I'd say. They seemed to be having a problem with their mother and her care assistant.

'Well,' says one of them, 'I know for a fact there was ten pounds in the biscuit barrel, so where's it gone?'

'But, Bee,' says the other, 'you know what Mam's like. She put her remote in the fridge. That tenner could be anywhere. So I don't want to go making any accusations. What if it turns up?'

Bee said she thought they should install a secret camera. She said, 'I know why you don't want to say anything, Bran. It's because she's foreign.'

'She's Irish. That's not foreign.'

'She's Lithuanian.'

'From Ireland.'

'That's still foreign. You've heard her, jabbering on her mobile. She could be saying anything. She could be talking to her accomplices.'

BISCUIT BARREL THEFTS: POLICE EYE BALTIC GANGS.

She said, 'They come over here, taking our jobs, they should learn English.'

Bran said, 'Her English is all right. It just throws her when Mam speaks Welsh.'

Bee said, 'I still think a camera's the answer. You can get them in Argos.'

A hidden security camera. That was something Philip hadn't got round to yet in his bid to keep Mum safe. Of course, Mum doesn't have a care assistant and she doesn't keep money in her biscuit barrel. Even if she did she'd never agree to a camera because what if it caught her in nothing but a longline brassière and big knickers? It could end up on Facebook. Elder porn.

We did try Mum with a cleaner, many years ago, after she'd had a dizzy spell while she was up her step-ladder. That didn't work out. The cleaner skipped dusting the tops of the wardrobes two weeks in a row.

I remember saying, 'Mum, how do you know?'

'Because I watched her,' said Mum. 'Through the crack in the door. And I'll tell you another thing. She didn't put my dressing-table doilies back in the right positions.'

Doily misplacement. Passive aggression, or what?

So then my sister-in-law Yvonne, of blessed memory, said sod it, she'd do the step-ladder stuff, but let the record show that in her opinion everybody should get built-in cupboards, right up to the ceiling. She used to go across once a fortnight for picture rails, light bulbs and wardrobe tops. Knowing my mother, she probably checked on Yvonne through the door crack, too. Just because a woman has been the salvation of your only son, just because she's given you two lovely grandchildren, well, two relatively okay grandchildren, doesn't mean she might not help herself to a cheeky squiff of your Lenthéric Tweed. No, Yvonne only got herself promoted to the ranks of the faultless by dying. And after that our mother's housekeeping standards were left up to Philip. Mum could have moved into a nice cosy council bungalow by now. It's not my fault she insists on staying put with a load of old utility-issue dust traps.

Philip always says, 'You can understand it. It's the family home.'

And I always say, 'It's not bloody Chatsworth.'

Bee and Bran moved on to discussion of some unnamed male who wasn't pulling his weight. A brother, probably. That's one thing I can't say about our Philip. *Au contraire.* He might say it about me. 'My sister. Never lifts a finger.'

The thing is, I would, if it was necessary, if it ever came to bottom-wiping and stuff. But Mum doesn't need anything like that, not yet. She certainly doesn't need her kids duelling over who hauls her wheelie bin into the street. She's absolutely fine.

A man came in, ordered something, looked around for a table. His options were to share with a woman and two grizzling toddlers or with me, Bee and Bran. A no-brainer, really, though I will say Bee could have been more gracious about moving her bags. He was wearing a hat with earflaps. He was quite nice-looking, but he hadn't shaved, which makes some men look surly.

It can feel a bit odd, sitting opposite somebody at a small table and not speaking. Unless you're married to them. I did have a book in my bag but I didn't feel like whipping out *Unleash Your Inner Giant* in public. He had a newspaper.

Bee said, 'I tell you what I'm thinking, Bran. I'll put another tenner in the biscuit barrel. See what happens.'

Bran said, 'That won't prove anything. If it disappears it could still be Mam meddling and forgetting where she's put it. It'll just be money down the drain.'

I said, 'You know there's stuff you can get, like an invisible dye. To put on banknotes. If you think somebody's stealing from you.'

They looked at me.

I said, 'Sorry. I couldn't help overhearing.'

They wanted to know what the stuff was called.

I said, 'I don't know. You'd probably have to send away for it.'

Bran said, 'There you are, Bee. Ask your Gethin to look it up on his computer. Wouldn't it stain, though? Wouldn't it ruin your towels?'

'I think it wears off. I don't know. I've only read about it.'

Mr Earflaps said, 'You need black light to see it.'

'Black light? What's that when it's at home?'

'It's a special torch.'

'Oh, yes? And I'll have a jar of elbow grease and a left-handed hammer while you're about it.'

'Please yourselves,' he said, and opened his paper.

They put their rain hats on and gathered up their bags. One of them turned back when she got to the door. She bent down and whispered in my ear, '*Crimewatch*, right? I knew your face was familiar. I've been puzzling and puzzling. You haven't been on for a while, though.'

I gave her a smile.

She said, 'Terrible what happened to Jill Dando.'

Mr Earflaps watched her go. He said, 'Nutcase?'

'No, just a case of mistaken identity.'

'Lucky you,' he said.

His sandwich arrived. Sausage, white bread, no butter, brown sauce and a black decaf.

I said, 'Why?'

'Why what?'

'Why am I lucky?'

'In my business you get people recognizing you all the time. You can't go anywhere.'

I took another look at him. I said, 'Why? Who are you?'

He laughed, but he wasn't amused.

'If you're somebody famous, I'm sorry. I don't get out much. The last film I saw was *Pirates of the Caribbean.*'

He pretended to read his paper instead of giving the sausage sarnie the attention it deserved. The smell of it was making my mouth water.

'So you're not going to tell me who you are? Does the woman behind the counter know?'

Silence.

'I'll ask her.'

'Don't you dare. I'm here incognito.'

'Okay. Well, you definitely are incognito to me. I don't have a clue who you are and I wouldn't even be interested if you hadn't made a big deal about it.'

He ate his sandwich, said nothing. So now he was really annoying me.

I said, 'You started this line of conversation. As far as I'm concerned, you're just a scruffy-looking guy in a stupid hat.'

Grunts.

' "In my business." I wonder what that could mean? You look like you're in pretty good shape. Are you a sportsman? I don't follow any sports so I wouldn't recognize you.'

Withering look. He had a Botox forehead. Shiny. You can spot it a mile off.

'I think you're an actor. Or a model. Are you one of those guys who models for catalogues? Shirts and stuff? They must get recognized all the time. "Hey, didn't I see you in your Y-fronts? Holding a big spanner"'

Still nothing. I mean, if he didn't want to converse with me he could have scoffed his food and walked away. The rain had stopped. Almost stopped.

I said, 'I suppose you must be on the telly, then.'

He didn't say he wasn't.

I said, 'Well, your secret is safe with me. I don't watch it. It's all rubbish.'

He put his newspaper down. 'You never stop, do you?' he said.

But, as I recalled, he was the one who'd opened the conversation. And he trod on my little umbrella, going off in a huff because I didn't recognize him. Sad creature.

He'd left his newspaper on the table but I didn't pick it up. I'd decided not to check the papers for at least five days, to give the story time to gain some traction once the alarm had been raised.

FEARS GROW FOR MISSING TV CHEF.

Who would make the first call? My money was on Louie. He knew what it was to feel overwhelmed, to want to just run away and hide. He'd go back over our last conversation and think, Lizzie was really despondent the last time I spoke to her. I shouldn't have hurried her off the phone. I should have been a better friend. Yes, Louie was definitely the one.

4

The time Louie went missing there was a major flap on because it was the day for his astrology slot and he didn't turn up for makeup. The PA phoned him every two minutes and Louie never answered. I was doing a fondue demo but I kept losing my thread, worrying about him. They had viewers phoning in. 'What's wrong with Lizzie Partridge today? And what happened to the horoscopes?'

They replaced Louie with a back-up piece they had on tape, about some woman running a bird hospital on her kitchen table, and I remember thinking, Is that really an advisable thing to do? Mending a bird's wing? Surely that bird's going to be disabled the rest of its days and there's no disability allowance in Bird World, no special consideration. The other birds see you hobbling around, they're going to say, 'Hey, look at Gimpy. Let's nobble him.' If you're a bird and you have mobility issues I'd say your fate is sealed.

I went straight round to Louie's flat after the show. He wasn't there. I was on the front step, wondering what to do next, when the press arrived and started ringing all the bells and peering through windows that didn't even belong to Louie's flat. That was when I found out he'd been in court that morning. He'd been caught playing doctors in the Handsworth Park toilets and spent the night in the cells because he wouldn't give the police his name. The magistrates had fined him £50, he'd paid up and disappeared.

It was in the local paper, of course, but by a stroke of luck there was an electrical fire at a workshop in Aston, a lot of smoke, no casualties, and the Duke of Gloucester came to town to unveil some plaque so, what with one thing and another, the story about Louie got relegated to the bottom of page five.

For three days I heard nothing from him. I was going out of my mind. Then a letter came. He was hiding out at a cousin's house in Rustington. Cousin Ralph had never married and he'd been in a similar spot of trouble himself many years earlier, so Louie had found a safe haven with him. It was February before he reappeared.

In those days Meredith was our editor. I'd asked him if they were dropping Louie but I never got an answer. Then one Sunday the phone rang and it was Louie himself. He said Mercury was in Gemini or some such baloney and I should expect an old friend to walk back into my life. He was on top of the world. Not only was he coming back on the show but one of his exes had read about the court case and got in touch with him. That was Chas. And they've been together ever since.

'Bad publicity is salt to a flagging career, Lizzie darling,' he said. 'You should see the letters they've had. It's the older women. They love me. Bring back Louie! they cry. So they have.'

There had been a few viewers who thought he should be strung up but, like Louie said, their voices were drowned out. His brush with the law had transformed him into hot shit.

★

On Friday morning the soil managers checked out and a message appeared on the board in the hotel lobby:

WELCOME TO FURSONALITY 2010.
Meet'n'Greet 7 p.m. in the Terwyn Price Room.

I wondered who Terwyn was. I wondered what you had to do to get a venue in a budget hotel named after you.

I bought a newspaper. I'll admit it, I was itching to read what they said about me. Louie would have become concerned I wasn't answering my phone. He'd have asked around. People's indifference would gradually have given way to worry. By Thursday night somebody would have reported me missing.

I went to a different café and ordered a full Welsh: eggs, bacon, tomato, mushrooms, toasted laverbread loaf. There was nothing in the paper. Absolutely nothing. I went through it three times. Then I realized there might be a delay because Louie wouldn't know who to contact. Not Tom, because he knew Tom and I weren't an item any longer. And he wouldn't have Ellie's number, or Philip's. He probably didn't even know what names they'd be under. Did he know I was née Clarke? Yes, I think so. And he might remember Ellie works for a big law firm in the city centre and, as it happens, she didn't change her name when she got married. She and Nat combined their surnames, with a hyphen, because she doesn't see why a woman should surrender her identity to a man and Nat agrees with her. Of course if your name was Smellie or Daft you might be eager to surrender it.

So my grandson is Noah Partridge-Hurst, poor little sod. Or is it Hurst-Partridge? I can never remember.

Laverbread is seaweed. It's good for you, they say. I could do something with that. A St David's Day special. Slow-cooked lamb with laverbread? Might work. Whether the West Midlands are ready to eat seaweed I couldn't say, but as I don't have a cooking gig any more it doesn't really matter.

I turned my mobile on. Still no messages. Not one anxious enquiry. Great. I'd been gone four days and nobody had missed me. That meant sweating it out for another week at least. The hotel receptionist said in that case would I please settle my bill to date. Well, what the hell? Stick it on the plastic.

It was a dry day so I caught a bus to Barmouth. It was a pretty little place. Not a lot to do, but attractive. I could have bought fudge, or got a tattoo. I have acres of skin. But in the event of losing my mind and making a desperate bid to look cool, fear of pain would stop me actually proceeding.

My dad had a tattoo, from when he was in the army. It was supposed to be a four-leaf clover but you'd never have known. Just a blue smudge. It must have been done after lights out. And Ellie has one, acquired when her chief ambition in life was to piss me off and her nose stud had failed to send me into orbit. Well, a piercing soon closes up if, say, you get fed up with people telling you you've got snot on the side of your nose. A tattoo, though, that could be the cause of lifelong regret. She doesn't flaunt it nowadays, of course. Fortunately it's in a place not generally on view in a court of law.

Barmouth has a proper sandy beach, not shingle like Aber. I sat for a while, nodded at a few elderly walkers, spoke to a few dogs. I felt like crying but the tears were stuck somewhere in my chest. I've been on my own, on and off, for a long time. Twenty years since Alec left. Can it really be? There were boyfriends. No, there weren't. There were men in blazers, sent by that dating agency. I think once you'd signed up and paid they were contractually obliged to find you a certain number of dates. Anything between the ages of fifty and ninety and still breathing.

Then Tom came along. That was a serious relationship, but I apparently fucked it up because he left and Tom is a saint. Everybody says so.

I do have friends. A few. There's Lynette, from childbirth classes. I haven't heard from her in a while. Years, actually. She's got a bunch of grandchildren keeping her busy. And Susan Carter. She kind of latched on to me after I became a celebrity. Hi, remember me? Lansdowne Road Infants? She always was a bit needy. Then there's Big Rita, from Philip's street, and Little Maureen, they've always been friendly. I should make more of an effort. Have people over. I'd need to tidy up a bit first. Get rid of the mouse.

When I got back from Barmouth I sat in the hotel lobby for a while, hoping to see some furry costumes, but there was nothing doing. Just unremarkable-looking people arriving with big suitcases, mainly guys. They could have been soil executives, arriving on the wrong day. Soil Management Redux.

I caught the lift with a smiley couple. It was a squeeze because they had a lot of luggage.

I said, 'Costumes?'

'Oh, yes. You can't travel light when you're a furry.'

I remarked that it looked like being a fun weekend.

'It'll be smashing. Your first time, is it?'

I said, 'No, I'm not here for . . . I'm just an ordinary guest.'

40

I think they felt quite sorry for me.

She said, 'We're Merv and Mavis.'

As they got out of the lift I said, 'I'll look out for you.'

'You do that,' said Merv. 'But I bet you won't recognize us.'

Just after seven I went downstairs to see what was going on. Plenty, that's what. There were furry folk everywhere. Lions, rabbits, some kind of blue thing with perky ears and big paws. I went for a quick peep into Terwyn's memorial room and a six-foot canine on the door said, 'Well, good evening. Come on in for some Fur-bulous fun.'

I said, 'I was just looking.'

'That's okay,' he said. 'This is an open event.'

'But I'm not one of your crowd.'

'I can see that. But you can still come in. Nobody cares what you're wearing. They only care about what *they*'re wearing.'

'Are there other people in there not wearing costumes?'

'Sure to be.'

'I can't see any.'

'Then be the first. Open the flood gates.'

'Are you a wolf or a dog?'

'I'm a raccoon. I'm RJ.'

'I'm sorry?'

'I'm RJ from *Over the Hedge*. Bruce Willis did the voice.'

'I didn't see it.'

'It's okay. A raccoon, it's not mainstream. I'll probably be the only one here. But please, do go in, circulate, admire. Try our specially commissioned non-alcoholic cocktail. It's called a Harmless Beast.'

I said, 'I'm just on my way out. I might look in later.'

'Have a nice evening,' he said. 'At 10 o'clock there'll be Musical Chairs followed by an All-comers Cuddle Fight but I'm afraid that's a closed session.'

I went to the Chinese. I'd been living on sandwich dinners, to economize, and I had a real hankering for lemon chicken. There was an A-board outside with a paw print drawn in chalk. It said 'WELCOME ALL FURIES'. There was nobody else in so I got the big greeting. Where would I like to sit? The choice was overwhelming.

'Are you expecting a lot of furries tonight?'

'Oh, yes.'

I said, 'How do they eat in those costumes?'

'Not eat. Just drink beer, with straw,' he said. 'Very thirsty. Other customers like this furies. Is real good fun.'

Real good fun. I caught sight of myself in a mirror. The lone diner waiting for her lemon glop. Why hadn't I gone in to the furry gathering, had a quick drink? The man on the door couldn't have been more friendly. Merv and Mavis had seemed like nice people too. What possible reason did I have – solitary female, nowhere else to go, nothing else to do – what reason to say no? I'll tell you. When the raccoon on the door invited me in, the first thought to flitter across my mind was, You'll end up on a mailing list. You'll end up getting pestered.

So, it had finally happened. I had turned into my mother. A woman who can be relied on to see the downside of every-thing. Go with Winnie and Lilian to Seniors' Bowls? Oh, no. Next thing you know they'll have put you on the tea rota. Invite people round? What, and have them dropping crumbs?

Have them traipsing dog mess in on their shoes? 'Traipsing' is one of Mum's words. It conveys a horrible inevitability. Guests, shoes, dog shit. It's very Muriel.

I don't know if Dad was sociable. I don't know anything much about him, except that he did as he was told. 'Go and shave'; 'Throw a bit of slack on that fire'; 'Not that shirt, Wilf.'

He used to wink at me sometimes. Signalling. 'I'm still in here, Lizzie. I do as I'm told, but I'm still in here.'

In spite of my mother's warnings I used to be a sociable person. When I was married to Alec we used to have dinner parties. People did in those days. We drove a beat-up old Riley but we had Rosenthal dinner plates and a Georg Jensen teapot. We'd invite people he worked with, mainly. It was fine. I liked to cook, he liked to schmooze. Sometimes we'd get invited back and we'd do a critique while we were driving home.

'Hat-trick,' I'd say. 'Pâté, beef casserole, chocolate mousse. Winner of this month's all-brown dinner award.'

'Fucking Lambrusco,' Alec'd say. 'I take him a bottle of Gruaud Larose and he serves us fucking Lambrusco. What a tight-wad. And he earns more than I do.'

The way I met Alec, I'd been doing a catering course at the Tech and I'd just jacked it in because it was all about portion control and kitchen hygiene. There was hardly any cooking. So I went to work at Dauber's, learning how to make Kugelhupf and brioche, and if we weren't busy in the kitchen I'd help in the shop. Alec used to come in occasionally, to buy a slice of strudel, and that was where he first saw me, in my whites, with flour on my nose.

We were a great team, me and Alec, until we weren't any

more. He started travelling. It was for work, all quite legit, for a while. I'd quite have liked another baby but he wasn't keen. Funny how that panned out for him. With Alec away more and more, I was getting bored. Ellie went to a playgroup and you had to do your turn as a helper. It wasn't really my thing, singing 'Row the Boat', negotiating with three-year-old ankle-biters.

I'd catered a few dinners before we had Ellie. It was a Mrs Fox who got me started on that. She was a Dauber's customer too. So when the playgroup was having a fund-raiser, I offered to cater it. I knew I could do it. Everybody was blown away by it. They were easily blown away, but even so. Word got round and most weekends I was doing dinners for locals. I loved it. Leave me alone in a kitchen and I was a happy woman. The only trouble was I didn't have a head for business. By the time I started driving out to the upmarket folk I was barely covering my costs. That used to make Alec mad.

He'd say, 'It's not a goddamned soup kitchen, Lizzie. Put your prices up.'

I just hated asking people for money and, somehow, the more they had the harder it was to talk about it. I remember a woman with a six-bed detached out in Bromsgrove querying the price of Stilton. She said, 'Danish Blue is a lot cheaper.'

I said, 'There is a very good reason for that.'

I never worked for her again.

I catered a big Christmas party for some people out in Shirley and things really took off after that because I got a radio gig through one of their guests. He said I had a good voice for radio. He was three sheets to the wind when he came into the kitchen looking for a backside to squeeze, but he was right. I did sound pretty good on radio. And then I got Hegarty, agent to the also-rans, and Hegarty got me *In the Kitchen with Lizzie Partridge*. That was good money. But Alec was gone by then.

Alec left me in stages. At first he'd just come home late and jump straight into the bath. Then he started going on business trips that required swimming trunks and strawberry-flavoured condoms. It wasn't that I'd let myself go. But if you offered Alec anything – cup of tea and a Hobnob, a bacon sandwich, a blowjob in an office cupboard – he'd take it, and the girls he worked with were offering plenty. He was good-looking. Kind of Jon Bon Jovi without the ratty hair.

I never knew the names. He never cried out 'Mandy!' or 'Chelle!' in the night. He probably didn't keep track of their names. Then Nikki came into our lives. That was when he actually moved out. Alec didn't know what had hit him. He packed his bags, cried a bit, made Ellie a bunch of promises and went. I think he saw it as a temporary arrangement with lots of lovely sex, but Nikki said, 'No, pal, it's marriage or nothing.'

I didn't fight it. The bank was transferring him to their Boston office, and if I was invited, nobody asked me how I felt about it. Would I have gone with him? Probably. I didn't have any other plans. But we got divorced instead and Nikki had her dream beach wedding in St Lucia. Ellie attended, paid for by Daddy, who was doing okay in those days. She actually laid aside her Doc Martens and wore a dress. She liked Nikki. There wasn't so very much of an age difference between them.

When I saw a photograph of the wedding I felt the tiniest twinge of sympathy for Alec. A sweating middle-aged man going to his doom in a rented white tuxedo. He wasn't really a beach person. Nikki looked exquisite, of course. Spaghetti-strap silk, bare feet, a Tiffany pendant. No bunions, no flaking shins or bingo wings. Now it's Nikki I feel sorry for. Left in the lurch with twins to raise.

Ellie was at university, first year. I got a call from Alec's sister. I never got calls from his sister, even when we were married. When she said, 'This is Moira,' I couldn't think who it was. Then she said, 'Lizzie, he's dead. Alec's dead.'

She said he'd been in an accident but that wasn't quite the case. He'd just pushed himself too hard on a crunch-bench.

BRIT BANKER IN BOSTON GYM TRAGEDY.

He was fifty-four. His boys weren't even in kindergarten.

I drove over to Warwick to break the news to Ellie. She took it very hard. And then, of course, she wanted to go to the States for the funeral, and she was in such a state I didn't feel I could let her go on her own. It was a deeply weird experience. In the chapel at the funeral home Ellie sat with Nikki and the twins and I sat behind them. The fifth wheel. I really wanted to cry but it didn't seem quite right. Crying over the love rat who left you for a child bride? I could have been crying for Ellie's loss but she was grieving without any help from me. The day her daddy left us he became Mr Wonderful. The only thing he ever did to annoy her was expect her to continue living with me, the Benighted Nazi Mother from Hell. Maybe I just felt a generic kind of sadness for people dying too young. Maybe I was jet-lagged.

So there I was in the Aber Chinese, still the lone diner. It was eight o'clock, the lemon chicken was gone, the tea, the recycled orange quarters and the fortune cookie were consumed – *He who desires fruit must climb tree* – and I was feeling quite regretful that I hadn't plunged into that room full of Tiggers and bunnies. There might have been some interesting people there. Except how would you know? Maybe a person who goes to Aberystwyth specifically to dress up as Scooby Doo is, by definition, interesting.

When I got back to the hotel the only person in Terwyn's memorial room was a girl with a broom and a dustbin sack. The party was over.

She said, 'You looking for the furries, is it? They'll be in the Aneurin Pugh.'

5

This is perhaps the moment to say something about me and men. I wasn't looking to hook up with anybody in Aberystwyth. I'd kind of given up on that scene. You know that body dysmorphia thing anorexics get, where they look in the mirror and see a disgustingly obese walrus? Well, I suffer from a related condition. When I look in a mirror I see a moderately attractive thirty-five-year-old brunette but I know the rest of the world sees a woman the downhill side of sixty, with frown lines and reading glasses.

After Alec left, it winded me for a while. It was at least a year before I went on what might loosely be described as a date. His name was . . . Was it Alan? Not Alan. Adam. We used to see each other in the newsagent's, got chatting, eventually. Then one Sunday morning he suddenly asked me out for a drink. He was a biologist, a bit shy. I liked that. He came on very strong all of a sudden. Took me to a pub that had more than eighty different beers but no toilet seat in the Ladies. Tried a bit of a fumble on my doorstep but wouldn't come in to take things any further. He disappeared off the radar for a few weeks, then popped up again. He invited me to see his lab one weekend. It was interesting. I tried to ask intelligent questions. Then we went for another half of Old Dog Slobber, or some other murky brew, and he told me I was definitely his type and he really liked older women but he didn't feel quite ready to have a relationship. Maybe I hadn't shown enough interest in his Petri dishes.

Yvonne was to blame for what happened next. She filled in a form for a dating agency and put my name and address on it. The first I knew about it, I got an information pack from Crème de la Crème – Introductions for Discerning Singles. I think Yvonne felt I made the place look untidy, being unattached. If you gave her a bunch of daffs she'd trim the stems till they were all exactly the same length.

I binned the brochure, but then I got the hard-sell phone call from Tonya. She had a smoker's voice. Frankly, I only went along for the complimentary no-commitment chat to get Yvonne off my case. If Crème de la Crème had some decent men on its books, fine, if not, *sayonara*, and in future leave me to blunder along on my own. But that wasn't Tonya's MO.

It wasn't a chat, it was an interview. I didn't even get to look at any photos because Tonya was by no means ready to take me on. I mean, I was on television, for crying out loud. Not a big name, admittedly, but it surely added some interest to my profile. She said I needed to tone down the earrings. My lovely parakeets!

Then she got to work on my list of interests. She said her best-sellers among the mature clientele were golf, bridge and tennis. So we drew a blank there.

She wasn't impressed by my belly-dancing. She said it might send the wrong message.

SEE MY HIP SHIMMY, STOP. ADMIRE MY PEL-VIC GYRATIONS, STOP.

What else could I say about myself? That I could pop bubble-wrap for hours?

'My advice, Lizzie,' she said, 'is to avoid anything wacky. You are selling yourself and wacky is a minority taste. Keep it mainstream. Keep it badminton and Andrew Lloyd Webber.'

She gave me the number of her hairdresser. And not only did I cave in to the supercilious bitch and get my hair done, I also had a lash tint and lost two pounds on the Crème de la Crème Hip and Thigh Diet. I put them back on again, and some, after I'd dated Terence, fifty-one, divorced, no dependants.

I was a fool not to realize Tonya would have titivated his personal profile too. It said he liked the theatre but it turned out he'd seen *Showboat* in 1970. What really got Terence lit up was orienteering. He said he could talk about orienteering until the cows came home, and he did. We had the worst Indian meal ever and then, because I can never rest until I've turned a minor disappointment into a total bloody disaster, I picked up the bill. He did reach for his wallet but not with any real intent.

He said, 'Well, it's been very nice.'

Thirty quid for poppadoms, beers and a couple of shoe-leather curries with a man who hadn't snipped the price tag off his blazer. Maybe he planned on taking it back, getting a refund. Five feet eleven sounded about right and he did indeed have blue eyes and silver hair but, as I recall, his description made no mention of weasel features and the habit of saying, 'Ta.'

After Terence came Bernard. He'd made a mint in pest control and was actually quite attractive in a seedy Jack Nicolson kind of way. He'd managed to slip past Tonya the fact that he was 'technically' still married. 'Technically' that didn't bother me. I wasn't looking for another husband, just a bit of company, a bit of action. But I was 'technically' a bit concerned about basic levels of candour.

On our fourth date he picked me up in a Ratattack vehicle instead of the Merc. That was when I twigged that he was still cohabiting with Mrs Bernard. He didn't have a love nest, though I'm sure he could have afforded one. He thought we'd have sex in the back of his van.

I said a hotel room would be a nicer idea. He said the van would be more fun, like being teenagers again. Of course I didn't want to feel like a teenager. I wanted to feel like a loved-up woman, then have a hot shower and wrap myself in a big fluffy towel. But Bernard was determined to have van-sex. It was round the back of some industrial estate. The kind of place people turn up murdered. He enjoyed it. He said so, several times.

Tonya was disappointed in me. She said Bernard was very keen to continue the relationship.

I said, 'I'm sure there's somebody out there for him. It's just not working for me.'

She sighed and said she'd go back to her files. From the look on her face, you'd have thought I'd asked her to fix me up with Sean Connery.

I said, 'No, I mean me and the agency. The whole thing. It was my sister-in-law's idea but it's not my thing.'

She said, 'Well, I hope you realize there can be no question of a refund.'

★

So that was pretty much my mid-life dating record, until I met Tom. Funnily enough, that was because of Yvonne too, indirectly. She might not have made old bones but she made things happen, even when she wasn't trying. Even when she was lying in a hospital bed. But I'm not going to talk about Tom because he hasn't looked for me, hasn't left an anxious message in a whole week. He's too busy running errands for somebody called Sally.

I found the Aneurin Pugh Lounge. Another Aber big-shot immortalized by a function room with sticky carpet. There was a handwritten sign on the door, 'HEADLESS ZONE. STRICTLY NO PHOTOGRAPHY', and there were furries sitting around in their costumes, but minus their heads. I peered in, looked around for the raccoon. No sign. I wasn't even sure I'd recognize him. The head is everything with those outfits. Then someone was cooee-ing, waving to me. It was Mavis of Merv and Mavis.

I said, 'I'm not sure I'm allowed in here.'

'Course you are,' she said. 'You've caught us with our heads off, mind. We're just cooling down.'

They were both flushed and there was a sharp whiff of stale sweat. Their costumes looked a bit tiger-ish, like on the Frosties box, but I wasn't sure what they were supposed to be. Merv's was red and blue, Mavis's was green and pink.

I said, 'I've just been out to the Chinese for dinner. They're hoping to get some of you in later on.'

'Not us,' says Merv. 'It'll be room service for us, eh, Mave?'

They'd brought Cup-a-Soups with them, for convenience, and plenty of Jaffa Cakes. Mavis said they didn't generally go out in public in their costumes, except once a year for charity, to raise money for muscular dystrophy. They'd had a son.

I admired their paws. Merv cracked a joke: 'All Mave's handiwork!'

They were from Stoke-on-Trent. He'd been a bus driver, she'd been a school dinner lady. They were both retired but she said she missed the company.

He said, 'We keep busy, though, don't we, Mave? Working on our costumes and whatnot.'

They'd been furries for five years. Old-timers, they called themselves.

Merv said, 'Most of them here are youngsters. You can see for yourself.'

Mavis said, 'And a lot of them are, you know . . . That way.'

'Not that we mind,' says Merv. 'We take people as we find them and furries are very nice.'

'Well,' said Mavis, 'let's say, most of them are.'

Interesting. Could it be there were a few mean hearts beating underneath all that fur? Costume-envy possibly? There seemed to be a preponderance of dogs in the room. Mavis said you'd find that at any of these events. She said, 'I'm not being funny, but a lot of them think dogs are cuter. It depends, though, on the head. If you get the head wrong a dog can be quite frightening. Anyway, me and Merv couldn't be dogs because it would upset Henrietta and Charlotte.'

Henrietta and Charlotte were their cats.

'And as for that lizardy thing over there,' she said, 'I hope he's not planning on going around town like that tomorrow because he could cause a panic. You could get people stampeding. If you ask me, he doesn't even belong here. Lizards aren't furry. There ought to be rules.'

LIZARDS TO APPEAL CONVENTION BAN: FURRIES ACCUSED OF DISCRIMINATION.

'You here on your own, Lizzie?'

'Just for a few days. Getting some sea air. Do you all know each other? Is it the same crowd every time you meet?'

'Mostly. Those two puppies are Dom and David. They run a bed-and-breakfast so they only come to events in the winter, when they're not busy. That duck, what's his name, Merv?'

'Orville.'

'No, what's his *name*? I think it's Ken. His wife died. Cancer. Very sad. She was a duck as well. But there again, should ducks even be here?'

I said, 'Do you know RJ? The raccoon who was on the door at the welcome party?'

'Raccoon?' says Mavis. 'Is that what he's supposed to be? I thought he was a panda. No, we don't know him.'

I wandered back to the lobby, had a look at the notice board to see what was scheduled for Saturday.

10 a.m. till 3 p.m.: Costume & Accessories Fair in the Terwyn Price Room.

7 p.m.: Photo Call in the Aneurin Pugh Lounge.

9 p.m. till late: Fursuit of Happiness disco in the Rhodri Ellis Banqueting Suite.

A voice said, 'See anything that interests you?'

I said, 'Are you the raccoon I spoke to earlier, or some other raccoon?' He still had his head on.

'I told you, I'm the one and only raccoon,' he said.

'I was just talking to a couple in the headless zone.'

'Then you saw them at their worst. Flushed faces, flat hair.'

'A bit smelly.'

'Oh, yes. It's uphill work to stay fresh when you're suited. Tell me, honestly, can you smell me?'

He lifted his arm.

'I can smell baby powder.'

'Phew!'

'What's your name?'

'RJ. I told you.'

A pale blue bear stepped out of the lift. It said, 'Hi, RJ. Are you going out for street hugs?'

'What, now? No. Friday night, I don't recommend it. Getting poked and prodded by drunks. I'm just going to hang out till the fun starts.'

The blue bear said it was going to see if anybody else was brave enough to go out.

I said, 'The fun. Is that the Musical Chairs?'

'Yes. It may not sound like much but it gets pretty ruthless. Especially for those of us with tails.'

I hadn't noticed he had one. 'Can I watch?'

'I'm afraid not. Strictly no fleshies allowed.'

I was longing to see this man's face.

I said, 'Are you going to take your head off?'

'No,' he said. 'I prefer to remain a raccoon of mystery. What's your name?'

'Lizzie.'

'Okay, Lizzie. Raccoons don't really shake hands but you can scritch me if you like. Behind the ears.'

6

I couldn't sleep for thinking about that damned raccoon. He was probably no more than a boy, mid-thirties say, like the puppies who ran a B-and-B. Still, he was the one who'd come up and spoken to me. He could have slipped by me, not said anything. Was he hitting on me? No. It was out of the question. I wasn't looking my best and, anyway, he had to be gay. They all were, apart from Merv and Mave and Orville the Widower Duck. What was it Louie called me? A fruit fly. Did I gravitate to them or did they gravitate to me? A kind of mother-figure. Ellie would laugh at that.

I suppose it's our job to mortify our children. Wearing tartan tights. Coming last in the mothers' egg and spoon race. Sending cauliflower pakoras for the school picnic instead of something normal, like crisps. Okay, the tights were a mistake.

Between the ages of thirteen and seventeen, life with Ellie was one long eye-roll. She schlumped around in an oversized black sweater, sighing at every word I uttered. Then she changed. It seemed to happen overnight. She came back from visiting Alec in the States and announced she was going to be a lawyer, and when the school told her she didn't have a snowball's chance in

Hell of getting into university, she picked up the gauntlet, told her boyfriend goodbye and knuckled down to revising. Credit to her.

GOTH ZOMBIE IN A LEVEL RESULTS SHOCK.

Since this personality transplant she's become a single-minded perfectionist. Graduated with first-class honours, trained with a firm everybody wanted to join, admitted to the roll of solicitors in record time. Criminal defence is her thing, magistrates' courts mainly but she's getting a few Crown Court cases. Yet another respect in which she doesn't resemble me. I'd be a prosecutor. Ellie's big on mitigating circumstances and rehabilitation. I'm more a lock-'em-up-and-throw-away-the-key person.

Ellie's husband's a psychiatrist, so you could say they both tend towards the soft and squishy, empathetic side of human nature. They're vegetarians too, vegans almost. It seems to me a poorly considered position to take. What the heck are we going to do with all those boy cattle if we don't eat them?

When Nat and Ellie got married I offered to cater the reception, seeing as I wasn't required to wear a big hat or offer advice on Married Love, but Ellie had already arranged for some mobile vegetarian outfit to deliver wholewheat wraps and carrot cupcakes. My mother wasn't happy. She kept buttonholing people and saying, 'When Elizabeth got married to Eleanor's father, we had a proper reception.'

Actually, we had a cold buffet at the Glamis Hotel and a two-tier sponge because Alec hated raisins. Hardly a champagne blow-out. The thing was, we thought I was pregnant. We were on the way to the register office when I found out I wasn't, so we went ahead anyway. It was too late to cancel the buffet.

I think Mum's problem with Ellie's wedding was that she didn't understand wraps. That you were supposed to eat the whole thing. I kept telling her it was just a kind of sandwich.

'Well,' she said, 'if that's the case they've been very sparing with the butter.'

My daughter, whose stock response in her teens was 'Whatever. Quit stressing', now has a plan for every eventuality. She timed her pregnancy so that Noah would be born in October. Apparently October gives you the jump educationally on kids whose parents were careless enough to give birth in August.

I think it was touch and go whether they'd have children at all, because of her career. It's a tricky one. Leave it until you're earning enough to pay a Norland nanny and you might discover your eggs are all past their lay-by date. Nat took paternity leave so she could get back to work ASAP. Such a pity, I thought. I mean, the one time in your life you have every excuse for lolling on the sofa and wearing your slippers all day, and Ellie was squeezing herself into her court suits. She'd be up at some unspeakable hour pumping breast milk and reading briefs. I offered to go over and help but she turned me down. She said, 'Thanks all the same but we have to get Noah into a routine and I know what you're like.'

I said, 'And what does that mean?'

'You'd be carrying him around all day. Picking him up the minute he whimpers.'

'How do you know?'

'Nana told me that's what you did with me.'

My daughter decided to subscribe to the Muriel Clarke

School of Baby-rearing. How well I remembered that. Our Philip bellowing for an hour because it wasn't time for his bottle. No wonder he grew up to be a human food-compactor, everything consumed at speed, without query or comment.

Yvonne used to say, 'He'll scoff anything, as long as he don't see how it's spelled.'

But I was saying about the raccoon. It seemed to me my only hope of seeing what was inside that costume was to pay for a hotel breakfast, sit in the dining room, Godfather-style, with a clear view of the door, and hope I recognized the walk. Breakfast was served from 7.30 till 10.00 which was a long time to linger over a pot of tea and a croissant, but I decided there was no need to be down there before 9.00. People would sleep in. They'd all be exhausted from playing games in their fur suits. I set my alarm for 8.00.

I'm not really a morning person. When I was presenting *In the Kitchen* Tiffany used to spend ages doing my eyes. 'The main thing,' she used to say, 'is to emphasize your sockets. You can never go wrong with taupe.'

I rummaged through my bag. No eyeliner and absolutely nothing taupe. The best I could come up with was a paste made from coffee granules and a black biro.

'Blend, blend, blend.' That was Tiffany's watchword. She had more brushes than Leonardo Frigging da Vinci. Nice girl, though. I wonder what became of her? When I left the show, she was expecting. That child must be in secondary school by now. Tiffany's probably got a little business, doing makeup for brides. Have brushes, will travel. Blend, blend, blend.

A word of warning. Don't ever try to blend instant coffee

into your eye sockets with a toothbrush. You'll look like a Hallowe'en lantern, plus you'll have to buy a new toothbrush. And don't, under any circumstances, use a cheap, blobby biro as an eyeliner, but particularly not when you've become obsessed with a raccoon who is undoubtedly gay and possibly young enough to be your son.

I washed off as much as I could and went downstairs. There was hardly anyone in the dining room: a single man, too short and too fat to be RJ, and a spoony young couple. The waitress insisted on giving me the breakfast tutorial. This is the toaster. Here we have a selection of juices. Kippers are available, to order. I started with prunes. When I was a kid prunes were more a threat than a foodstuff. Dad tended to be a bit costive so we kids were both assumed to have inherited the sluggish Clarke bowel. But later on I used to do lovely things with prunes. Devils on horseback. Rabbit with prunes. Prune and Armagnac ice cream.

Merv and Mave appeared around 9.30. They headed straight to the table next to mine. Of course they did. They didn't know I was raccoon-spotting and needed to concentrate. Mave said most of the furries got room service or skipped breakfast altogether, but for her it was part of the luxury of staying in a hotel. They both had the works: bacon, sausage, beans, mush-rooms, fried eggs.

I said, 'No laverbread?'

'Not on your life,' says Merv. 'You ever heard of Sellafield? It's just up the coast. I wouldn't fancy anything that comes out of the sea around here.'

I'd just started on my kippers.

There was a sudden influx, all men, all in jeans and sweat-shirts, some youngish, some not so. Any one of them could have been a raccoon in plain clothes. None of them gave me a second look. I was trying to study them without appearing to and at the same time be polite to Mave, who was showing me pictures of their cats.

I said, 'At an event like this, do you recognize furries when they're not wearing their costumes?'

Merv said, 'Oh, yes. Because you see them in the headless zone, so you get to know who's who. See the chap over there, at the cornflakes? He's Brave Heart Lion. Out of the Care Bears? And the one pouring juice? He's Bingo the Gorilla. Mind, we don't know everybody. There's some don't like to be seen without their head. When they get too hot they go up to their room for a breather, in private, like.'

'Or,' said Mave, 'they've got in-head fan ventilation, so they can stay suited for a lot longer. I wouldn't want it, though. You've got batteries and wires, and the noise. Any road, we like to be sociable, don't we, Merv? We like to take our heads off and have a natter. That's how you make new friends.'

They were going to the costume fair. Mave wanted to buy new paw pads for her feet and a travel-size glue gun, but they were also tentatively in the market for resin eyes. Just looking.

It was Saturday morning. My grandson would be going to Toddler Yoga and then to Water Babies. Louie and Chas would still be in bed, arguing about whose turn it was to get up and make the eggs Benedict. Tom would have been out for a paper. Maybe he was with this Sally, whoever she was. Boy, he hadn't let the grass grow. It was only five minutes since we'd split up.

Well, five months. He never did hang about, though. Now I think of it, the first time he chatted me up his wife was still breathing.

I was sitting in the League of Friends café at the hospital, waiting to go in and visit Yvonne, and he recognized me from the telly. Told me he very much liked my recipe for marmalade ice cream. Never thought I'd see him again. Then I bumped into him after his wife had passed away. He was bringing a box of chocolates for the nurses, to thank them for everything. We just clicked. And now it appeared he'd clicked with somebody else.

I checked my phone for messages. Nothing. How could that be? How long would it take before somebody said, 'Whatever has happened to Lizzie?'

It was a brilliant morning. I went out for a walk along the promenade, and down by the marina, who should I see but Mr Earflaps, sitting on a bench.

I said, 'Hello again.'

He shot me a and-who-the-fuck-are-you look.

I said, 'The tearoom, the other morning? We shared a table with two ladies and you were telling them about black light.'

He said, 'Are you following me?'

'No. Do you ever take that hat off?'

He was looking pretty rough.

I said, 'Are you still on the run? Has anybody recognized you?'

He didn't answer. I sat down beside him. Offered him a mint imperial.

Silence.

I said, 'Have you been reported missing? I haven't. I've been gone nearly a week, my family haven't missed me and no member of the public has recognized me, except that woman in the café who thought I was on *Crimewatch*. See? We're soon forgotten. What did you say you were in?'

'I didn't.' He looked at me. He said, 'Did you do a *Casualty*?'

'No.'

'*Morse*?'

'*Midlands This Morning*. I had a cooking slot. But it's been a while.'

'I did a *Morse*.'

'Which one?'

'*Sleep of the Dead*.'

'Were you an actual actor or an extra?'

'Doesn't matter. You wouldn't remember it.'

'Were you a corpse?'

'No.'

'What were you?'

'College porter.'

'So just an extra.'

'No. I had lines.'

I asked him what else he'd done. A soap. *Cloverfields*. That seemed to be the biggest feather in his cap.

'So why are you hiding in Aberystwyth?'

'Why are you?'

'I asked first.'

'I'm being written out.'

'And you thought you'd beat them to the punch? Jump before you're pushed.'

'No. They need to understand, they can't just dump people.'

'Yes they can. They do it all the time.'

'There'll be an outcry. Especially when people find out I've gone missing. There'll be concern. I've got a lot of fans.'

'But not around here apparently.'

'I have fans everywhere.'

'Is that why you're wearing that hat? So your fans won't recognize you? So they won't say, "oh it's okay, he's not missing after all. He's skulking around Aberystwyth looking like a dipstick." What's your name?'

'They can't write me out. It's not a good time. I've got negative equity. Craig Eden.'

'I'm Lizzie Partridge, by the way. I got fired too. I've been fired lots of times. And I've got vermin. At home.'

Suddenly I couldn't stop laughing. I was apparently chairing a meeting of Scrap Heapers Anonymous on a seafront bench in Aberystwyth. I thought he was laughing, too, but when I looked he was crying.

I said, 'Well, Craig Eden, I'm sorry for your troubles but I'd like to thank you for cheering me up.' I gave him a tissue. Men never have tissues. My son-in-law carries organic baby wipes but he's the exception to many a rule. Nat actually wore Speedos under his trousers when they went to the hospital, so he could get into the birthing pool with Ellie.

Craig said, 'What do you mean, cheered you up?'

I said, 'You've made me see how deluded I've been. Nobody's looking for me. And my bet is nobody's looking for you. You're sitting here, looking like a total pillock in that hat. Take it off. Nobody's going to recognize you. Nobody's going to run up to you and say, "Craig Eden, thank God you're okay." Same for

65

me. Global don't give a toss. Interpol haven't been alerted. Even the damned mice probably haven't missed me.'

'Who's Global?'

'Doesn't matter. The point is, we've got to pick ourselves up. You'll get another gig. So will I. Something'll turn up. Do you have an agent?'

'Obviously. I've been in the business since I was seven.'

'Really? What were you in?'

'I was the Joop Loop kid.'

'I don't think I ever saw that.'

'It was an advert. Joop Loops. Breakfast cereal. They tasted of fruit.'

'Did you have freckles?'

'Yes.'

'I think I may have seen you. Sounds to me like you shouldn't have any problem finding more work.'

I was lying, of course. If you're a household face at seven you're very likely to hit the buffers by the time you're forty. Unless you're Shirley Temple.

He said, 'You don't know what you're talking about. If you get written out of *Cloverfields*, you're tainted goods.'

'Not necessarily.' I told him Louie's story. He said he'd never heard of Louie Doyle. 'Nevertheless,' I said, 'he's proof that there can be life after a setback.'

He said *Cloverfields* had been good money.

I said, 'These things hardly ever last, Craig. So now your feet are back on the ground you can think about what to do next. Get real.'

'Says you.'

'Says me. Do you know what I've been doing this week? Spending money I can't afford on a hotel room, waiting for somebody to report me missing. Checking my phone for messages every half-hour.'

He yawned. Maybe he'd been sleeping rough. He did look a bit grubby.

'And, since yesterday, I've been entertaining romantic fantasies about a guy dressed as a raccoon who is almost certainly gay. The guy, not the raccoon. How pathetic is that?'

All he said was, 'You're a fucking nutcase,' and he was gone, earflaps a-flapping. Well, I tried.

7

I decided I'd go home on Monday. Try travelling on a Sunday and the words 'essential engineering works' and 'replacement bus service' spring to mind. Besides which, I was still quite keen to unmask RJ before I left. Go home on Monday, Tuesday buy mouse traps, extend one last tentative olive branch to Tom, and call the people who published the *In the Kitchen* spin-off, see if I can sell them a follow-up. *Back in the Kitchen with Lizzie? Still in the Kitchen? Anyone for Seconds?*

Food fashions have changed. This could be a problem. When we compiled *In the Kitchen* nobody had heard of quinoa. Not that you'll find it in any of my recipes even now. When Stuart was producer he was always on at me to go easy with the butter and lard. Now they're all the rage again. Of course, Stuart had his reasons. He never really lost his baby weight. One spoonful for Tabitha, one for Daddy, open wide, here comes an aeroplane, oh, another spoonful for Daddy. Time to buy some forty-two-inch-waist trousers.

When I got back to the hotel a group of furries was mustering outside, preparing to hit the town. I could see RJ's friend, the blue bear. He was wearing a T-shirt over his fur suit. It said:

'HUG A BEAR TO FREE A BEAR. NO DONATION TOO LARGE.'

I asked him what bears he wanted to free.

He said, 'Dancing bears, zoo bears. Asia, mainly. Want a leaflet? Want a hug?'

I was trying to find my purse.

'No, no,' he said. 'First you get the hug, *then* you donate. Depending on your satisfaction with the quality of the hug.'

His name was Blue Baloo and, I will say, he gave a really good hug. I used to get the occasional snot-cuddle from Noah but these days he mainly runs away from me. If you had ever told me that I'd allow a stranger dressed as a bear to embrace me in public I'd have laughed. But it was Aberystwyth. Nobody there knew who I was, or cared. Maybe that was why I started blubbing. Maybe it all came together in that moment. Lonely, lost, out-of-work woman, far from home, tired of hotel existence, troubled by thoughts of vermin, destitution and somebody called Sally.

Blue Baloo said, 'Mind the suit, mind the suit. Ten nine, ten nine. Waterworks. Request back-up. Group hug required.'

Next thing I know I'm in a fur-suit scrum and getting a strong dose of armpit odour. I stopped crying, bunged Blue Baloo a fiver and ran inside the hotel. The raccoon was sitting in the lobby with a wolf and a kind of owl-type bird. He raised a paw at me.

I told the girl on Reception that I'd be checking out on Monday morning.

She said she hoped I'd had a pleasant stay, and would I like to fill in a customer-satisfaction questionnaire?

I said, 'Sure. You see that man dressed as a raccoon over there? What room is he in?'

'Oh, I couldn't say,' she said.

I don't think she even knew who I was talking about. I don't think she knew the difference between a raccoon and a wolf and a cartoon bird.

I went along to the Terwyn Price Room, to take a look at the costume fair. There were stands selling shag fur and foam and buckram by the metre for the do-it-yourselfers. There were grooming tools and cooling devices and body parts – eyes, noses, growls, squeaks, paw pads, hoofs and claws, lots of claws. And there was a girl in a kind of lizard-skin bomber. She had a white streak in her hair and a portfolio with pictures of custom-made suits.

I said, 'How's business?'

'Not bad. Quiet, actually.'

'I love your jacket. Is it real lizard?'

'Synthetic.'

I looked through her photos. Dragons seemed to be her main thing.

I said, 'This crowd seem more into fur than scales.'

'Yeah, they're on the older side. They like their fur. Are you press?'

'No. I'm just a time-waster. These are amazing costumes, though. How much do you charge?'

'Depends. They start around two thousand. The black dragon was nearer three. I work with my clients to realize their dreams. I do do fur, if that's what you're interested in.'

'Did you get any commissions today?'

'People take my card, then go away and think about it. It's a big investment. What kind of fursona did you have in mind?'

And a voice said, 'I think she'd be a fox. What do you think, Min?'

It was the raccoon.

I told him I did not consider that a compliment. I knew somebody once who raised a fox cub, kept it in the house. It smelled really rank.

He said, 'I meant clever like a fox. Cool and clever. How about coming to the disco tonight? It's open to fleshies.'

'How can you dance in that suit?'

'Very easily, thank you.'

He walked away. The girl rolled her eyes.

I said, 'Do you know him?'

'Sure,' she said.

'What's his name?'

'RJ.'

'I mean what's his human name?'

'I'm not allowed to say. He prefers to be just RJ when he's suited up.'

'Well, he keeps hitting on me and I think I'm entitled to know what I'm dealing with. Is he old, is he young? Has he got hair? Has he got teeth?'

'He's okay. For his age.'

'Is he gay?'

'He's my dad.'

'So he's, what, fifty, fifty-five?'

'A bit older, actually. Quite a bit.'

'Your mum doesn't come to these things?'

'She's in Alicante. They're divorced.'

So, suddenly things were looking up. I had the possibility of a Saturday-night date, if you could call a casual invitation to a disco from a mystery man in a faux-fur suit a date. Trouble was, I didn't have a damned thing to wear. I scooted down to Darkgate Street and bought a palette of eye shadow, for socket enhancement, mascara, a cheap pair of flats and a floral dress that I regretted almost before I'd left the shop. When I got back to the hotel and tried it on again, my suspicions were confirmed. It made me look like a two-seater settee.

The disco started at nine. I stayed in my room till ten, reading *Unleash Your Inner Giant* and lining my stomach with crisps and KitKats to protect it from the effects of half a bottle of nerve-steadying pinot grigio. Maybe a bit more than half. I could hear the thud of the music.

I said, 'Right, Lizzie. You're going to wander nonchalantly into the disco, survey the scene, locate the raccoon. He probably won't even be there, or he'll be dancing with some cute bunny. In which case, leave. But casually. Like you've seen what you came to see and you now have better things to do.'

I hadn't factored Merv and Mave into this plan. They claimed me the minute I put my nose inside the Rhodri Lewis Suite.

Mavis said, 'Come and join in. You can dance with us. That's one good thing about a disco. It don't matter if you're on your ownsome.'

Merv was quite a mover. I think it's called Gangnam. Mavis was more sedate.

'Bad back,' she yelled. 'I have to be careful.'

I felt a bit of a tit, frankly, dancing with a pair of Frosties tigers. Then something caught my arm and swung me round. It was RJ.

I said, 'How do you always manage to sneak up behind me?'

'It's a gift. Know something else raccoons can do? Walk down tree trunks head first.'

'Bet you can't do that.'

'No, but I'm working on it. Don't you like dancing?'

'I do. I'm more of a foxtrot person these days.'

'See? What did I tell you? You're a fox.'

We were shouting over the music. You're not expected to talk at a disco. We bopped around for a while. I was hot. I was a flushed and sweaty disaster and my shoes were killing me. We stepped outside. There was a table of bottled water so the furries could rehydrate. RJ drank through a straw.

I said, 'So that girl who makes the dragon costumes is your daughter?'

'She is. Min.'

'Is that her real name?'

'No. Her name's Maxine but she hates it. We used to call her Maxi, and when she threatened to sue us for cruelty we agreed to call her Minnie instead.'

'Did she get you into being a furry or was it the other way round?'

'I started it. She helped me make my first suit. She's very clever with her hands.'

'I could see that. I looked at her catalogue. Not much of a saleswoman, though, is she?'

'She hates that side of it. She's happiest when she's in her workshop. But you have to come to these conventions, else how are you going to attract new business? She's got a website now so we're hoping sales'll pick up. You got any kids?'

'One daughter. She's a lawyer.'

'Could be more useful than a dragon-maker.'

'I should tell you I'm also a grandmother.'

'So's Goldie Hawn.'

'Am I ever going to see your face?'

'Let's not rush into anything. What I'd love to know is, what are you doing here? I mean, Aberystwyth in November? It's not the holiday season. You're not one of us. You're on your own. There's a story there.'

'I'm having a nervous breakdown.'

'Are you? You're hiding it very well.'

'Do you wear that suit at home?'

'Only to build up my stamina. It can be very draining. It's hot, it's heavy.'

'But you love being a raccoon.'

'I do. Do you want to talk? About whatever it is? Your nervous crack-up.'

'Not really. It's just that everything was really shite last week. Shite to the power of ten. So I ran away. And nobody's missed me.'

'I bet they have. Elaborate. About the shite.'

'Well, I lost the remaining shred of my career. My ex is seeing somebody. Daughter's too busy to talk to me. My mother doesn't like me.'

'Your mother? No, I'm sorry but I can't accept that. Mothers always love their kids, even when nobody else does.'

'Well, let's say she's begrudging. She prefers my brother. Who is a twerp.'

'Ah.'

'He took early retirement. So now he has nothing better to do with his time than dance attendance on her. But she always preferred him anyway. If you're not going to take that raccoon head off I think you should at least give me some idea what you look like. Do you have a full head of hair?'

'Ish.'

'If someone was playing you in a film, who would they cast?'

'George Clooney. Not really. John Hurt. '

'Like in *The Elephant Man*?'

'More *Alan Clark Diaries*. I have to say, Lizzie, there's something familiar about you. I really feel like I've seen you somewhere before.'

'Where do you live?'

'Warwickshire.'

'Then you've probably seen me on television.'

'Seriously?'

'*Midlands This Morning*. I used to do their cookery slot. Lizzie Partridge.'

'I might have. I wouldn't usually see daytime telly, though.'

'I do home shows too. Used to. Cooking demos. And magazines. You might have seen my photo in *Teabreak!* Actually, I know what it is. I just have one of those faces. I'm Everywoman.'

'I don't think you are. I like your face.'

I said, 'What will it take to get you to show me yours?'

'You'll have to meet me some time when RJ's hibernating.'

75

'We could just go to the headless zone.'

'I don't do headless. For RJ it's an all-or-nothing-at-all thing.'

'I don't even know your name. Your human name.'

He paused.

'Okay,' he said, 'it's Rod. As in lightning, fishing and Dyno. So, Lizzie Off The Telly, how would it be if RJ took a nap and Dyno Rod showered and got dressed? We could go and find a pizza or a curry or something.'

I said, 'Do you hibernate?'

'Not exactly. I just sleep in late.'

8

'Well, well, Lizzie Off The Telly,' he said, 'whatever happened to that don't-mess-with-me face? How appearances can deceive.'

He was nice. Dark hair, greying a bit, pleasant-looking. Late fifties, early sixties, it's hard to tell with men. His face was a bit crumpled and he was slimmer than he'd seemed when he was RJ, but that's a full-body shag-fur suit for you. We'd finished the white and made a start on a screw-top red. You could hear the music still thudding away downstairs.

I said, 'If you want to go back to the dancing I won't be offended.'

It was a lie but if he was going to bolt I preferred him to think I was okay about it. He turned the bedside lamp on and leaned up on his elbow. He said, 'Abandon a lovely woman for a sweaty disco? What kind of a jerk do you take me for?'

'You came all the way to Aberystwyth for the chance to wear your raccoon suit. It'd be terrible if you went home with regrets.'

'It would.'

'I thought you might revert to type. You know, raccoon type. Need to get back out there, on the prowl?'

'You mean like going through people's dustbins? Urinating on tree trunks? No, you have to understand, RJ is asleep. When the suit comes off I'm Rod. And I don't screw and run. Not these days. These days, I can either screw or run but not both in quick succession.'

'Does everyone know about RJ? Do your neighbours know, and people you work with?'

'Not really. It's not that it's a big secret. I mean, everybody does something. We've got a neighbour who does battle re-enactments. Wouldn't interest me. People know about Min's business, of course. She's got a unit now, on an industrial estate. It has proper ventilation. But she still brings work home, if she's got a rush job on, so they've seen her unloading dragons from the back of her van.'

'And your ex?'

'Yes, she knows. Not that RJ had anything to do with us splitting up.'

'Why did you?'

'Oh, you know, things ran their course. She moved on, met a younger man. Spanish. It was no biggie. And I'm retired, so I don't have work people asking me what I'm doing for the week-end. Nobody enquiring where I'm going with a raccoon tail hanging out of my suitcase.'

'You're a bit young to be retired.'

'Let's say I'm taking a break. I wouldn't rule out working again, if the right business opportunity came along.'

'You had your own business?'

'Several.'

'What did you do?'

'This and that. Import—export mainly.'

'And you sold your business, so now you're free to be a part-time raccoon.'

'Exactly. Part-time raccoon, part-time sex predator who hangs around seaside hotels in the off-season. Don't keep pulling the sheet up under your chin. I'm enjoying the view.'

'I'm sixty-four.'

'I'm still enjoying the view. So how did you get into cooking and telly and everything?'

'The long way round. In the slow lane. Left school, worked in a bookshop, picked up a cookery book and got the bug. Started a catering course, jacked that in. Worked in Dauber's, made apple strudel. You know Dauber's?'

'In the arcade near the cathedral?'

'That's the one. Got married, had a baby, did a bit of cooking for pin money. Dinner parties. I got my first proper gig through somebody's dinner-party guest. He thought I had a good radio voice and a squeezable backside.'

'He wasn't wrong. So much for studying hard and getting your O levels. All you needed was to be in the right place at the right time, with the right bum.'

'It's true. And to think old Whiskery Warrington told me my only hope of advancement in life was teacher-training college. I couldn't have been a teacher. You're not even allowed to whack them now.'

'No. But they're allowed to whack you. How unfair is that? Whiskery Warrington? That's a memorable name. Could that possibly have been at Peakirk Secondary?'

Well then I got this lurchy feeling in my stomach, like when you realize you've just locked yourself out of the house. I was in bed, with a total stranger, except that now it seemed he might not be. Which was worse?

'Lizzie?' he said. 'Were you at Peakirk?'

I was suddenly stone-cold sober and I wished I knew where my big knickers had landed in our haste to get into bed. He rolled onto his back and stared at the ceiling.

He said, 'I knew I recognized you. Didn't I say?'

'I don't recognize you. And I never knew anyone called Rod.' Truth of the matter was, I didn't pay much attention to boys when I was at school. They were just spotty idiots, always wrestling with each other.

He said, 'My God, I know who you are. You're Swanky Clarke. You are, aren't you? Don't look at me like that. I'll tell you who I am and then we'll be evens.'

Rodney Pooley. He was Rodney Pooley. Who had a briefcase when everybody else had a duffel bag. Whose mum used to drive him and his sister in a big black Morris when nobody else even had a car.

I think I may have groaned. Maybe it was just an inner whimper of mortification.

'Lizzie,' he said, 'why did they call you Swanky?'

'Because in Home Ec one time I called serviettes table napkins.'

'Why did you do that?'

'Because I didn't like words that end in -ette. I still don't. And then at Christmas I gave out cards with Carpaccio's *Flight into Egypt* instead of funny Rudolph ones. So that was that.'

'Tarred and feathered. Poor old Swanky.'

'And La-di-dah. They called me that too.'

'Bitches.'

'They were. Do you remember Janet Coleman?'

'Yes.'

'She was the Alpha Bitch. She started the "Swanky" name. And the thing was, we'd been really good friends when we were at Lansdowne Road. She used to have fits and I was always the one who sat with her till her mum came to take her home. She turned on me after we went to Peakirk. I don't know why. I'm sure I never did anything to her.'

'Envy? Inferiority complex?'

'About what?'

'Perhaps she sensed you were going to become a mature sexpot.'

'And whatever she decreed, the others all followed her.'

'Sheep, as well as bitches. Bitch sheep.'

'Janet Frigging Coleman.'

'Maybe she wasn't quite right in the head.'

'Could be. She used to say I'd marry somebody like you and have a hostess trolley and serve After Eight mints. It was the worst insult she could think up. Feeble, really.'

'Quite inventive though. Did you? Get a hostess trolley?'

'No. But we got one of those coffee percolators that looked like something out of a chemistry lab.'

'Cona. Yeah, we had one of those. Who did you marry?'

'Nobody you'd know. Alec Partridge. He was older than me, went to King Ed's. He's dead now. Coronary.'

'I'm sorry.'

'No need. We were divorced. He'd upgraded to a newer

model by the time he keeled over. Had another family, had another life. Who did you marry?'

'Janet Coleman.'

I thought we'd both die laughing. Every time we stopped and tried to speak it welled up again, and the only thing I could find to dry my tears was my tights.

I said, 'Very good joke. Great timing. So who did you marry really?'

He looked at me.

'You're not serious?'

But he was. Rodney Pooley had married Janet Frigging Coleman.

'Were you interested in her, when we were at school?'

'No. I was interested in Sturmey Archer 3-speed bike gears.'

'So what happened?'

'I grew up. I was a late developer. Woke up one morning and "Hey! Girls!" She had great legs, Janet.'

'I don't remember her having good legs.'

'No, I probably shouldn't have said that. They were average legs. Very average. Nothing special.'

'Did you get a hostess trolley?'

'I think we did, as a matter of fact. Never used it, as far as I can remember. Anyway, legs are not a good basis for marriage.'

'Nice for a table or a chair.'

'Right.'

'So how long did you last?'

'About nine years. We had a couple of years of guerrilla war-fare. Then she ran off to Greece for a while, looking for lurve. Rhodes. It was after we'd been to see *Shirley Valentine*. But that didn't work out. She came back and we went for marriage guidance counselling. You ever do that?'

'No, we skipped it. I just gave in. It was a relief when he went. Like having a tooth pulled. You dread it, but you want the dull throb to end. Then what happened, after the counselling?'

'We went to Spain for a holiday. I got sunstroke and she met Chucho. So that was that.'

'And your daughter stayed with you?'

'We spent a lot of money on plane tickets but, yes, mainly Min lived with me. Janet's never been very settled. Always moving apartments. The grass is always greener.'

'She still with what's-his-name?'

'Chucho? No. He didn't last long. She always seems to have a bloke in tow but I think they're just drinking buddies. I'm afraid she's a bit of a barfly, these days.'

And did it give me any pleasure to hear how my old enemy had ended up? I'm afraid it did. Just a bit.

Rod was leaving after breakfast the next morning. He offered me a lift. It wouldn't have been much out of his way. I turned him down, told him I'd bought a train ticket for Monday, which was true, and that I was going to stop off in Shrewsbury to see an old friend, which wasn't. I didn't much fancy three hours cooped up in a car, reminiscing about Peakirk and Janet Coleman. I wasn't even sure I'd want to face him again. That's the trouble with impetuous sex. You can get a paralysing attack of morning-after embarrassment.

He said, 'I do realize it was the RJ mystery that seduced you. It's a card you can only play once.' He offered me his number.

Wrote it on the little pad by the telephone. He said, 'But don't take it just to make me feel good. I won't be crushed if you don't call me. Not much, anyway.'

It doesn't get any easier, the whole boy meets girl, TV has-been meets retired business-tycoon thing. RJ had definitely oiled the wheels. If Rodney Pooley had been attending the soil management conference and chatted me up in the lift, I reckon I'd have dismissed him. Just another chancer in a cheap sports jacket.

I said, 'I will take your number but I don't know when I'll call you. It's only fair to warn you my life's been a bit of a mess lately. Did I tell you I have mice?'

'I believe you did mention it.'

'So I've got that to deal with when I get home, and a front door that won't open, and I need to find some work. And talking of messes, does the name Craig Eden mean anything to you?'

'Was he at Peakirk?'

'No, he's an actor in some soap and he's in town having a breakdown because they're not renewing his contract. Cracking up? Do it in scenic Aberystwyth! He thought he'd go missing, make them worry about him and offer him his job back. They won't, of course. That only happens in fairy stories.'

'I've never heard of him. What's he in?'

'*Cloverfields*. I've never seen it. He's been mooning around all week, pretending he doesn't want to be spotted but nobody's recognized him so now he's really depressed. It bucked me up no end, talking to him. It put things in perspective.'

'Perspective can be a very useful thing. I'm going back to my own room now, Lizzie Off The Telly. Let you get some sleep. I'm afraid I can't manage encores, these days.'

I let him go. I have a feeling I sleep with my mouth open. I have a feeling that in repose I look like that painting by Edvard Munch.

I slept very well indeed. By the time I went downstairs the lobby was full of furries in plainclothes, their fursonas packed away till the next gathering. Clacton, in March. The circus was leaving town and Rodney Pooley had already checked out.

9

I always go to Mass on Sundays. I'm not Catholic, and probably never will be, but I like to keep the possibility in play. Tom used to say I was just playing hard to get with God. He's a relaxed agnostic himself, an attitude I find baffling. I mean, either go all out and call religion a load of old wishful thinking or get down on your knees and quake. I can't understand the intermediate position.

There was a Catholic church in Aber but they seemed to be temporarily between venues so I wandered along to the Anglicans. They were friendly. A bit hand-squeezy, and I don't care for synthesizers in church, but it was them or chapel so I endured.

There's not a lot to do in Aberystwyth on a winter Sunday. I bought all the papers, a family-size bag of chocolate-covered raisins and a magazine that had an article on how to look fabulous in your fifties. They never go beyond the fifties, those articles have you noticed? After fifty-nine you fall off the edge of the world. You stand waiting to pay for a bottle of shampoo and they don't even notice you. Shop-lifting probably gets easier.

On the plus side, when you get into your sixties you don't need to shave your legs any more. You may grow a moustache but your legs are as hairless as a baby's bum. And, it turns out, you can get unexpectedly and very satisfactorily laid by someone you haven't seen in fifty years.

I was feeling very good about the Rodney Pooley episode. We'd handled it well. No promises, no regrets, and a great post-coital laugh. Very grown-up. But then I had a horrible thought. What if he told Janet about it? Exes do confide sometimes. I remember Alec telling me what a fuss Nikki was making about her pregnancy. It was his cack-handed way of paying me a belated compliment. The discarded wife who at least hadn't been a diva about heartburn and swollen ankles. And, to be fair to Nikki, she had been expecting twins. But I didn't want Janet Coleman Pooley knowing my business, even if she was a sun-damaged old soak.

I went through all the papers and there was still no mention of a nation-wide hunt for me or for Craig Eden.

I packed my bag and went to bed early to make the morning come sooner. Farewell, Aberystwyth. Farewell, grey, gritty beach. Farewell, Terwyn Price, Aneurin Pugh and Rhodri Ellis, whoever you were.

When I got off the train at New Street I didn't go straight home. I went round the shops and bought Berry Naughty nail varnish and some not quite so big knickers.

I'd been away a week but there was nothing in the letterbox apart from Special Offers junk.

GET YOUR WHEELS BALANCED IN TIME FOR THE FESTIVE SEASON!

Nothing in the fridge either, except milk that had turned to curds and whey, and one egg I wasn't sure I wanted to risk. The light was flashing on the phone, though. Four messages. So I had been missed after all.

Hawthorn Dental Practice. 'Mrs Partridge, you missed an appointment with the hygienist.' Damnation. They'd bill me for that.

And then Tom. Would I be in later? That was Wednesday. Would I kindly let him know when I'd be at home? That was Thursday. Hellfire, Lizzie, don't you ever listen to your messages? That was Friday.

Well, what was another hour? I disinterred a mysterious ice-clad item from the freezer. It turned out to be fish fingers, bought for Noah and never eaten. On the rare occasions he sets foot in my house he brings his own crudités. Ellie doesn't want him acquiring bad eating habits. This is the girl who used to add brown sauce and melted cheese to a perfectly good bacon sandwich.

Fish fingers with malt vinegar and tinned peas. That is a winning combination. There are times when you just have to shove the balsamic where the Emilia-Romagna sun don't shine.

I called Tom.

He said, 'You took your time.'

'I've been away.'

'I got those bait-boxes you wanted.'

'Did I ask you to get them?'

'Yes. Several times. You left messages. You were in a panic about mice.'

'Sorry. I forgot. Do you want me to pick them up?'

'No, I'll drop them round. Unless you're going away again.'

'If you're coming today could you bring me some milk? And bread.'

'Anything else?'

'Eggs, chocolate digestives.'

'On a health kick, are we?'

You can always tell when Tom's annoyed. His voice goes all tight.

It was dark by the time he came. Straight down to business. Where did I think the mice were? I showed him where I'd seen something move. He was down on his knees with a bait-box. He said, 'I can't smell mice. You can usually smell them.'

'Maybe it was a spider. A very big spider.'

'A bait-box won't deal with spiders.'

'I definitely saw something move.'

'It was probably this.'

He had something in his hand.

'What is it?'

'A ball of fluff and hair and general crap. Look at it. It's like tumbleweed. When was the last time you cleaned the floor in here?'

'I don't know.'

'Not since I left by the look of it. It's disgusting, Lizzie. I'll put these boxes down but I don't think you've got mice. I don't think any self-respecting mouse would move in.'

I offered him a drink but he was driving.

'Have you been somewhere nice?'

'Wales. I needed to get away, do some thinking.'

'Oh, yes? Did you reach any conclusions?'

'That my life isn't over yet.'

'Good. Then you'll have time to push a broom over this floor.'

'How's Sally?' I thought I might as well get it over with. Find out if it was Goodbye For Ever or See You Around, Maybe.

'Sally?' he said. 'Why do you ask?'

'Because the last time I spoke to you, you were out shopping for her and you got a parking ticket.'

'That's right. Two minutes and I'd have made it back to the car. Bloody dog.'

'What dog?'

'Sally. Tessa and Simon's. She's still a pup.'

'They got a puppy while they're staying with you? That's cheeky.'

'Well, they'd already paid for her. They were committed. We thought their building work would be finished by now.'

'Their building work won't ever be finished. You're saddled with them for life, Tom. Them and their dog. You'll be in your grave and they still won't have a roof on their house. Well, they will. They'll have yours.'

'One thing about you, Lizzie, you always think the best of people. That's a very sexy colour you've painted your nails. Is there something you want to tell me?'

'Such as?'

'A new gentleman friend?'

'Would you mind if I did?'

'Of course not. Well, a bit. So, have you?'

'No. Just new nail varnish. Want to stay for scrambled eggs?'

'I shouldn't. Simon's away, Tessa's working late and I've left the dog. She chews things.'

'What brand is she?'

'Beagle. You know my leather chair?'

'Chewed?'

'Ruined.'

'Why do you put up with it?'

'What else can I do?'

'Tell them to bugger off to a pet-friendly hotel. That'd speed up the building work.'

'You never liked Simon. I got along with Ellie but you never liked either of my boys.'

That wasn't strictly true. I didn't mind Christopher, although he's a bit of an oddity. Doesn't date girls, doesn't date boys. The only thing that gets him excited is cycling. He goes all round the country, pedalling like a demon. Never sees anything of interest because he's always bent over his handlebars. Sometimes he does sponsored rides in aid of Cancer Research, in memory of his mum. He's all right. But Simon's a different matter. He's got his eye on his dad's money. Not that Tom's got much, but there'll be the house. If Tom and I had ever thought of getting married, Simon and Tessa would have found a way to queer it. Tom can't see it but they're banking on a nice fat legacy and they don't want him dipping into their mess of pottage.

'How long have they been living with you now?'

'I'm not discussing it. You have to help your kids if you can, even when they're grown-up. You'd have Ellie here if she needed a place to stay.'

'Ellie would live in a tent in Cannon Hill Park sooner than move in with me.'

'I don't think so. Well, seeing the state of this kitchen, per-haps you're right. How's Noah?'

'Oh, you know. Playing first-chair tambourine in the crèche orchestra. Solved Fermat's Theorem during his afternoon nap. He's been offered a place at Cambridge only they don't have any booster seats.'

'You're lucky to have a grandchild. Have you done some-thing different? Is it your hair?'

'It needs cutting.'

'Looks okay to me. Did you change your pancake?'

Pancake! Tom's so old-fashioned sometimes. He has a com-puter. He can do emails and everything but he calls tights 'stockings'. He calls a jacket and skirt a 'costume'.

I said, 'Nobody wears pancake, these days. It's called founda-tion. But no. I was in Aberystwyth. It's probably the sea air. It perks you up.' But more likely, I thought, what you're noticing are the effects of being wooed, seduced and royally laid by Rodney Pooley.

'Aberystwyth?' he said. 'An interesting choice.'

'Like I said, the location didn't matter. I just needed to get away.'

If Tom wanted us to give it another try, would I? I might. He's a very decent man. Not complicated. You'd look at him and think, There's an old geezer in a cardigan, but he's in good shape. He's got a rowing machine. It was the first item he brought when he moved in here and the first item he took back to his house when we split up, and it weighs a ton, so I knew he really meant it, about leaving.

Why did he go? He said my sneery attitude to people got him down. He said when he met me I came across as a very different person. That was because he'd seen me on the telly before he ever met me in person. You're all eyes and teeth and energy in front of the cameras. You have to be. The viewers don't know it's taken an hour in Makeup to get you looking halfway human. They don't know how deep you've had to dig when your husband's just left you and the producer's given your Buttery Chicken the slot immediately after a piece on heart disease.

It was the meringue incident that really hooked Tom. Meringue-gate. And not only Tom. I got some very appreciative letters after that, and quite a few X-rated ones among them. I know some people think the whole thing was planned. It wasn't. You could plan something like that but viewers would sense it. They're not stupid. Well, I suppose by the law of averages some of them must be.

It was my last show so they'd put me in the final slot, for a nice chummy Gather Round 'n' Taste while the credits were rolling. Chocolate and raisin refrigerator cake, a mocha ginger pavlova and a chocolate rum mousse. Valerie Tobin had been on earlier with her Bikini Action Plan Diet. Not a great advert for skimpy beachwear, our Valerie. She had no breasts. Just a prominent sternum and a very scraggy neck.

She didn't even pretend to try my desserts. Not a nibble. She was such an ungracious bag of bones. Kim was presenting that morning and she lived in fear of putting on an ounce, but even she went through the motions. Tobin could have put a sliver in her mouth and run straight to the loo to upchuck as soon as we were off the air. But, no, she had to steal the moment, making a little speech about healthier eating. And before I knew it I found myself stealing the moment right back. I intended to sock her in the mouth with a forkful of cake but I missed and just clipped her nose, enough to draw blood.

I didn't expect her to retaliate. I wouldn't have thought she had it in her. Damn me if she didn't knock out two of my teeth. Well, that did it. I had nice teeth. Everybody said so. After that it was all a red haze but apparently I smashed her face into the pavlova. Kim tried to pull me off her, the floor manager pulled Kim off me, and I succeeded in squashing dear Valerie's face up against a camera in those last few seconds while it was still rolling. I gave a face full of mousse to anyone in range, too, but sadly that happened off air. Security were called. They were laughing but they still incarcerated me in the Green Room for ages. Then the police came. Tobin wanted me charged with assault. Kim talked her out of it, pointed out that sometimes bad publicity can turn out to be very good publicity. She knew the switchboard was flooded with calls. The viewers had enjoyed our little scrap.

I'd asked the PA to contact Hegarty for me but he wasn't answering, sleeping off a heavy meeting, no doubt. When they finally let me go it was Tom who was waiting for me in Reception. He was still in his carpet slippers. After he'd seen the fight he'd come straight to the studio to drive me to a dentist or wherever I wanted to go. He thought I was brilliant.

'Serve that Tobin woman right,' he kept saying. 'I wouldn't be surprised if they offered you your job back.'

But they never did.

Anyway, Tom and I ended up in bed that very night, me with a fat lip and a temporary bridge. But at least I didn't have a sternum like an emaciated pheasant's.

10

My first thought about the raccoon was that I wouldn't phone him. I'd let him make the next move. My next thought was, how could he? I hadn't given him my number. Could he get my number? Am I in the phone book? Do people even have phone books any more? So then I thought I would call him, but only after a few weeks, or definitely no sooner than one week. I'd keep it light and casual, no expectations. And in the meantime I'd put his number away, somewhere out of sight, lest I got tempted in a moment of weakness and gave completely the wrong impression. That was when I discovered I didn't have his number.

I was fairly certain I hadn't left it on the pad in the hotel. I thought I remembered tearing it off. Where had I put it? I turned out my suitcase, my bag, my pockets, the kitchen bin, my bag again. Nothing. One way of looking at it was I'd been saved from myself. It had been a brief encounter, seasoned with mystery, nicely rounded off with a surprise and a good laugh. An unlooked-for little bonus for a woman with a bunion and midriff bulge. But, no, I couldn't let it rest. I wanted to have his number or some other information about him, some remnant, fragment, to make him real and then forget about him. Perhaps.

I abandoned Operation Clean-up and called my mother. I said, 'I'm sorry I haven't phoned. I've been away.'

'Have you? Did I know?'

'It was spur-of-the-moment. Aberystwyth.'

'Your dad and I went to Abersomewhere once.'

'I remember. Aberglaslyn. In the three-wheeler. Thirty miles an hour top speed. There must have been tailbacks behind you all the way to Oswestry. Wilf Clarke, Road Hog.'

'Mrs Sanderson passed away.'

'So, another funeral.'

'There'll be nobody left to come to mine. Philip's not feeling too good. He had the flu jab. I told him not to.'

'Why? You should have one as well.'

'I don't want one. You don't know what's in them.'

'Do you remember the Pooleys?'

'Who?'

'A family called Pooley. They had a boy my age, Rodney, and a girl a bit younger.'

'No. I don't remember them. Now listen to this. Mrs Sanderson is having a cardboard coffin.'

'Very sensible. A lot of people are doing it.'

'Well, I think it's disgusting. You'd better not put me in one.'

'Your coffin is nothing to do with me. You said you were leaving all that to Philip. The Pooleys had a car. Actually, they might have had two because Mrs Pooley used to drive the kids to school and back.'

'And then listen to this, they're taking her all the way out to Leominster to bury her in a field.'

'Are you sure it's not a woodland memorial grove?'

'It's not a proper cemetery.'

'You mean it doesn't have neglected tombstones and dead chrysanthemums? Sounds lovely.'

'Sounds barmy to me. Of course, she always had to be different.'

Oh, yes. Hilda Sanderson, *enfant terrible*. The first woman on Glenville Close to wear slacks. The first to get an eau-de-Nil front door.

'So you don't remember the Pooleys?'

'No. Why?'

'I bumped into him while I was away. Rodney. Will you go to Mrs Sanderson's funeral?'

The exasperated sigh of a woman who thinks funerals should be vanilla. *Abide With Me*, ashes to ashes, etc., but she can't bear to miss one, even when the coffin's made of cardboard. 'I suppose I shall have to put in an appearance. Eleanor was going to come to see me on the weekend but I told her not to bother.'

'Why?'

'Her little one does run about so.'

'His name's Noah.'

'I know what his name is, thank you very much. Andrew would have been a nice name, or John.'

My mum has four great-grandsons and there's not an Andrew or a John among them. Philip's daughter Kayleigh has been the main purveyor of babies and it's possible she's not finished yet. I doubt Ellie plans to have another child, what with her career and everything, but I think the onward journey of some of the Clarke genes is safe in Kayleigh's hands. There's Scott too, although he's not breeding yet.

They were young when Yvonne died. Scott was eight or nine, Kayleigh was twelve going on twenty. We all did what we could to help because Philip was floundering, but they needed their mum and they couldn't have her. Yvonne had shaped those kids. Scott, being male, was presumed to be helpless. He was a tough little nut. I think he knew, deep down, that he wasn't helpless but what can you do when your mother keeps rearranging your hair and tutting? After she died he stuck to his dad like glue. Philip could hardly go to the toilet without Scott waiting for him outside the door. They were two boys drowning in shallow water.

Kayleigh was different. When Yvonne was alive they used to go shopping together every Saturday, buying clothes that were too young for Yvonne and way too old for Kayleigh. For the first year after her mum died Kayleigh had a go at replacing her, telling her dad what needed doing, remembering which day the bins had to be put out. Until she discovered boys. Mainly the kind that rides his bike with no hands and looks old enough to buy cigs and Strongbow without any questions being asked.

You name it, Kayleigh did it. She gave her dad a few years of hell, skipping school, hanging out with one loser after another. Then Wendy clickety-clacked into Philip's life and that seemed to give Kayleigh a cold shower. Wendy was happy to leave ring marks on the kitchen counters and let a cleaning woman deal with them once a week. This reawakened the Inner Yvonne in Kayleigh. There was a brief power struggle, J-cloths at dawn, then Kayleigh walked away and set up her own establishment with Kev, who is an all-round diamond geezer and CORGI-certified gas engineer.

Kev and Kayleigh have three boys now, all with names that perplex my mother just as much as Noah's does: Reece, Ryan and Brandon. And Kayleigh has become her own woman. She runs a tight, well-scrubbed ship and she has all her Christmas shopping done by 1 October, but in the raising of her sons she's discarded her mother's ideas. She doesn't believe the Y chromosome necessarily causes helplessness. Reece, Ryan and Brandon were all making their own beds by the time they started school. You could send any one of them to SPAR and they'd know the difference between skimmed and semi-skimmed. Unlike their granddad Philip. Yvonne would be very proud of her.

I said, 'Noah's a very fashionable name, these days.'

'I wouldn't know about that,' said my mother. 'I don't keep up with trends. All I know is he dashes about and I'm worried he'll fall and hurt himself.'

It's her furniture she's concerned about really. She started off with two little side tables and over the years they've multiplied. As soon as she turns out the lights and goes to bed they're at it, propagating. Getting from one side of her living room to the other is like a slalom course.

'You needn't worry about Noah. He's made of that hard kind of rubber they use for balls. I reckon if you bounced him he'd hit the ceiling.'

Given the opportunity to move, Noah grabs it. It's because he spends so much of his life strapped into the back of a car. Top-of-the-range kiddie seat, Toyota built like a tank. He sees the world flashing past his shatter-proof window and he wants a slice of it. So the minute he's freed he's jumping around like a flea at a fair.

'And you know Eleanor won't allow him to have a biscuit. She says sugar is a drug. I know she went to college but I do wonder where she gets some of her ideas.'

My daughter, the former spliff-puffer and jelly-baby scoffer, now surveys us from the dietary high ground.

'I know. To listen to Ellie, you'd wonder how the human race has flourished for so long.'

'I told her, when we had the rationing, you'd have killed for a bit of sugar. Your father and I had to make do with a cardboard wedding cake. You don't mean the Pooleys who lived on Carisbrooke Road?'

'Possibly. I only knew one lot of Pooleys. What do you remember about them?'

'Nothing. They had that detached house. He was probably some type of higher-up. They weren't people me and your father would have mingled with.'

Sometimes my mother's choice of words fills me with joy. They can be so brilliantly wide of the mark. Let us be clear, my parents didn't mingle with anyone, ever. Mingling was what people did at cocktail parties. 'I'd better go and mingle'; 'Don't just stand there, Wilf. Mingle!'

In fact, as a family we were actively anti-mingle. We kept ourselves to ourselves. A lot of people did in those days. It was a precaution. At some point in her life my mum had learned that social mingling can lead to all kinds of unwished-for consequences, the most terrifying of which was people getting too close, too presumptuous. You have a friendly word with someone over a glass of sherry and the next thing you know they'll be on your doorstep wanting to borrow a shilling for the gas meter.

I said, 'Just remind me, what kind of people did you mingle with?'

'I can hear that tone in your voice. We didn't need to mingle. We were all right as we were. Your father had a very delicate stomach. He couldn't have coped with banquets and swarees.'

'He used to eat pork pie with piccalilli for his breakfast on Christmas morning. That's not for the faint-hearted. Did you ever go to any parties? I don't recall you ever going out in the evening.'

'How could we? Your dad worked shifts. We used to see your Auntie Edie and Uncle Cyril. And there was Jean and Dennis, next door. We were neighbourly with them.'

'Jean and Dennis? Don't bring their names up. He was a flasher.'

'I don't know what you mean. He certainly was not.'

'Mum, he showed me his willy and paid me half a crown not to tell anyone. How many times have I told you?'

'I'm not listening.'

'Fine, don't listen. You know it's true. I can remember it like it was yesterday. *Housewives' Choice* was on the wireless, Guy Mitchell was singing "She Wears Red Feathers And a Huly-Huly Skirt" and Uncle Dennis showed me his organ. And it was in full working order. As I now realize. Still, the half-crown hush money was welcome.'

'Goodbye.'

Click.

I mean, they say it's best to tell somebody about these child-hood traumas, get them off your chest instead of lugging them around with you all your life. I don't think I was too scarred by watching Uncle Dennis jerk off but I might have been. Bad enough I had to witness it without being called a liar into the bargain.

So, the Pooleys lived on Carisbrooke Road, which was substantially superior to our street. They had proper front gardens. I bet the chipper van never turned down that way.

My mother called me back later. I apologized for upsetting her about Uncle Dennis. I don't know why. Not my fault he couldn't keep his old todger to himself.

Mum said, 'I'm not going to talk about that. Now, I spoke to Doris Green. She said the Pooleys left under a cloud.'

'Really? What do you think she meant by that?'

'There was talk.'

'About anything in particular?'

'She didn't say.'

'Okay. Did you phone her specially?'

'No. I'm getting a lift with her to Mrs Sanderson's . . . send-off. Doris's son's going to drive us.'

Muriel Clarke, arbiter of funerary arrangements. If you're in a wooden box it's a funeral. If you're in a carton it's a send-off.

11

I called Chas.

He said, 'Louie's up north. He started rehearsals yesterday. There's a landline in the place he's staying.'

Louie does have a mobile but he hardly ever answers it. He thinks it's infra dig to be so available. Sometimes I think he's right.

A woman answered. She said she thought he was in bed but she'd go and see. It was only nine o'clock. I heard him shuffling to the phone.

He said, 'Lizzie, I'm dead.'

They'd had him dancing all day. He had two numbers to learn. One with Cinderella and then a big ensemble piece for the finale when he'd have to sing and dance at the same time.

'Too many clotted-cream teas?'

'Fuck you, too many cream teas, Lizzie Partridge. I'm not overweight. I'm compactly built. These dances are just ridiculous. I'll be a wraith by January.'

'Who was the woman?'

'Girl, dear. A child, practically. She's one of the chorus. They're all very young and they all have very long legs. I was going to soak my poor bod in Radox but the bathroom's full of dripping Lycra. I might have to make other living arrangements. I think I'll spring for a little place of my own. It's an allowable expense.'

'Are they all girls?'

'Two of each. The boys are divine, of course. So fit. And they depilate.'

'Does Chas know?'

'That I'm living with oiled and hairless beefcake? No, and he doesn't need to. When he comes up to see the show we'll kip at the Whitley Bay Ritz. So what's new with you?'

'Well, since you ask, I ran away. I tried to disappear from my shitty life but you didn't notice.'

'Gosh, I'm sorry. I thought I spoke to you recently. How long were you gone?'

'A week.'

'Not long enough. Unless you're on Twitter. If you were tweeting every five minutes you'd be missed a lot quicker. But I'm sorry I didn't worry about you.'

'You weren't the only one. Actually, not one single person noticed I'd gone. I spent a week skulking in Aberystwyth and nobody wondered where I was.'

'Aberystwyth? Now I feel really terrible.'

'Good. So you should. But I'm feeling much better now. And I did get unexpectedly laid.'

'Whoa! Rewind to "skulking in Aberystwyth".'

'Have you ever heard of fur-suiters?'

'No, but I can't wait.'

'They dress up as animals and cartoon characters. They have conventions and weekend get-togethers.'

'Why?'

'So they can hang out, compare costumes.'

'I'm still listening.'

'I was staying in this hotel where they were having a fur-suit convention, and there was a guy dressed up as a raccoon. A cartoon raccoon.'

'Oh, my goodness, where is this going? Did you . . . ?'

'Let me finish. So, he seemed interested in me but I thought he must be gay because they nearly all are . . .'

'Now I'm really listening.'

'But he wasn't gay so, yes, we did, eventually, and then afterwards, post-coitally as you might say, I discovered we used to go to the same school.'

'You mean when he took off his raccoon mask?'

'No, no. You don't wear those costumes in bed. They'd get ruined. I didn't recognize him because I hadn't seen him in fifty years. He was a pimply berk when we were previously acquainted. Not even acquainted, really.'

'Heavens. And now he's a senior citizen who dresses up as a cartoon character. Gosh, Lizzie, you do find them. Is he married?'

'Divorced.'

'Makes sense. It wouldn't be every marriage that could accommodate a raccoon.'

'And the funny thing is, I knew her too. His ex.'

'It's a horribly small world.'

'I mean, if I'd known who he was I probably wouldn't have . . . But he was great in bed.'

'Did he take a pill?'

'I don't think so.'

'I bet he did. A guy his age.'

'No, it was a chemically unaided performance made possible by my surprising reserves of sex appeal.'

'Okay. Well done, you. And now you're going to tell me you're thinking of getting a furry suit. How about being Benny the Ball? I can coach you to do the voice.'

'The thing is, I've lost his phone number.'

'That's okay. He'll find you if he wants to.'

'You don't think I should try Directory Enquiries?'

'No. Play it cool. But. Lizzie, you're full of surprises. And poor old Tom. Ousted by a raccoon.'

'No, he wasn't. He'd already ousted himself, and now he's stuck with non-paying, ungrateful lodgers and a beagle that chews. And don't say, "Tom was so nice."'

'Well, he was. And I'm not sure if I like the sound of this dude. What the heck is a raccoon anyway?'

'It looks like a cross between a fox and a panda.'

'Thank goodness you're no longer breeding. That would have taken miscegenation a step too far.'

'Shall I come up for the show? Can you comp me?'

'Darling girl, I'd love to see you, but don't decide yet. If I have many more days like today I'll be a stretcher case and they'll have to get some soap-opera nobody to step into my dancing pumps.'

'Speaking of which, have you ever heard of an actor called Craig Eden?'

'No.'

'He was in Aberystwyth too. Just got written out of some soap, feeling unappreciated, worried about his Visa bill. He was hoping to raise a hue and cry, too, but nobody seemed to be searching for him. Sad, really. How are they billing you on the posters? Does it say Former TV Astrologer?'

'It doesn't need to. I'm a household name. And I'm not sure I like you talking about my billing and an out-of-work basket case in the same breath.'

'So you don't think I should try to find Rodney?'

'Who's Rodney?'

'The raccoon.'

'You mean follow his paw prints? No. Let him do the tracking. It's what males like to do.'

I did try Directory Enquiries. It's not my fault if Louie regularly fails to give me the advice I want to hear. I thought if there was just one R. Pooley in the Nuneaton area I'd get the number and put it somewhere safe but I wouldn't call him. At least, not straight away. But it turned out there were quite a few Pooleys and he might not even have been one of them. He might be ex-directory. And, anyway, what if I was misremembering everything about him, except that he used to be a berk with a briefcase?

My brother called. Philip always sounds like he has a cold. He has this range of expressive sniffs. The weary snuffle. The angry, sharp intake. And his favourite: the long, slow, more-in-sorrow-than-in-anger nose sigh.

'About Christmas,' he said. 'I wish you'd have a word with your daughter.'

Mid-November and the battle lines were forming.

I said, 'I have no idea what Ellie's doing for Christmas.'

'Not coming here, that's what. Can't even spare an hour or two to spend with her nana on Christmas Day. Nor Boxing Day.'

'So you've already spoken to her.'

'Somebody had to. You weren't answering your phone.'

'I was away.'

'You should tell me when you're not going to be around. What if something happened to Mum?'

'Well, it didn't. I've spoken to her, she's fine. And what's so urgent about Christmas?'

'Wendy needs to know what size bird to order.'

'And Ellie has said they're not coming, so now you know. That's three helpings less. Or two and a quarter.'

'It could be Mum's last Christmas.'

'It could be anybody's last Christmas. Anyway, I don't think Mum will mind. You'll have Kayleigh's boys there. And you know she finds Noah very tiring. Kids his age are better off staying at home. They get overexcited. Ellie's not coming. Fine. Untwist your knickers.'

'How about you?'

'Do you really want me?'

'It's not a question of *wanting* you. It's a question of doing the right thing.'

'Tell you what, I'll have Mum if you like. She can come here for a change.'

'I don't think so. She does enjoy her turkey and I know what you're like. You always have to be different.'

WOMAN ROASTED OVER CHRISTMAS GOOSE.

'I can give her a nice Christmas.'

109

'No, you won't. You'll do something fancy.'

'You don't know that. I might do sausage and mash.'

'She's coming here, Lizzie. We don't know how much longer we'll have her.'

TRAGIC PENSIONER DENIED LAST TURKEY DINNER.

'Fine. How about if I come over for a couple of hours in the morning? Or even after dinner. You don't have to feed me.'

It wasn't that Wendy was a bad cook. It was just such a squeeze around their table, and I always seemed to end up sitting on a kiddie stool.

'Well,' he said, deep sniff of disgust, 'I suppose we shall have to be grateful, if that's all the time you can spare.'

I told him to count me in for dinner.

The best time to catch Ellie is between 9.30 p.m. when Noah finally gives up the fight and falls asleep and 9.45 when she starts checking her evening emails. She kept yawning.

I said, 'You sound tired.'

'Yes,' she said. 'I have a three-year-old.'

I said, 'Funny, I didn't lose much sleep when you were that age. It was when you were fourteen you kept me awake. I gather Philip's spoken to you about Christmas.'

'Did he? Oh, yeah. He makes such a bloody fuss about it. About not being there for Nana. She doesn't care.'

'That's what I said.'

'Anyway, we're going to Nat's parents.'

'But they don't do Christmas.'

'What do you mean?'

Nat's people are Jewish. Not Jewish in the yarmulke-and-two-kitchen-sinks sense. But I don't think they eat pork, and when the grandfather died there were no funeral flowers. They're kind of selectively Jewish.

I said, 'Jews don't keep Christmas. Why would they? It's a celebration of the Messiah's birth and they're still waiting for Him to turn up.'

'Why must you be so literal?'

'Not my fault that they missed the boat. And they crucified Him.'

'That's racist. Nat's mum and dad acknowledge their roots. Doesn't mean they have to be all holy about it.'

'Does your son know he's half Jewish?'

'He's three.'

'Yes, but he's very bright. He notices things. Like, do you have a seder for Passover? Why is this night different from other nights? Has he ever heard that? Does Daddy wear a little hat with kirby grips? Not that I've ever seen.'

'Are you being like this because we're going away for Christmas?'

'Being like what? And I know for a fact you didn't have him circumcised.'

'You know nothing about any of this.'

'If you say so. I'll change the subject to something I really and truly don't know about. On a computer, if you wanted to find somebody's address or phone number, how would you go about it?'

'Who are you looking for?'

'I bumped into an old school friend. Only I've mislaid their number.'

'There's People Search. You probably have to pay to get a phone number. Or you could try Facebook. You get some older people on there.'

'I've heard of Facebook. Do I have to fill in a form or something?'

'Mum! Nobody fills in forms. You can just log on and look.'

'How do I log on?'

A sigh worthy of her Uncle Philip. 'Do you want me to look for you? What's her name?'

'It's a him. Rodney Pooley. So you do this Facebook thing?'

'Of course I do. He might be on LinkedIn as well. What's his profession?'

'I don't know. Businessman. Import and export.'

'Is he local?'

'Nuneaton. Somewhere around there. We were at school together.'

'And is this, like, casual interest? Where did you bump into him?'

'Aberystwyth.'

'Where?'

'It's in Wales.'

'I know where it is. What were you doing there?'

'Hiding. Seeing how long it'd be before anybody missed me.'

'Are you drunk?'

'Not yet. I was staying in a hotel, and he was there at a fur-suit convention. He was a raccoon.'

'You are drunk.'

'Two glasses. I could walk a line. He gave me his number and I lost it.'

'Are you and Tom definitely finished?'

'We still speak. He was here a few days ago.'

'Tom's nice.'

Everybody says that. Tom's a treasure. You shouldn't have let that one get away. Not at your age. Good men don't grow on trees.

I said, 'Yes. Nice but annoying. He washes plates before he puts them in the dishwasher. He'll drive three miles to get tea-bags a penny cheaper.'

'Nat wouldn't even know how much to pay for teabags.'

'And if he sees somebody selling the *Morning Star* he doesn't just buy a copy, which is bad enough unless you want it to line the cat's litter tray. He stands and has a friendly chat with them.'

'What's wrong with that?'

'Everything. If he must talk to them he should ask them what they've got to say about Stalin and all those other Com-mie bastards. So you reckon Facebook is the place to look?'

'Yes. And when you search, specify UK because there are probably dozens of people with that name.'

'I'll go to the library. They have computers there.'

'Why don't you get yourself a laptop?'

'Why don't you get a proper coffee-maker instead of run-ning down the street holding a cardboard cup that's cost you two quid a pop?'

'Are you going to Uncle Philip's for Christmas?'

'Yes. It's that or win the Least Considerate Daughter award

three years running. What should I get Noah? Not a book about Baby Jesus, that's for sure. How about *Hebrew for Toddlers*?'

'Get him some Lego.'

'Okay. I'll be interested to hear what you get for dinner at the Hursts.'

Their name was Hirsch originally but they changed it a couple of generations back. Pity, really. Noah Hirsch would have been a great name. Full-on Old Testament.

Ellie said, 'You're not the only person who can cook, you know. And frankly I couldn't care less what we get.'

'No burned chipolatas with your turkey. No Uncle Philip sweating over the carving like it's brain surgery. "Scalpel, retractors, swab. Swab, Wendy!" Maybe not even any defeated sprouts. You lucky, lucky girl.'

She laughed.

12

Today's mission: to buy my grandson a tasteful and worthy Christmas gift. Also something to take to Philip and Wendy's on Christmas Day. But what? I gave them a really nice panettone one year, but by the time they'd had it checked out by sniffer dogs and opened it, it was stale. If I take wine, I'm the only one who drinks it. Philip's tipple is zero-calorie cola and Wendy nips at a perpetually replenished gin and orange while she's cooking. She gets quite rosy and devil-may-care.

NAIL TECHNICIAN IN MAGIMIX HORROR WAS TWICE OVER LEGAL LIMIT.

You used to be able to find something suitable in Rackham's food hall. Quail eggs or smoked eel or a nice piece of Stilton. But it's not Rackham's any more and it's not really a food hall. It's a Food on the Go concept.

I decided on the retro, gently ironic route for Philip and Wendy. A box of Christmas crackers, the cheap ones, a tin of Quality Street and a bottle of Irish cream liqueur. If it's sweet and creamy my mother doesn't consider it to be the demon drink, and I dream that some day, under the influence, she'll surprise us all. She might flout my brother's health and safety regulations and get up and boogie.

I bought Noah a kind of construction kit. It said suitable for ages five to eight but Ellie says he's way ahead of his peers. It must be tough raising a genius. And I do wonder how popular my daughter is at the crèche gate.

The library was my last stop. The computers were all in use. They said I'd have to wait my turn so I went for a mooch around the bookshelves. They had a copy of *In the Kitchen* and it hadn't been taken out since 2007. It's definitely time to relaunch my career.

One of the computers was vacated. I asked the librarian whether there was anyone who could help me with it but she said computers weren't her job. I felt sorry for her, really. She was old enough to remember a time when libraries were silent and lined with books. All she had to do was stamp the date, ker-chunk, and maybe put you on the standby list for the latest Denise Robins. Now the place is full of mouth-breathers with bottles of energy drink. There's a tepee, too, and a dressing-up box and a kids' events co-ordinator. When I was a child a library was a welcome alternative to the crushing boredom of Glenville Close but you have to lure them in now. You have to offer them An Event.

I sat down at the computer. The guy next to me was playing a card game. I asked him how to turn it on.

He said, 'Already on.' Didn't even look away from his screen.

A girl slid into the station the other side of me. She reminded me of Ellie before she got so serious-minded. Crimson hair. Droopy sleeves. Chewing gum.

I said, 'Do you have five minutes to help an idiot?'

'Sure,' she said, and pulled up her chair. She said I had a lot of windows open.

'Is that like saying I have a screw loose?'

'No,' she said. 'You've just been clicking too much.'

So I told her the story – chance encounter with someone from school days, lost phone number – and she was rattling away on the keyboard. She had Facebook on the screen in about two seconds. How do they do that?

She couldn't find Rodney Pooley. Not the one I was looking for at any rate. 'Anybody else?'

I said, 'His daughter has a business. She makes costumes. Animals.'

'What's her name?'

'Minnie Pooley. Might be Maxine. Her business is called Dragon something.'

Rattle, rattle, click, click.

'Dragon Dreams, Bedworth. That her?'

And there she was. Minnie, in the same lizard bomber jacket but the streak in her hair was blue.

'That is dope,' she said. 'Does she make this stuff for, like, films?'

'She might do. But mainly for people who like dressing up as dragons.'

'Radical. Let's see if her dad's a Friend.'

He wasn't. But Mave and Merv were.

I said, 'I know them. I didn't realize they were friends with her.'

'They might not be. You can be a Friend on Facebook. Doesn't mean you actually know them. So do you want to message her? Ask her for her dad's number?'

'I'm not sure. Will everyone be able to see what I write?'

'Depends. On her settings.'

I didn't know what to do. I hadn't expected it to be that easy. I said I'd think about it. She swung back to her own computer, left me staring at the screen. Did I or did I not want to contact Rodney Pooley? I never seem to get it right with men. Either they run a mile or they're all over me like Virginia creeper.

She said, 'Tell you what. She's got a website. Click on the link, see, like this? Bring up the contact page. There's her mobile. You could just call her. Get her dad's number. Right?'

I said, 'You've been very helpful.'

''S okay,' she said. 'My nan's a bit twilight about computers too.'

So, I had Rod's daughter's business number, written down and tucked into my wallet. And as soon as I was that close to being able to call him, I didn't desperately want to any more. Louie was dead right. Let the raccoon do the hunting.

I got the address for Izzard Sykes while I was in the library too. They published *In the Kitchen*. It was high time they heard from me. Tom used to say I'd allowed things to slide. Rested on my laurels. 'You're very talented, Lizzie,' he used to say, 'but so are a lot of other people. If you want to get back into television you're going to need sharp elbows.'

But in those days I was enjoying being a couple again. We'd go off for mini-breaks. We'd get up on a Monday morning, Tom'd say, 'Fancy a few days in Kent, try some oysters?' or 'Look. Flights to Nice from £4.99' and off we'd go. I couldn't have done that if I'd had a cooking gig. You may only be on for seven minutes but you're there for hours, setting up, getting dicked about over the running order, waiting for Makeup to have an empty chair. It was fun. I liked talking to the camera. It's much easier than talking to real people. I didn't even mind feeling sick as we came out of the commercial break, in case I forgot what I was supposed to say. I never did forget. And after you've finished you feel great. You're floating, flying, and ravenous. Louie and I used to go for a big fry-up in the studio canteen after the show.

So the question was, what to propose to Izzard Sykes? The Mediterranean diet is old hat. They say Scandinavia is about to have a moment but I wouldn't have anything to offer there. Very big on dill, the Scandinavians, that's all I know. Maybe something English? Old-fashioned English comfort food. Steak and kidney. Bread-and-butter pudding. Men like that stuff. Or cooking for one. There are a lot of divorcees around nowadays. People can get fed up with the ping of the microwave. That was it. Cooking for one.

I was pretty sure Alec's old typewriter was in the attic. The trouble was, so were several tons of other forgotten junk. The first thing that happened was the opening rod for the loft door came away in my hand. I was standing on a step-ladder trying to coax the trapdoor open when I heard somebody calling, 'Anyone at home?'

My son-in-law, Nat.

He said, 'I just picked Noah up from Sensory Play. Thought we'd pop in and say hello. What are you doing?'

'Trying to get into the attic.'

'It looks rather dangerous.'

'You're supposed to say, "Move aside, leave it to me." '

'Sorry. I'm not very good on ladders.'

'Where's Noah?'

'Asleep in the car. Shall I bring him in? Or?'

Just what I needed. A jammed loft door and a grizzling three-year-old. 'I'll put the kettle on.'

'Not for me. Unless you've got rooibos?'

Noah was red-faced and extremely pissed off about being woken. We laid him on the sofa and he went back to sleep.

'What's Sensory Play?'

'Squishy bags. Sand foam. It's an exploring experience. Nothing too structured. So how are . . . things?'

Then I knew this was no chance drive-by on the way home from squishy bags. Dr Nat had been instructed to make a house call and ascertain whether I'd finally lost my mind.

I said, 'Things are fine. Apart from not being able to get into my attic. I thought I had vermin but it turned out I just had fluff balls, so that was nice.'

'Ellie mentioned you'd been away.'

'Yes. Wales. The seaside.'

'Feeling a bit low, were you?'

'No, I wouldn't say "low". I'd say I was feeling rock-bottom miserable. Worried about money, lonely, unappreciated. I never hear from my daughter, my brother drives me nuts and my mother is like a humungous black hole of . . . stuff. Joy, affection, stuff.'

'Mm, mm,' he said. He kept nodding. They probably have a whole class in nodding and mm-mm-ing in psychiatry school. They probably have a whole module.

He said, 'Ellie does work terribly long hours. But I hear what you say, Lizzie. We should see more of you. It's just the weekends are so busy.'

'But it's okay. I'm feeling much, much better now.'

'That's good. That's great. A change of scene can be so beneficial.'

Noah opened one rheumy eye and glared at me.

'Has he got another cold?'

Erk. Loaded question. Shouldn't have said 'another'.

'It's catarrh.'

'Like his great-uncle Philip. He had his adenoids done when he was a kid but it didn't make a lot of difference. He still sounds like an elephant with its trunk in a knot.'

'It's just that Ellie wondered . . . She thought you seemed a bit . . . When she spoke to you. A bit . . .'

'She thought I was drunk. I wasn't. Do they still take out adenoids?'

'I don't think so. '

'So while I was in Wales I ran into an old friend, from my school days. He dresses up as a raccoon. It's his hobby.'

'That's interesting.'

'I hadn't appreciated there are grown men who do that but it takes all sorts.'

'It does indeed. It's a well-documented fetish.'

'It's not a fetish. Not in his case at any rate. One thing he definitely doesn't do in that suit is sex.'

Noah rose from the sofa like the Toddler from the Black Lagoon. 'Dat,' he said, pointing his chubby little finger at my chocolate biscuit.

Nat lunged for his Noah Survival Pack and brought out the rice cakes. Noah took one and promptly dropped it on the floor.

'Want dat,' he said, concentrating on my biscuit. That boy can go from drowsy to fully locked-on in seconds.

'But we don't eat those, do we?' said Daddy.

Noah nodded solemnly.

'Because they're full of sugar and sugar is nasty. We eat rice cakes because we want to grow up strong and healthy.'

Noah slid off the sofa and came and stood about an inch from me. I crammed the forbidden fruit into my mouth and took a sip of tea. He transferred his gaze to the biscuit tin.

I said, 'Would it be the end of the world, Nat? I won't tell if you don't.'

'Now, now, Granny,' says Nat, 'we know the rules.'

He scooped the discarded rice cake from the floor and broke out a fresh one. 'Noah,' he said. 'Look what Daddy's got.'

But Noah was trying out his powers of telekinesis on my Chocolate Digestives. His face turned pink, then red, then a kind of damson colour, and when the biccies still didn't jump out of the tin he screwed up his eyes and did a huge, room-clearing poo. Maybe it was by way of protest. Maybe he just needed to go. That child has a considerable through-put of dietary fibre.

Nat sighed and looked around for a suitable place to do the clean-up. I suggested the bathroom floor. I knew for a fact I'd wiped it recently whereas the living room, well, it had been a while. He carried Noah out of the room like a roll of lino, rigid but still yelling, 'Want dat.'

I moved my sugary poison out of sight and fetched the

construction bricks I'd just bought for him. Hell, he didn't know it was only November. Happy Christmas. Happy Hanukah. Happy Not Allowed One Sodding Biscuit Day.

When they returned Noah was chugging on a sachet of organic parsnip and apple gunk. As soon as he saw the Build-a-Bunch the parsnips went the way of the rice cake. 'Mine,' he said, and up-ended the box. So that was him sorted.

Nat said, 'So, Lizzie, you're feeling okay? Generally? That's great.'

'You're wearing your doctor hat again.'

'No.'

'You sound like you are.'

'Ellie was just a bit concerned. When you live alone it must be easy to . . .'

'Please yourself?'

'What I meant was, one could . . .'

'Lose touch with reality? Drink too much? Neglect personal hygiene? One could. But one hasn't.'

'No. Good.'

'I realize my daughter finds me exasperating. You must see a lot of that, as a shrink. Daughters, mothers.'

'No. I mean yes, family relationships can raise issues. But Ellie doesn't feel that way about you.'

'Yes, she does. The same as my mother exasperates me. It's okay. It's more a feature than a problem. I'd probably miss it if it ever stopped.'

'My mother doesn't exasperate me.'

'Sons are different. Ellie won't have this problem with Noah.'

'We're raising Noah to be gender-neutral.'

'Well, good luck with that. So, in brief, then you can close your file on me: I had a bad week. I was feeling sorry for myself. I went away, to see if my nearest and dearest missed me. They didn't. But I did meet some interesting people, including the guy dressed as a raccoon who, it turned out, used to be married to an old frenemy of mine. And now I'm fine.'

'Married to a what?'

'Frenemy. One minute she's your best pal, next thing you know she's calling you names. It's another thing girls do.'

'Was there a particular reason you were trying to get into the loft?'

'I was looking for Alec's old typewriter. I've got an idea for a cookbook. I need to write a letter.'

'A typewriter? Won't it need a ribbon or something? Do they even still make such things?'

'Why wouldn't they?'

'If you draft the letter I'm sure Ellie could get one of the secretaries to type it for you.'

'Don't worry. I'll figure it out. I should take a look in the attic anyway. Have a clear-out. God knows what's up there.'

'I think you should get someone in to fix the trapdoor. And maybe bring the stuff down for you. You shouldn't be climbing ladders.'

'Why not?'

'What if you fell?'

'What if I didn't?'

'You should have your mobile on you at all times.'

'What if you catch your hand on my gatepost and get a splinter, which leads to tetanus and cardiac arrest? Nat, this is not a good attitude. And neither is making Noah wear a helmet when he rides his trike.'

'A child's skull is very vulnerable.'

'You do know Ellie ran away to America when she was sixteen? Nicked my credit card, booked a flight, made her own way from Boston airport to Alec's place. She rode on the subway till she got to the end of the line, then asked some total stranger and quite possibly psycho murderer to phone her dad for her. She didn't get the nerve to do that by wearing junior kneepads.'

'Things were different then.'

'No, they weren't. The world's always been the same. Nice people, evil people, wonky ladders, sabre-tooth tigers. You can't spend your life in a safety harness.'

Noah presented me with his first construction. 'Yocket.'

Daddy told him it was really, really excellent. It wasn't. It was average, as yockets go. If they carry on like that Noah is going to grow up with a very inflated sense of achievement.

Nat said, 'You know, there's a man we got in to assemble our flat-pack shelves. He didn't charge much. Latvian, I think. I could arrange for him to come over. Clear the loft for you.'

'I don't know. I don't like getting men in. A woman on her own, you never know what they might try.'

He blushed.

I said, 'Now you really think I'm deluded. Further evidence for the prosecution.'

'Absolutely not. You're wise to be cautious. Rapists don't care about age or sexual attractiveness.'

'Thank you.'

'But do bear in mind what I said about your phone. You might think of getting a personal alarm too. Ellie has one.'

He started tidying away Noah's yocket.

I said, 'You might as well take it with you. Take the whole kit. I probably won't see you again before Christmas and he'll no doubt get a mountain of presents on the day so he might as well have this now.'

Noah gave me a snotty kiss, as instructed.

I whispered, 'When you're older you can come to my house and play with fire.'

13

The contents of my attic: an old suitcase of mildewed baby clothes, two moth-eaten rugs, a Betamax VCR, stacks of records, Bananarama, *Motor City Soul*, *Now That's What I Call Music*, volumes 3, 4 and 5, a squash racket that must have been Alec's, ditto a ski suit, although we never went skiing, a chest-expander contraption, probably dated from when he decided to get himself bedroom-ready for some tasty young thing; a Fisher Price cash register, a SodaStream, a small, odd-shaped and completely useless piece of linoleum, a Girl's World head customized with felt-tip pens, a broken roller blind, a Cabbage Patch doll that might be suitable for a grandson being raised gender-neutral, and a cracked dressing-table mirror.

I remembered how that had happened. It was Ellie's birthday, eleventh, I think. We were supposed to take her and a couple of her friends ten-pin bowling and Alec was more than an hour late, said something had come up at work. I think we all know what exactly came up.

I didn't make a fuss. I didn't want to ruin Ellie's day, embarrass her in front of her friends. I waited till bedtime to throw things at him. I was never much good at ball games. The only thing that hit him was a little alarm clock and he just laughed. It was the bottle of aftershave that hit the mirror.

> *Out flew the web and floated wide.*
> *The mirror crack'd from side to side.*
> *'A curse has come upon you,' cried the lady.*
> *'That's your lot.'*

It wasn't, though. Things continued to 'come up' at the office for quite a while before he moved out. And the bedroom stank of Paco Rabanne for weeks. Sometimes I think I can still smell it.

I lugged the attic contents downstairs. The car wouldn't start. It didn't even raise my hopes with a feeble cough. It was as dead as Queen Anne.

I called Tom to see if he'd take all the junk to the tip for me. As soon as I'd done it I realized it was a mistake because Tom loves a jumble sale. He came over and started appraising everything. Vinyl is coming back. Cabbage Patch dolls are collectable. You could sell the ski suit on eBay. That's a perfectly good suitcase.

I said, 'Take it all. Sell it, incinerate it. I just want it out of here.'

'So you're getting the loft insulated. About time too.'

'I'm thinking about it.'

'Do you want to come with me?'

'To the landfill?'

'Yes.'

'You mean to, like, to say goodbye to the SodaStream?'

'I thought you might like to get out for an hour. We could go to the Jumping Bean, get a cup of coffee.'

'Is this a date?'

'No.'

I dry-shampooed my hair while he loaded the car. I looked rough. Changed my shirt, twice. Still didn't look great.

We were sitting in the Bean waiting for our order when it suddenly dawned on me.

I said, 'Shit.'

'You've thrown something away and now you wish you hadn't.'

'No. The whole reason I was in the loft, the whole point of risking life and limb climbing up there, was to find Alec's old typewriter. But it wasn't there.'

'A typewriter?'

'Why does everybody say "typewriter" like that?'

'Because typewriters have gone the way of corsets and collar studs. What did you want it for?'

'To shell peas. What do you think I wanted it for?'

'If you need to write something you can do that on my computer.'

'And then?'

'And then what?'

'How does it get from your computer into the post box?'

'You can email it. Or if you want to send it the old-fashioned way you can print it off, sign it, put it in an envelope . . .'

'You have a printer?'

'Yes.'

'In your house?'

'Yes.'

'Why?'

'Why not? I use it a lot. I can print interesting stuff for the U3A group. I can print my boarding pass, if I'm flying anywhere.'

'Are you? Flying somewhere?'

'Cyprus. For Christmas.'

'Nice. Are Simon and Tessa going with you?'

'Lord, no. They're going to South Africa and I didn't fancy being on my own and lumbered with the dog. So I booked Paphos. The dog's going to the kennels. How about you?'

'I'm avoiding the doghouse. Going to Philip and Wendy's. Because.'

'Your mother.'

'Yes.'

'She'd probably be just as happy staying in her own place.'

'She would. But it's got nothing to do with happiness, Tom. It's about keeping everything the way it's always been. Have a sherry, wear your paper hat, eat your bloody pudding, fall asleep. Philip's Rules. She's eighty-nine, you know. When she goes he'll be in pieces.'

'So do you want to write your letter on my computer? Or I can do it, if you tell me what you want to say.'

'I want to write to my old publisher. I've got an idea for a new book.'

'That's great. I'll bet you've still got a lot of fans out there. What's the theme?'

'Well, I was thinking about all these older people, end up

living on their own. Even not so old ones. You know? They used to cook for a family, they've probably got casseroles big enough to feed the Household Cavalry. Gets to around six o'clock and they think, Bugger it. I'll just make a bit of toast.'

'I don't. I always make a proper meal.'

'That's because your Barbara was useless in the kitchen.'

'Who says? I never said that.'

He did. When I first knew him he used to say Barbara's idea of cooking was microwaving a macaroni cheese from the chill cabinet. Usually when somebody dies they start off on a pedestal. Then, bit by bit, the truth about them gets re-established, but in the case of Tom's wife the sequence has been reversed. It wasn't a particularly happy marriage but it wasn't an unbearable one. Like getting your teeth descaled, probably. You'd rather be doing something else but you know you need to be sensible. Raise the kids, pay the bills. He was more relieved than grief-stricken when she died but now he seems to remember her quite fondly.

I went back to Tom's to type my letter. The beagle was in a cage in the kitchen. Sally. She went crazy when she saw us. Tom said he'd set me up at the computer, then take her out for some exercise. He'd been gone half an hour when I heard a key in the door and Tessa, the daughter-in-law, walked in.

'Oh,' she said.

I said, 'I'm just using Tom's computer. He's taken your dog for a walk.'

She hovered. She said, 'I didn't know you and Tom were still . . .'

'Friends?'

'I thought you were finished.'

'Some things are never finished. Like your building work, from what I hear.'

She went to the downstairs loo and did a very angry-sounding pee. The paper got snarled up in the printer. Tom came home. Sally slunk back into her cage.

I said, 'Tessa, in my opinion your dog is depressed.'

She ignored me. She was looking at the items Tom had salvaged from my clear-out. The records, the kiddie cash register.

I said, 'Beagles are hunting dogs. They need to be out in the countryside sniffing for stuff to kill.'

She said, 'What's all this?'

'From Lizzie's attic,' says Tom. 'I'm going to put it on eBay.'

She turned to me. 'Are you moving?' she said. 'Are you selling your house?'

Tessa is one of those people whose neck turns pink when she's excited. If I was selling my house she'd be eager to pounce. Properties new to the market were catnip to Tessa. But then, what if I was reconciling with Tom and planning to sell up and make a move on her husband's inheritance prospects? That could give you neck-flush too.

I said, 'No. I'm staying put. It's not much but it's what I know. You and Simon must be longing to go home.'

Tom fetched a bottle of chenin blanc from the fridge.

I said, 'I mean, there's the expense, quite apart from anything else. Paying a mortgage on a place you can't even live in, plus the building work, plus paying your way here.'

Tom shot me a warning look.

I said, 'What is the going rate for lodgers, these days? I've no idea. Obviously you probably wouldn't charge family the commercial rate but, still, it must mount up. For food and heating.'

Tom said, 'Glass of wine, Tess?'

She said she was going out again. She had two properties to show and she didn't know what time she'd be back. He said he'd prepared a lasagne and did she want Simon to wait and eat with her?

'Whatever,' she said.

Tom unsnarled the printer.

'Well done, Lizzie,' he said. 'Now you've upset my daughter-in-law. She'll tell Simon and he'll be pissed off with me. You're such a mischief-maker.'

'I gather they're not paying to live here.'

'Drink your wine. I think I've got some olives.'

He read what I'd written.

He said, 'You're not serious?'

'You said it was a great idea.'

'The idea is good. It's the title I'm querying.'

'It's just a proposal.'

'Okay. But how well do you think this is going to sell if people have to ask for a book with the F-word in the title?'

'Like I said, it's just a suggestion. It's to get the publisher's attention. Titles are negotiable. How long has it been since Simon and Tessa moved in?'

'I can't remember.'

'Yes, you can. You left me in February, came back here, and

about five minutes later they moved in. That's nine months. You can create a new human life in that time. Single cell to fully functioning baby. All you've got to show for it is a ruined leather chair.'

'They pay for the dog's food. Simon brings in a couple of bottles if he's passing SPAR.'

'Incredible. You're a fool, Tom.'

'So I've often been told.'

'You will be glad when they go? You don't actually like having them here?'

'They're okay.'

'Really? No petty annoyances? Because you are quite an easy chap to annoy.'

'So you say.'

'On a scale of Using the Last of the Toilet Roll and Not Replacing It to, say, Playing Led Zeppelin After Lights Out, where would you put them?'

'In the middle.'

'Somewhere around Never Washing the Grill Pan?'

'They don't use the grill pan.' He smiled. 'Okay. She picks at her feet. The hard skin.'

'Like, when she's watching TV?'

'Or at breakfast even, when she's reading the paper.'

'That's gross. What else? What about Simon?'

'He hums.'

'That can be annoying. Is it always the same tune?'

'It's not really a tune. That's the thing about it. It's just a sort of one-note pom-pom-pom. I don't think he knows he's doing it.'

'Should be a capital offence. What time does he get home?'

'About half six.'

'I can help you get rid of them.'

'They're family, Lizzie. I don't want them to feel unwelcome.'

'After nine months of free lasagne and hot baths? What does Christopher think about it?'

'He hasn't said anything. I don't think he cares. You know Christopher. Did I tell you he's in training to cycle the Inca Trail next year?'

'If Barbara were still alive, what would she say?'

'She doted on Simon. We nearly lost him, you know. When he was born.'

'You didn't nearly lose him. From what you've told me, they cot-nursed him for a couple of days because he was a bit flat after the delivery. He still is, really. Flat. Not very lively. I think what we should do is go up to your room, just before Simon gets home, and as soon as he's in the front door, pretend to have really noisy sex.'

Tom put his glass down. 'Well,' he said, 'if we're going to the effort of climbing the stairs, why pretend?'

14

On 21 December Tom came round. 'Early Christmas present,' he said.

It was a laptop computer. He said he'd bought it with the money he got from flogging my junk. I couldn't believe he'd made that much but he swore he'd only needed to top it up with a few quid.

I said, 'It's very kind of you, but do I really need it?'

'Yes. To write your new book.'

'I haven't heard back from Izzard Sykes.'

'You will.'

He set everything up for me, showed me how to blow the cobwebs off my email account. I didn't quite see the point. Who would I email?

'You can start with me. Send me videos of cats doing funny things. And there's Ellie. I'm sure she uses email.'

I said, 'If I start corresponding with Ellie through a computer I'll see even less of her. Have the Parasites moved out yet?'

'Only to go on holiday. I drove them to the airport yesterday.'

'Get the locks changed while they're gone.'

'I'm off tomorrow myself. Early flight.'

He likes a bit of winter sun, does Tom. I asked if he was going on his own but he didn't answer me.

He said, 'I didn't get you a printer, Lizzie. They take up space, and if you need to print something you can always drive over and use mine.'

I'd have invited him to stay for dinner followed by possible complimentary extras but I was having a few people round for drinks. It was part of a Getting My Shit Together project: hoover the carpet, polish the wine glasses, make some fabulous canapés. Admittedly the guest list wasn't sparkling. Mrs Allen from next door, who owns the Maltese yapper, the young couple from the other side, who moved in during the summer, Yvonne's old pals Little Maureen and Big Rita, and Meredith, who used to be the editor on *Midlands This Morning*.

I see him occasionally in Aldi. He's come down in the world, does a bit of local radio now. I only asked him because I needed another male. That's a lie. I asked him because I couldn't think who else to invite. Lizzie No Friends. I couldn't invite Susan Carter even though I always get a card from her at Christmas. She was one of the Lansdowne Road crowd and I'd have had to wear a Hannibal Lecter mouth restraint not to ask her if she knew Janet Coleman was now a lush propping up bars along the Costa Blanca. A couple of vinos and I was liable to blurt out that I'd been getting it on with Rodney Pooley.

I'd thought of making angels on horseback but I couldn't get oysters. As with guests, you have to work with what's available, so I made dried figs and goat cheese wrapped in Parma ham, some little lamb and aubergine kebab-y things, crab balls with wasabi, walnut brittle, and some spinach fritters because I had this feeling the young couple might be vegetarians.

A quarter to seven, and I was rueing the whole idea. The tree lights were jammed on seizure-inducing flicker, the spinach fritters had flopped and I had no idea what to say to anyone. Alec was brilliant at parties. He could work a room, charm, joke, bullshit. Tom was pretty good too. Road works, weather, Aston Villa, storage heaters. He could run with anything. Preparing food and then hiding in the kitchen, that's my forte.

Mrs Allen was first. I knew she would be. Anxious to get the occasion over with probably. She doesn't go out much. When I invited her she'd looked quite startled. Then it turned out she doesn't drink. I hadn't thought of that. All I had to offer her was a very old can of Sprite. She toyed with a kebab and we talked about wheelie bins. Her dog was barking just the other side of the wall but she appeared not to hear it. I suppose you can get used to anything.

Deep and Pari brought me a poinsettia and a bottle of sparkling water in case I didn't have any. Nice couple. Deepak and Parinaaz, they both work in some government office doing property valuations.

Mrs Allen said, 'You two'll like them meat things. They're ever so spicy.'

Pari said they didn't cook much, too tired by the time they got home from work. They usually had a pizza delivered. I'd seen the guy on a moped.

Mrs Allen said, 'My husband used to like an Indian. He'd get a battered sausage with chips and curry sauce from Cod

Almighty but, you'll laugh at this, I used to make him eat it out in the sun lounge, to stop it stinking the place up for days.'

The Allens' sun lounge, so-called, used to annoy Alec. He complained about it to the council but they measured it and said it was within building regulations, just. It's like a small greenhouse tacked onto the back of the house. It faces north and the only things in there are two folding chairs and a tomato-plant graveyard so it hardly warrants being called a sun anything but Mr Allen used to spend hours sitting there. You'd smell his pipe. Actually, I think he died out there. I hope he enjoyed one final battered sausage before he went.

Pari said they'd got their house for a good price because it needs a lot of work. Jim, who used to own it, never did anything with it. He kept piles of old newspapers in there, which people said (a) was a fire hazard or (b) would topple over some day and bury him alive, neither of which happened. He died of *C. diff* on Men's Surgical. The first time in his life he allowed himself to be guided by health experts and he ended up in long-term storage in the mortuary until some distant relative could be found to get him cremated.

Pari said the properties on the street that have sold since they moved in have gone for £10,000 more than they paid. And so, as we approach the Blessed Nativity of our Lord, people gather together, as is the custom, to discuss house prices.

Mrs Allen said, 'Of course, this street used to be all white.'

'Yes,' said Deep. 'Neighbourhoods do change, don't they?'

She said, 'So where was you born then?'

'Me?' says Deep. 'Dudley Road Hospital.'

SEND 'EM BACK POLICY BACKFIRES ON PENSIONER.

Little Maureen and Big Rita were late. They said the taxi got lost but I reckon they'd been priming the pump in a pub somewhere. I was playing an Einaudi CD, nice tinkly background music. Rita said we needed something we could dance to.

Little Maureen said, 'I don't think it's that kind of party, Reet.'

Rita said, 'Yeah, we're a bit short of blokes but it don't matter. Instead of us handbags we can dance round Deep.' She put on the Buena Vista Social Club.

Deepak was very genial but he said they really couldn't stop. They were expecting a phone call because Pari's sister was having a baby, due any minute.

'See what I mean?' said Mrs Allen, the minute they'd gone. 'They breed like rabbits.'

Rita said she thought Deepak was a bit of all right. A great connoisseur of the male body, is Rita. When we all went to see the Hunkies, Rita was first in line to get her photograph taken with one of them and hold a suggestive pink balloon in front of his dick.

Maureen said, 'We never see you over our way these days, Lizzie. You fallen out with the new wife?'

'No. I'm invited for Christmas dinner, actually. Wendy's okay.'

'If you say so.'

'Philip seems happy with her.'

'You know she's had the front garden dug up? It's all concrete now. So she can park her car off the street.'

'Sounds like the kind of thing Yvonne would have approved of. You can give concrete a hose-down. So you don't like Wendy?'

'We haven't set foot in that house since she come on the scene, have we, Reet? When I think of the hours we spent there, after Yvonne passed. Helping him with the kiddies. Now all you get is a half-baked wave. If you're lucky.'

Meredith was a no-show. Well, he was and he wasn't. Eleven o'clock, I'd bundled Maureen and Rita into a taxi and I was in my dressing-gown with a cup of tea and the walnut brittle, which nobody had touched. The doorbell rang and there he was, looking the worse for wear.

'Sorry,' he said. 'Busy night. Lot of parties.'

I told him to clear off but he got his foot in the door and he was talking so loudly I was afraid he'd wake Mrs Allen. I know she sleeps at the front of the house so as not to miss anything. I could imagine how her account of the evening would go down at the Seniors' Club.

'We've got foreigners at number 39 now. And her next door to me, she has men coming and going at all hours. Of course she used to be on the telly, so she probably takes drugs. It used to be such a nice quiet street.'

The cab company said there was a minimum two-hour wait for a car so I had to let Meredith in. He finished the crab balls, the brittle and the Ferrero Rocher Maureen and Rita had brought me. We talked about old times. He said Valerie Tobin had made a fortune out of her fitness merchandise. He said, 'Course, the bottom's fallen out of the video business now.'

I said, 'Valerie didn't have a bottom. The back view of her leotard was like two perished balloons.'

'Very good,' he said. 'Perished balloons. That's right. She was very slim.'

'Thin, Meredith. She was a bag of chicken bones. Imagine having the nerve to flog a Bikini Diet and Exercise Plan when you've got nothing to put in a bikini.'

'You two never really hit it off. I remember that. What about what's-her-name?'

'Dear old what's-her-name? Do you mean Kim?'

'Kim Kendrick. What's she doing?'

'No idea. Louie's doing pantomime.'

'Who?'

'Louie Doyle. Used to do the horoscopes.'

'Oh, yeah. The fake. Stuart's done all right, though.'

Stuart used to anchor with Kim. Not one of television's most magnetic partnerships. He'd come from presenting *Let's Play!* It was a show for the pre-literate demographic. He was New Man, suede ankle boots and stripy sweaters. Kim was a mixed message in an Alexis Colby suit. She'd wear backless shoes that screamed 'boudoir' but she always wanted to present the heavier stuff – homelessness, domestic violence, sick children with oxygen tanks. She wanted to be taken seriously, with that little crease of concern between her eyebrows. Until she discovered Botox.

I knew Stuart was still in television. I'd seen him doing a programme about narrowboat holidays one time when I was at Mum's. He'd developed one of those walk-and-talk-to-camera styles where they wave their hands around too much. In my humble opinion.

I said, 'And what about dear Sandie?'

'Who?'

'Sandie Mulholland. You gave her my job. You were screwing her.'

'Are you sure?'

'I can't think of any other reason she got hired. Bit of a one-trick pony, Sandie. Jerk chicken, jerk pork, jerk goat.'

'What did she look like?'

'Big earrings.'

'No, doesn't ring a bell. Mind you, I was getting a lot of totty in those days.'

'An all-you-can-fuck buffet.'

'God, yes. Not that I go short, these days, mind you.'

'Perish the thought.'

I went to the kitchen to top up his glass. By the time I came back he was asleep, mouth wide open. I threw a duvet over him, turned out the lights and went to bed. It was still dark when I heard him on the move, opening cupboard doors in the kitchen and saying, 'Fuck, fuck.'

He was looking for paracetamol. I made coffee.

He said, 'Great party.'

He was studying me, trying to work out where he was.

I said, 'It's Lizzie. Partridge. This is my house.'

'Yeah,' he said. 'I took a leak out the back.'

'Not on my raspberry canes, I hope.'

'Didn't want to disturb you.'

'You'd had a few by the time you got here last night.'

'Still, great party.'

'I'm going back to bed. When you leave, close the door quietly. Actually, go out the back way. The front door sticks.'

'Got it.'

He slurped his coffee.

He said, 'Did we . . . ?'

'You and me? Are you serious?'

'No, right. Thought I'd better check. Morning after and all that. Didn't want to appear a cad.'

'No, you're in the clear. We didn't. I wouldn't. Not if you paid me. Well, I might if you paid me a lot. You should go home.'

And off he went, a hopeless, hung-over, middle-aged guy in a leather jacket. Mrs Allen's Maltese let the whole street know.

We never get carol singers nowadays. We get people trying to sell new window frames and we get trick-or-treaters, so a front door that can't be opened does have its advantages. But no rosy-cheeked carol singers. I went to St Anne's for a carol fix but they seemed to have lost the plot. I was looking for 'Hark, the Herald Angels' not 'O Christmas Tree'. Even 'Little Donkey', I'm sorry, but for me that's borderline. So it was back to Mary Immaculate on Christmas morning. I prefer my Christian worship straight up.

I got to Philip's about twelve. By the smell coming from the kitchen I estimated we were at least two hours off eating. Kayleigh and Kev and their boys were already there. I see Kayleigh very rarely and each time it's more and more like seeing Yvonne, risen from the dead. Kev and their eldest, Reece, were putting the extender piece in the dining table. There's a knack to it and it always defeats Philip. I suspect he starts worrying about it as soon as they get back from their summer holiday, beginning of September. By the time Christmas morning comes he's completely lost it. But Kev can do it. Very handy is Kev. And now Reece is on the job too. A fourteen-year-old bonsai of his dad.

He knows his way around a box of drill bits. Fettling his granddad's table extension is just one more step to manhood for him.

Mum was on the sofa sandwiched between Ryan and Brandon.

'Elizabeth,' she said. 'Look at me. I'm learning how to Goggle.'

15

Kayleigh and Kev had bought my mother a tablet computer.

I said, 'That's very nice. But how are you going to use it when you're at home?'

She said, 'It runs on electricity, Elizabeth. Don't you know that? I can just plug it in.'

'But you need a connection as well. An Internet connection.'

'Oh, the boys will sort it out for me.'

Then Philip piped up, 'It's already sorted, Mum. It's all in your bundle.'

'Is it?'

'Your phone, your telly and your Internet. I told you. I got you a better deal, remember?'

I couldn't begrudge Philip his moment. He needed to bounce back from his table-extension humiliation.

I said, 'Well, congratulations. There can't be many people your age with a computer. Just mind what you get up to with it. No looking at sex videos.'

Ryan sniggered.

Kayleigh said, 'How come you're not on Facebook, Aunty Lizzie? I'd have expected you to be on it.'

'Why? What's the point of it?'

'So your fans know what you're up to.'

Her sons all looked at me. Fans? Who was this odd relative who not only saw no purpose in Facebook but who might also have fans?

Kayleigh said, 'Your aunty Lizzie used to be on the telly.'

'A very long time ago,' chimed in my mother. 'And it was only once a week.'

Likelihood of developing a swollen ego in the presence of Muriel Clarke? Negligible.

I went to the kitchen to bother Wendy. She was drinking orange juice with a little added something. The windows were steamed up and so was Wendy.

I said, 'The computer was a masterstroke. She's so fascinated by it I doubt she'll even set foot in here.'

'Good. I know how to roast spuds without her giving me advice.'

'I did invite her to my house, you know. To give you a break.'

'Philip wouldn't hear of it. Any road, don't worry. As soon as she's fallen off her perch we'll be going to the Toby Carvery for our Christmas dinners. You're not back with that Tom, then?'

'No. Did Philip get you something nice for Christmas?'

'Slippers. I shall take them back.'

He always buys her slippers. One of these years he'll get the size right.

I put the cranberry sauce into a dish, taste-tested the brandy butter, counted out the knives and forks. 'Nine of us, right?'

'Eleven. Scott's coming, with his girlfriend.'

I saw even less of my nephew Scott than I did of his sister.

He'd been a sad little tyke after his mum died. I'd tried to be there for him a bit, and so had Little Maureen and Big Rita, but he'd gone very buttoned-up and silent. I think he did it to keep his dad company in his misery because once Wendy came on the scene he was back out on the street, kicking a ball around and annoying the neighbours like any other lad.

'What's the girlfriend's name?'

'Can't remember. We have met her but he's had that many.'

Philip helped me set the table. He doesn't really help. He follows you around and adjusts the position of a spoon or a glass by a millimetre.

I said, 'I saw Maureen and Rita. They came over for a Christmas drink.'

'Oh, yes?'

'They were saying they never see you, these days.'

'Why would they?'

'Because they live just down the street? How about, because when Yvonne was ill you couldn't have managed without them? And afterwards. They were very good neighbours.'

'They were pushy. Always in and out, bringing dinners.'

'They did it so your kids wouldn't have to live on cornflakes.'

'Kayleigh could cook.'

'She was still a kid.'

'And they were always talking about Yvonne. Always bringing her name up.'

'I think it's okay to talk about people when they've died. It might even be a good thing.'

'Well, it got on my pippin.'

Poor Rita and Maureen. They say, don't they, that no good deed goes unpunished.

'Still, it wouldn't kill you to be neighbourly.'

'I'm not avoiding them. I'm pretty busy, you know. Seeing to Mum. I don't have a lot of time for leaning on the front gate gossiping.'

Ryan and Brandon had showed Mum a game she could play on her new toy. It was called Candy Crush.

I said, 'Uh-oh. Now the rot will set in. The ironing'll be piling up, the sink'll be full of dirty dishes.'

'No,' she said. 'I'm going to put it away now. I don't want to use it all up.'

Brandon rolled off the settee, laughing.

'Gan,' he said – they call her Gan. It's kind of short for great-nan. 'It don't get used up. It's always there. For ever and ever.'

She said, 'Well, I'm still going to ration myself. I'm used to rationing.'

To hear my mother, you'd think the war ended last week.

Brandon said, 'What's rationing?'

'It's when there was a war on,' said Mum. 'When there was shortages because of the U-boats. We had to make do with less.'

I could see that making do with less might be a difficult concept for a boy born in 2004. But Mum was on a roll.

'Four ounces of bacon a week, that's all you were allowed.'

'What's rounces?'

'Ounces. It was how we weighed things. Philip, how much would four ounces be?'

'Hundred grams.'

'Then you could have a shilling's worth of meat.'

'Granddad, what's shillings?'

'A shilling was five p. Of course it'd be more in today's money.'

'Two ounces of cheese, two ounces of lard.'

'What's lard?'

Ryan said, 'Lard's what Miss Akubele's arse is made of.' Then he rolled off the settee as well, laughing at his own wit.

Mum said, 'Lard's what you fry your eggs in.'

Brandon said he didn't like eggs.

She said, 'You'd have been all right in the war, then. You only got one egg a week. That's why everybody kept chickens.'

'Yay! Chicken McNuggets. Mum, can we go to McDonald's?'

'It's Christmas, you numpty. We're having a turkey dinner here.'

'Can we go tomorrow?'

I said, 'When your great-nan said people kept chickens during the war, she didn't mean to eat them. She meant so they'd lay eggs.'

Brandon ceased flailing his legs and looked up at me.

I said, 'You only ate the chicken when it got too old to lay.'

He contemplated this with a finger up his nostril.

I said, 'You do know where eggs come from?'

'Yeah,' he said. 'From Tesco's. In that war, who were the baddies?'

'The Japs,' said my mother.

I said, 'And the Germans. They started it.'

'What's Japs?'

Mum said, 'Japanese. Your great-granddad Wilf was nearly took prisoner by the Japs.'

In his life a lot of things had nearly happened to my dad. He nearly died of scarlet fever when he was a baby. He nearly won a fortune on the Treble Chance football pools in 1957. If only Accrington Stanley had drawn that Saturday, we'd have been millionaires, lording it in Solihull, brushing our teeth with Babycham. There was also a hint dropped by his sister Phyllis, on one of her rare visits to the old country, that he nearly didn't marry Mum.

I was warned from a very early age not to give credence to anything Aunty Phyllis said and, of course, that included the whisper that Dad had had a war-time thing with a girl in the Women's Auxiliary. He was in Rangoon, with the 14th Army. A steamy place, from what I've read. Anything could have happened and it probably did. It was just never mentioned in official Clarke family dispatches.

BURMA VET TAKES SEX SECRET TO GRAVE.

Brandon said, 'Did he kill them Japs with his laser blaster?'

I said, 'I think all your great-granddad had was a knapsack and a penknife.'

Mum said, 'Don't listen to her. She doesn't know anything about it.'

There was truth in that. My dad never talked about the war.

'I lived to tell the tale,' he used to say. What he should have said was, 'I lived not to tell the tale.'

Ryan asked Philip what he had done in the war.

'Wasn't even born,' he said. 'I remember when they used to test the air-raid sirens, though. A couple of times a year.

Remember that, Lizzie? To make sure they were still working.'

We were the generation that arrived when it was all over, a bit like Meredith. You could see there'd been a party, dregs in glasses, crumbs on the floor, and you could see there'd been a war – everybody on our street had an Anderson shelter in the back garden – but we'd missed the action.

I said, 'You haven't asked Gan what she did in the war.'

Brandon stopped picking his nose. Ryan sat up.

'What?' they said.

'Do you think she sat at home filing her nails?'

'Don't know. She couldn't be a soldier.'

So much for having equal opportunities rammed down their throats with their baby cereal.

I said, 'Your great-gran wasn't always an old lady, you know. She'll tell you.'

Oh, then I got a warm, two-sherries smile. I can be an apple-polisher when it suits me.

'Well,' she said. She put down her new toy. 'I did war work. I was at the BSA, in Small Heath.'

'What's BSA?'

'Guns. We made machine guns and rifles. I was a checker on the Lee-Enfields. When the barrels came off the lathe, I had to check them.'

'Why?'

'Because you couldn't send a rifle out if the barrel wasn't perfect. You could have cost a soldier his life. We worked seven days a week, day and night. I generally worked the day shift and that's why I'm sitting here today.'

'Why?'

'Because one night the factory got bombed. And the girl who sat in my seat on the late shift was never found. Only bits of her apron. Ida. Her name was Ida.'

Wendy emerged from the kitchen. 'Who was Ida?'

'The girl who copped it instead of me when they bombed the factory. Fifty dead in one night. And when we tried to get to work the next morning you couldn't fathom where to go. Everything was flattened. Just broken glass and water everywhere, where the main was hit. Blummin' Jerry.'

'Who's Jerry?'

'The Germans.'

'Why?'

'Why what?'

'Why is the Germans called Jerry?'

'I don't know.'

'Look it up on your computer. It's not just for games, you know. Goggle it.'

'What – just like that?'

Kayleigh showed her how.

' "Jerry. A nickname for German troops dating from the First World War. Origin unknown. Possibly refers to the shape of German helmets, which resembled a chamber pot or jerry." What's a chamber pot?'

I said, 'Okay. Time for you to complete your education. When your dad and I were kids we only had an outside toilet, so if you needed to go in the night, you used a potty. A chamber pot. A jerry. You kept it under the bed.'

'Didn't it pong?'

Philip said, 'Yes, it did. And in the morning you had to carry it downstairs, without splashing, and empty it in the lav.'

'That's right. Except you never did. I had to empty yours. It was considered girls' work.'

Wendy said, 'But what's that got to do with Ida?'

Gin and a hot kitchen can play havoc with a person's concentration.

Mum said, 'She worked on the same belt as me. Only she worked nights because she had a little boy and she couldn't get anybody to mind him in the daytime. Her husband was away in the forces, you see. So that was a terrible thing. I've often wondered what happened to that little chap. How old would he be now?'

'Seventy odd.'

'I suppose he would. And the thing is, if I'd been doing the night shift instead of Ida, none of you would be here.'

'Why?'

I said, 'Think about it.'

'What?'

'If Great-Nan had been killed in 1940, Granddad Philip would never have been born. If he hadn't been born, your mum wouldn't have been born. And if she hadn't been born there'd be no Reece, no Ryan, no you.'

Brandon mined his nostril a bit more. 'Why?'

And so much for compulsory junior-school sex education.

We were about to sit down to eat when Scott and his girlfriend arrived. Great-looking girl. India. I could sense my mother preparing one of her stage whispers.

I said, 'Her name's India. Like the country. Do not say a word.'

I hadn't seen Scott since he moved to London. If I'd passed him in the street I wouldn't have known him. He's got a pony-tail. When Yvonne was still alive she always insisted on him having very short hair, so he wouldn't get nits. It was completely illogical because Kayleigh was allowed long curls, but Yvonne's word was law. That buzz cut made Scott look like a junior thug and sometimes he acted the part. He once gobbed on Tom's suede shoes, just to show what a hard little man he was. I used to avoid Scott, but when his mum died I felt differently. Poor kid, he had a sister who was grown-up beyond her years and a dad who hardly knew his arse from his elbow. Plus Rita and Maureen running in and out with meat pies and piles of ironing. And then Wendy. She wasn't a horrible stepmother by any means, but I don't think she found a lot to say to a ten-year-old boy.

He gave me a hug. He said, 'Don't say it.'

'What?'

'Don't say "You've grown." Where's Dad?'

'In the kitchen, preparing to meet his Waterloo.'

'Sweater off? The pre-carving limber-up?'

Kayleigh said, 'I don't know why Wendy don't get them easy-carve crown roasts.'

'Because,' says Scott, 'it wouldn't be Christmas without Dad squaring up to a hot dead bird. I think I'll go in there. See if I can hinder.'

Mum whispered, 'That girl, what's she got on her feet?'

India was wearing red crêpe-soled lace-ups.

I said, 'They're what we used to call brothel-creepers. I like them.'

'Has she got something wrong with her? Are they orthoptic boots?'

'No, they're a fashion item.'

'I don't think so. I think she's got bad feet. But don't worry, I won't say anything.'

I suggested to Wendy that we seat my mother at the opposite end of the table from Scott and India.

'Whatever,' she said. She was a couple of gins past caring.

Scott appeared eventually, with a big platter of passably carved turkey.

I said, 'What's the final score?'

'Dad won on points. His shirt's a bit of a mess but the turkey conceded.'

We had to go through the just-a-sliver-for-me routine with Mum. She feigns a sparrow's appetite, yet year after year she's the only one to have Christmas pudding *and* a mince pie. I could see her trying to catch India's eye. She intended addressing the far end of the table.

I said, 'Her name's India, she's a nice girl, and those shoes are in fashion. Don't start. Eat your dinner.'

She laughed. She said, 'Did you hear that? This is what happens when you get to my age. You get told to shut up and eat your dinner. I'm sure I'd never have spoken to my mother like that.' She waited till she was sure she had India's attention. 'Where are you from, dear?'

'Dorking. Surrey.'

'That's nice. Been there long, have you?'

'Well, I was born there and my parents are still there but I live in London now. Hackney.'

'I went to London once. We went to see *The Mousetrap*. It was quite good.'

'I believe it's still on. You could see it again if you wanted to.'

'Oh, no. Because I already know who did it. And the money they wanted for a cup of tea! We went to a Lyon's Corner House and I couldn't believe the prices. We'd have walked out only I needed to use the facilities. Now I'll tell you something that'll interest you. My husband was in Burma.'

Scott murmured something to India. Probably 'Humour the old noodle. She thinks you're Indian.'

India said, 'Was that in the war, Mrs Clarke?'

'He was under General Slim.'

'He must have had some stories to tell.'

'Oh, yes. He didn't like it there. He got terrible foot rot.'

Scott said, 'More bread sauce, anyone?'

Wendy roared.

I said, 'Why are you inflicting Dad's foot rot on India? She's eating her dinner.'

'Because,' she said, spearing a sprout on her fork, 'when you've got a newcomer to the family you try to find topics of conversation that will be of interest to them, to make them feel at ease. It's good manners, Elizabeth. I'd have thought you'd know that.'

India said, 'I'm afraid I've never been to Burma. I was in Thailand, on my gap year.'

'Well,' said Mum, waving the impaled sprout, 'Thailand, India, Burma, it's all the same neck of the woods.' And she gave me the kind of triumphant look you get from a dog when it keeps barking and you both know you that, short of super-gluing its muzzle, there's not a damned thing you can do to stop it.

16

We went for a walk later, me, Scott and India. The dishwasher was chugging away, Kev and Kayleigh had taken their boys home, and Mum, Philip and Wendy were all spark out. It was starting to get dark and it was bone cold.

India said, 'I hear you're a bit of a TV legend, Lizzie. The food fight incident?'

I said, 'I was, for five minutes. Unfortunately nobody recorded it. It wasn't like when Emu attacked Michael Parkinson.'

Of course she was too young to know about Emu.

'Still,' she said. 'I'm sure people remember it. Scott does and he didn't even see it. He said it was the talk of the street. Was it planned?'

'Absolutely not. As a matter of fact I'd intended to bow out graciously. It was my last show, you know. They'd sacked me, given my slot to some never-was. She was screwing one of the editors. I was really gutted but I hadn't planned to do anything vengeful. I'm not a violent woman. It was Valerie Tobin who pushed me over the edge.'

'She the never-was?'

'No, Valerie was the diet and fitness guru. Self-proclaimed, I might tell you. I'd made three fabulous desserts and she was turning her nose up at them, like I'd offered her a taste of dogshit soufflé. So, you know, I just lost it. Then Kim Kendrick joined in. She was one of the presenters. She claimed she'd been trying to rescue Tobin but I think she just wanted to be part of the action. Anyway, I bit her hand.'

'Cool. But you never went back into television?'

'Nobody asked me.'

'That's very surprising. What if they did ask you?'

'I'd do it. But it's not going to happen.'

Scott said, 'India works in television.'

She seemed so young. I thought she must be a gofer. He read my mind. He said, 'And she doesn't just fetch the coffees.'

I said, 'I never suggested she did.'

'No,' he said, 'but you had an oh-yeah? face. India's a trainee producer. That's why we came up today. She wanted to meet you.'

I said, 'Okay, I enjoy a bit of soft soap as much as the next woman, but you're here because you wanted to see your loved ones at Christmas.'

'You are joking?' he said. 'We could have gone to Marrakesh.'

'You mean you weren't reminded this might be your last opportunity to spend Christmas with your nana.'

'Yes, that was mentioned. But that's okay. Nana makes it bearable. She's great value. Burma. Foot rot. *The Mousetrap.*'

'Kayleigh's husband doesn't say much, does he?'

'Kev's all right. He's the strong, silent type, and he has a considerable toolbox.'

India said, 'I think you mean lunchbox.'

'No, toolbox. That's why Dad doesn't like him. Kev shows him up.'

'I wish I had a son-in-law with a toolbox.'

'Ellie's husband not the handy type?'

'Nat can't even manage a flat-pack bookshelf. He gets a Latvian in. But your dad can do stuff. He's always round at your nana's fixing things.'

'No, he isn't. He's always round there fiddling and making things worse. Then he has to get somebody in. He has to pay somebody to sort out the mess. And he won't ask Kev. Because that'd be like admitting he's a knob and Kev isn't. Has he said anything to you about Wendy?'

'Such as?'

'I think they've got issues.'

'She always liked a drink.'

'Not that. She's started going out a lot apparently, in the evenings.'

'You mean playing away? Is she seeing someone?'

'Well, she doesn't seem the type to go to yoga.'

Poor Philip. He'd never tell me, though. I'm the last person. And he's a great one for burying his head. When they sent Yvonne home from hospital, they'd told him there was nothing more they could do for her, but he didn't seem to take it in. He just kept bumbling along. She'll be better tomorrow. I see a bit of an improvement. That kind of thing.

'What did your dad say to you?'

'He didn't. Kayleigh told me. She knows somebody who knows somebody. It's the house Kayleigh's worried about. If

Dad and Wendy split up, if they got divorced, he'd have to sell. And then what? Where would Dad go?'

'Kev'd have to build an extension on the extension. It won't happen. If I know your dad, he'll turn a blind eye to whatever Wendy's up to. And if it did come to it, if things turned ugly, he could move in with your nana. He's round there nearly every day anyway.'

We'd almost reached the crematorium.

I said, 'Shall we turn back? See if the sleeping beauties have woken up?'

Scott said, 'That's where we had Mum's funeral.'

India put her arm around him.

I said, 'Yes. What a day that was.'

'Kayleigh sat between you and Dad in the car. I had to sit with Nana. It was a bloody great limo, remember?'

'Daimler, probably.'

April 18, 1996. I forget dates. I couldn't tell you what day Alec and I got married but somehow I always remember the date of Yvonne's funeral.

'There was a big argument about whether you and Kayleigh should even be there.'

'I definitely wanted to be there. I thought I'd get to see Mum. I thought she was going to wake up and come home. And do you remember Uncle Oojamaflip?'

'Uncle Bobby?'

Bobby was Yvonne's brother. His sole contribution to the sad proceedings was the dent he made in a bottle of Scotch.

'First time in my life I'd ever seen him, and I've never seen him since.'

'I don't think you've missed much. Your mum never talked about him.'

We turned back before we reached the gate to the crem.

He said, 'I can remember her smell more than what she looked like.'

'Me too.'

'What was it?'

'Fabric softener, One-Step Kleen 'n' Shine for Floors, and bleach. And whatever was on special from Avon. I think the house still smells of her. It's one thing Wendy's not been able to change.'

India said, 'I know what your signature pong would be, Clarkey.'

She doesn't call him Scott.

'Spearmint mouthwash and old trainers?'

'No. Dove for Men and day-old Burrito Bowl.'

I think India's good for Scott. I hope she sticks around.

She said, 'So if you ever have any ideas, Lizzie, daytime slots mainly, but even post-watershed, if there's anything you'd like to do, we're always looking for new stuff.'

I said, 'As a matter of fact I do have one idea. Not for me per-sonally, but have you ever heard of fur-suiters?'

She had. She thought it was a Las Vegas thing.

I said, 'You'd be surprised. Mr and Mrs Norman Average of Acacia Drive. Although a lot of them are Mr and Mr. It's the hobby the neighbours don't know about.'

Scott said, 'Something you'd like to share with us, Aunty Lizzie?'

I told them about the Aberystwyth furries. India was

interested. 'You think you can find me someone to talk to? With the suit and without it?'

'Yes. They love to talk. You'd just need to remember that when they put the suit on they become a different person. It's like being an actor.'

'And do they cross-breed?'

'In what sense?'

'Would a guy in a bear costume get it on with a guy dressed as Big Bird? For instance.'

'It's not really like that. They're more focused on their costumes. They're more interested in how they look than how anybody else looks.'

'Pity,' she said. 'Sex would have been a strong selling point.'

When we got back to the house Mum was watching *101 Dalmatians*, Wendy was in the kitchen making tea and Philip was surfacing from a well-earned turkey-carver's sleep.

Scott and India had a taxi booked. They were staying at a Travelodge, getting a train back to London on Boxing Day. I blagged a ride with them.

She said, 'What I'd really love is to see you back on daytime. Wouldn't it be great to get you on a couch with the ones you had the food fight with?'

'You mean for Round Two?'

'Not exactly. But you were all obviously fiery women. Of a certain age and now . . .'

'Now we're of a certain age plus fifteen.'

'But older women are hot properties in TV, these days. Look at Anne Robinson. And you have a track record. The TV cook who came out swinging and broke the switchboard. Think about it. I'll make a few calls. And if you know one of these fur freaks who'd be willing to talk to me I'd definitely look into it.'

Which gave me what I'd really wanted for Christmas: a copper-bottomed excuse to get in touch with Rodney Pooley.

17

I had it all planned. I wrote it down so I wouldn't wander off-script.

1. Call his daughter's business number. Remember she likes to be called Min. Or was it Minnie?
2. Mention conversation with India and the TV idea.
3. Leave my number.
4. Do not witter on like a nervous twit.
5. Get off the phone quickly.

When to call? She wouldn't be working on Boxing Day. If she was anything like the rest of the country she wouldn't be working till halfway through January. But that could be good. Everybody says I'm crap on the phone. So call and leave a message on her machine. I rehearsed it a few times. A lot of times, actually.

'My name's Lizzie Partridge. This is a message for Rodney. We met at the Aberystwyth convention and I mentioned it to a friend in television who'd be very interested in exploring the idea of a documentary. If he'd like to know more, my number is . . .'

I tried it crisp, tried it casual. In the end my voice started giving out and I sounded quite pleasingly husky. I dialled the number. Damn me if Rodney himself didn't pick up. That threw me for a loop.

I said, 'What are you doing answering your daughter's business phone?'

'Lizzie Clarke,' he said. 'What are you doing calling her business phone? I gave you my number.'

'I lost it.'

'Chucked it away more like. I answered Min's phone because I'm in her office. Also known as "the kitchen". Merry Christmas.'

'The reason I'm calling is—'

'Fancy a return match?'

'That's not why I'm calling. Maybe. Yes. Listen, I was talking to a friend who works in television. I told her about Aberystwyth and she was very interested.'

'I don't do threesomes.'

'I mean she was interested in fur-suiters. She thought it might make a good documentary. I can put you in touch with her if you like. Have a chat with her? It might not amount to anything, but if it did, it wouldn't do your daughter's business any harm.'

He took India's number and mine. He wanted to fix a date to see me. I told him it'd have to be after I got back from Whitley Bay. He whistled. 'Whitley Bay? You've only just got back from Aberystwyth, you globetrotter. And when will you be jetting in?'

I couldn't say because I'd only that minute decided to go up there. I wanted to see Louie, of course, but I wanted to sharpen

Rodney's appetite as well. Unavailability: the irresistible umami of sex.

'Not sure. It'll be after New Year. A friend's doing panto up there.'

'Anybody I'd have heard of?'

'Louie Doyle.'

'Don't think I know her. Was she in *Emmerdale*?'

'It's a he, actually. And, no, he wasn't.'

'Sorry,' he said. 'I don't move in your star-studded circles. But thanks for the documentary tip. I'll get in touch with this India woman. And when you get back from Hartlepool—'

'Whitley Bay.'

'Excuse me, from Whitley Bay, perhaps you'll give me a call. Or not.'

That's what I call a great result. I gave good phone, got him interested, then kept him hanging. I turned on my Tom laptop to find out how the heck to get to Whitley Bay. It appeared to have died. Tom was away and I'd hesitate to call him anyway. He'd just laugh and call me a chump. I tried Ellie, got her voicemail. Still enjoying a Jewish Christmas at the Hursts or, knowing my daughter, back at her desk dreaming up ways to get her lowlifes tagged instead of sent to jail. I called Chas. He was at a service station on the M5.

He said, 'You're an answered prayer. I'm sitting here in Road Chef feeling guilty for going home. Louie got a couple of iffy reviews and now he's in a real depression. I was thinking of turning round and going back but if you're going to see him that'll cheer him up.'

Chas said Louie was finding the dance routines too much. Also that Cinderella had taken against him.

'Does he have to lift her?'

'You mean like Baryshnikov? Lord, no. That'd finish him. No, it's just a personality clash. She says he hogs the stage when they're on together, being too campy, but that's surely why they cast him. If they'd wanted a shrinking nonentity they'd have hired one. I'm sure there's no shortage.'

He said I should drive there, that I'd do it in four hours, but Chas hadn't seen the comatose pile of rust parked outside my house. The alternative to driving was a train to Newcastle and then the Metro or a cab. Louie had moved out of the shared house into a small flat, so he could soak in the tub for as long as he liked and go to the kitchen without feeling obliged to be chatty. The new place had only one bedroom but there was a sofa.

I said, 'Don't worry. I'll bunk down with Louie. I've done it before.'

'Really?'

'Long before your time. He'd just broken up with somebody or I'd just broken up with somebody. Can't remember. We got so rat-arsed I couldn't drive home so we shared the bed. With a pillow and an old teddy between us, I might add. Like that was necessary.'

'Was it Teddy Bare? Between you?'

'No idea. I don't think we were introduced. Don't tell me he's still got it.'

'Of course.'

'With him, in Whitley Bay?'

'Louie never travels without him.'

'Then we'll be fine. No personal space will be invaded. But I am not sleeping on a sofa, not even for Louie.'

I went up on Wednesday. The understudy was doing the matinee so Louie could rest. He'd lost weight.

He said, 'Wardrobe's going crazy. They have to keep taking in my trousers. Well, that's their job. Nobody seems to realize I'm dying here.'

'But you're always saying you want to lose weight.'

'A gentle reducing regime before we hit the beach is one thing. Weight loss by dance-studio torture is quite another. I'm emaciated.'

'You're not. You look good.'

'Chas said that. He was just humouring me.'

'I'm not. Haven't I always levelled with you?'

He hugged me. 'Oh, Lizzie,' he said, 'what's to become of me? Is it too late for a change of direction? Do you think I could do Shakespeare?'

He could only eat something light before the evening show. I made him an egg-white omelette with spring onions and the tiniest whisper of smoked salmon. I said, 'I'm only cooking this abomination because I love you.'

'I know,' he said, 'but after the show we'll get cod and chips and a side of mushy peas. That'll count towards my five-a-day. Now tell me about the possum.'

'The what?'

'The new man. With the furry costume.'

'He's a raccoon, not a possum.'

'Isn't it the same thing?'

'Not at all.'

'What's the difference?'

'Never mind. I haven't seen him again but when I spoke to him he seemed keen.'

'He called you?'

'I called him.'

'Tsk-tsk.'

So then I told him about India. He put down his fork. 'Lizzie,' he said, 'never mind about getting the damned possum a telly gig. This is *your* opportunity. It's called networking, darling. Work it. Cosy up to this precious girl before she moves on from your nephew. Scott? Was he the one you used to hate?'

'It was more dread than hate. He wasn't a likeable kid but he's turned out great. He did City & Guilds electrics when he left school and now he's learning lighting, for TV and stuff. He's getting a few jobs but he can't be earning much. I reckon India must be bringing home most of the bacon.'

'Please don't talk about bacon when I'm being starved for my art. But seriously, Lizzie, this is an opportunity for you. Take that girl to lunch. Pitch her some ideas. Did I tell you about *Dirty Secrets*?'

He'd been asked to read for a TV pilot. People go into each other's houses to clean. Louie would be doing the voice-over, if he got it.

'Presumably these would be people with really disgusting, scummy houses? Much worse than mine.'

'Off the scale. But I wouldn't have to be there. I'd just do the post-production sarcasm.'

'Even better.'

'But why am I getting voice-over offers? Are they trying to tell me something? Is it time to get my jowls done?'

'Do not get your jowls done.'

'Television, though, sweet. It's bitch eat bitch. Even worse for you girls. They might ask you to have a bit of work done if you were going back in front of a camera.'

'I'd refuse.'

'Bet you wouldn't. How much would they have to offer you? Two K per show?'

'They won't. Why would they? We didn't get that kind of money on daytime.'

'That was a long time ago. And we were just sideshows, little filler acts. But Kim was getting good money, and for what? Sitting on a couch reading from a teleprompter. At least we had skills, you and I. Though much good it did us.'

'What skills?'

'You showed people how to cook scrummy grub. I did horoscopes. Okay, I made up horoscopes. But even that required a modicum of creative talent. What talent did Kim have?'

'She could do lots of faces. She had the Serious Social Issue face. The Tragedy Interview face. The Now for Something Really Wacky face.'

'What's she doing, these days?'

'Don't know. I asked Meredith and he'd lost track of her.'

'Who?'

'Meredith. Editor. *Midlands This Morning*. Remember?'

'That bastard with designer stubble and an Aston Martin? No, don't recall him at all. What dizzy heights has he risen to?'

'Local radio.'

'Ha! Bumping along the bottom, like so many of us. Didn't he have a personalized number plate?'

'What – like A1 NOB?'

'Yeah – 400K ME. Anyway, if you were to get offered something but it's on condition that you have a lid-lift you must do it. Then you can have me on your show. I think I'd make a rather brilliant agony aunt. Otherwise I'm doomed to be wheeled out once a year as Widow Twankey. I'll be competing with John Inman.'

'I think he's dead.'

'Is he? Oh, well, that's freed up one vacancy.'

Louie went round to the Playhouse just after six. He does his own makeup. I followed on later, had a glass of red in the upstairs bar. Everyone was talking about the Fairy Godmother. She was going through an acrimonious divorce, apparently. Is there any other kind?

PANTO STAR IN CIVILIZED AND FRIENDLY MARRIAGE SPLIT.

I asked the girl behind the bar what she thought of the show.

'Canny,' she said.

And what did she think of Buttons?

'Who?'

'Cinderella's friend. In the kitchen scenes. Louie Doyle? He used to do *Spin to Win*. He hosted it.'

'Never seen it,' she said. 'You his mam?'

'I'm a friend.'

'Lysette's belta. Purely belta.'

Lysette was the one Louie didn't get on with. Cinderella.

She said, 'He's right enough, your friend. He's friendly, like. He sweats, though, summat chronic. When he's dancing.'

She was right about that. I sat in row K and I could see it dripping off him. He fluffed one of his gags, too, but he turned it around, got a good laugh out of it. I thought he was great. No, I thought he was okay, but I wished he'd stop putting himself through this every year. I wished he'd retire, or do a few voice-overs, enough to cover his Groucho Club membership. Which he never uses anyway because he never goes to London. He doesn't just live in Cornwall. He lives in a part of Cornwall even Cornish people don't go to. Tom and I drove down there once. Nice sea views. Next stop, Spain.

We lay in the dark with the pillow and the bear between us.

He said, 'I was fairly crap, wasn't I?'

'Not at all,' I said, because he already knew. He didn't need a cold shower from me. 'But the point is, are you enjoying it?'

'No.'

'So give it everything you've got, finish the season, then call it a day. You don't need the money. Do you?'

'Not desperately. But what would I do?'

'Go on cruises. Do crosswords. Whatever retired people do. What does Chas do with his time?'

'Reads seed catalogues. Recycles.'

'So get a bike and go with him.'

'Not cycles. *Recycles*. He finds uses for things. Empty yogurt pots. You know his morning suit?'

'I never saw him in a morning suit.'

'It was his grandfather's.'

'Does he wear it?'

'He would. If we got married.'

'Do you think you will?'

'It looks like they're going to bring it in. I'd like to. Will you give me away?'

'Try stopping me.'

'You haven't really told me about the badger.'

'Raccoon. There's not much to tell. He was at the hotel I was staying in . . .'

'When you ran away and nobody missed you.'

'Yes. He was at this convention and he was kind of flirting with me . . .'

'Dressed as a raccoon.'

'Yes. But I thought he was gay. I thought it was just that older-woman thing some of you boys have.'

'Lizzie Partridge, the poor woofter's Liza Minnelli.'

'He invited me to the disco. It was called the Fursuit of Happiness.'

He groaned. 'And then . . . you . . . ?'

'Right.'

'At what point did you actually get to see him?'

'He went up to his room dressed as a raccoon and came back down as a human.'

'How did you feel when the lift door opened for the reveal?'

'Jelly-legs.'

'I can imagine. What if he'd been everything you didn't go for in a man?'

'I don't know. It didn't happen. He was nice. Attractive, really. But it wasn't until afterwards, when we got talking, that I found out I knew him.'

'Golly. After fifty years. And him being married, formerly married, to your arch-enemy. My God, Lizzie, this is the stuff of soap operas. And where's the ex now?'

'In Spain, drinking too much.'

'You should write a treatment. Give it to this TV girl you're neglecting to cultivate. It'd be like *Grange Hill* meets *Eldorado*. So the ex is off the scene. Face down in a pool of sangria. And he's good-looking.'

'He's improved since he was sixteen.'

'Encumbrances? Kiddies? Maxed-out credit cards?'

'Just the daughter.'

'Okay. So we have the daughter making suits and the father wearing suits. I may be running ahead of myself here but could this possibly be the reason the ex turned to drink?'

'I'm not sure about the chronology, but it doesn't matter. I'm not planning to spend the rest of my life with him. It'd just be nice to be adored on the occasional weekend.'

'I know,' he said. 'Of course, Tom adored you. And not just on weekends.'

I said, 'Why does everyone go on about Tom? Living together didn't work for us. He can be very pernickety. People don't realize. But we're still friends. He gave me a laptop for Christmas.'

'Did he, by Jiminy? That was very generous, considering he no longer has nookie rights.'

'Who says?'

He rolled over to face me. 'You are such a hussy.'

'Actually, he bought me the computer with money he got from flogging some stuff for me on eBay. But it was thoughtful of him.'

'It was. I really liked Tom.'

I said, 'Have you ever cohabited with somebody who washes your saucer while you're still drinking your coffee?'

I didn't get an answer to that. Louie had fallen asleep.

18

A letter from Izzard Sykes.

Dear Ms Partridge,

Thank you for sending us your proposal for What to Cook When You Really Don't Give a Fuck. *After due consideration we don't feel this is for us at this time.*

Best regards, etc.

Well, fine. I didn't particularly want to do it anyway. The trouble with cookbooks is you have to test everything a million times. If you're big, really big, I suppose you have elves to do the testing and raise any queries. Like, should the gherkin be roughly chopped and incorporated into the mayo of your fish-finger sandwich or thinly sliced and fanned daintily on the side?

The phone rang. I practised my maturely sexy voice before picking up, in case it was the raccoon.

It was Tom. 'You've got a problem with the laptop?'

'Yes. How did you know?'

'You left a message. I told you I was going away for Christmas.'

'How was it?'

'Very enjoyable. What's wrong with the computer?'

'Dead.'

'Have you charged the battery?'

'Yes. It's plugged in right now.'

'Will you be at home this afternoon? I'll drop round.'

He was very bronzed.

I said, 'Christmas Day on a sun-lounger, eh?'

'Yes. It got up to 20 degrees on Boxing Day.'

'Sounds unnatural.'

'It wouldn't have suited you.'

I don't do sun. I just look flushed and cross and my features go out of focus. My eyes kind of disappear. I definitely look better with a pale face and red lippy. I actually had this officially confirmed by Yvonne, years ago, when she was doing Colour Counselling.

'You're winter, but sallow,' she'd said. 'You need to stick to blue tones. Fuchsia, lilac, forest green. Stay away from yellows.' Which was a bummer because I'd just bought an orange jacket.

Tom looked at the laptop and looked at me. He said, 'It's the battery, Lizzie. I told you to check the battery.'

'But it's plugged in.'

'Yes, the plug's in but it's not switched on at the wall.'

'So you've had a wasted trip.'

'Never mind.'

'Sorry. Cup of tea?'

'Go on, then. A quick one. How was your Christmas?'

'Quiet. I went to Philip's. Did my daughterly duty.'

'And how was Muriel?'

He always called my mother by her first name. She liked it. A bit of a flirt around Tom, my mum. A bit sparkly-eyed.

'She got one of those little tablet computers. Kayleigh's boys were showing her how to use it.'

'Marvellous. How old is she?'

'About a hundred and thirty.'

'I'll bet Muriel won't forget to charge her battery.'

He was right. She'll mark it on her Scenic Switzerland calendar. Put out green wheelie. Mothers' Union. Charge computer.

'I went to see Louie in *Cinderella*. Whitley Bay.'

'That's a trek. How was he?'

'Struggling. Depressed.'

'What's he got to be depressed about? He's got Chas. They've got that lovely house.'

'Sagging jowls. Downward career trajectory. Dodgy prostate.'

'He's a bit young for prostate problems.'

'Well, he peed every two hours the night I was there.'

My mobile rang. If it was Rodney I didn't want to talk to him with Tom listening in.

He said, 'You not answering that?'

'They can call back. What are we like, these days? Bloody phones. We're like servants on the end of a bell pull.'

'I can go, if you need to talk.'

'Why would I need you to go?'

'You might want to have a private conversation.'

'I don't.'

'Okay.'

He started the very gentle whistling that signifies he's getting round to saying something you may not like. It's Beethoven usually. If it's the *Pastoral* it'll be some little thing, like you lined the kitchen bin with a colour supplement he particularly wanted to keep. If it's the Fifth, he's working up to something big. I made the tea, cut the last of the malt loaf and buttered it.

'So,' he said, casual, too casual, 'how are you?'

'I'm great.'

'Work picking up?'

'Not really. Izzard Sykes didn't go for my cookbook idea. There might be something else, though. You remember Philip's boy, Scott?'

'How could I forget him?'

'Yes, but he's no longer a repellent little hooligan. He's the new, improved, grown-up Scott with a very nice girlfriend, who happens to work in television.'

'Your patience as an aunt has been rewarded. That's nice. I hope it leads to something. I always thought you were great on television. Well, you know that. And ... are you seeing anybody?'

'Possibly.'

'I'll take that as a yes. I'm only asking as a friend, Lizzie. Seeing as we are still friends.'

'Sure.'

'Are you happy?'

'Too early to say.'

He was chasing crumbs round the rim of his plate. 'While we're on the subject, I'm seeing someone.'

'Oh, good. I'm glad.'

DISCARDED LOVER FAILS POLYGRAPH TEST.

'What's her name?'

'Geraldine.'

'That's nice. So you're Tom and Gerry.'

'Except she doesn't like to be called Gerry. We met at the U3A.'

'Is that like a dating agency?'

'It's the University of the Third Age. She gave a talk on post-war Vietnam.'

'That sounds fun.'

'It was very interesting. She'd been there, on a cycling holiday.'

I hated her immediately. I could just imagine her wearing one of those aerodynamic helmets.

'Did she go with you to Cyprus?'

'Yes.'

'So it's serious, then. It's moving right along.'

He said, 'I'm seventy-one, Lizzie. I don't have time for long courtships.'

'Courtship. Such a lovely old-fashioned word. Does that mean you'll be getting married?'

'Maybe. When I say "courtship" I don't mean anything offi-cial. I just mean . . .'

'Paphos, with a double bed. So have you taken up cycling?'

'As a matter of fact I have. It's good exercise.'

'Is it? Don't you get lungs full of traffic fumes? Don't you get over-developed calves? Christopher must be happy, though. You'll be able to have father-and-son bike chats.'

'Go ahead. Scoff. I'm only telling you because I hope we can still be friends, you and me. Geraldine does know about you, about us.'

Does she indeed? I'd love to know how that conversation went. Great girl, Lizzie. We were together for many years, on and off. Then why did you leave her, dear Thomas, dear Thomas? Because she puts jam jars back in the fridge with sticky bottoms. Because she forgets to use coasters. To name but two crimes against civilized cohabitation.

My phone rang again.

'Someone's very persistent,' he said. 'Anyway, I'd like you to meet Geraldine some time.'

'I'd be happy to,' I lied. 'I didn't know you were into that university thing.'

'Just keeping the old brain active. We've just had a talk on the Battle of Bosworth.'

'Who won?'

'Lancaster. Henry Tudor. Richard Of York Gave Battle In Vain.'

'Did he?'

'It's a mnemonic, for the colours of the spectrum. Red, orange, yellow, green, blue, indigo, violet.'

'Did you learn that at this 3A place too?'

'No, at school. Anyway, I must make a move. You've got phone calls to answer and Sally needs walking.'

'So the tapeworms are still living with you.'

He smiled. 'It's complicated.'

'Not really, Tom. It's glaringly simple to anyone who's not such a soft touch. But Geraldine'll help you sort that out. Because she probably won't want to move in with you while they're in residence. It'd put a bit of a dampener on the honeymoon, having Tess and Simon the other side of the bedroom wall. And she won't want her handbag eaten by the dog either.'

Off he went, my former live-in who now wants me to be his chum. Who now wants me to meet his new love. Only under no circs must I call her Gerry. I sat for a while, until I felt okay about things. Then I remembered my phone. Could it be I'd had two eager messages from the raccoon?

No.

First missed call was from Mum. 'It's only me. I just wanted to let you know that Thelma Cashmore passed away on that fancy cruise. I can't say I'm surprised. I said it'd be too hectic for her but of course her son insisted. Money to burn.'

OUTBREAK OF SCHADENFREUDE REPORTED IN W. BIRMINGHAM.

'I don't suppose there'll be a funeral. They'll probably bring her back in an urn. Anyway, I mustn't natter on. Cheery-bye.'

Second missed call.

'Hi, this is India. Lizzie, I have some rather exciting news. We've tracked down your two old sparring partners, Valerie and Kimberley, and they'd both be interested in meeting, to kick around some ideas. So give me a call and we'll set something up. Bye.'

What a day. Thelma Cashmore dead, Tom Sullivan spoken for, and a twitch of interest in me for television. The Lord may taketh away but sometimes he turneth right round and giveth.

19

The meeting with Vertical Hold was fixed for the following Thursday, at a hotel near Leicester Square, which seemed strange because Kim used to live in Solihull and Turtle Face was in Knowle.

India said, 'Yes, Kimberley is in Solihull but Valerie lives in Surrey now so London works better for her.'

I wondered who'd died and left her in charge.

'And what's with "Kimberley"? She always used to be Kim.'

'I don't know, but she's very thrilled about seeing you again.'

'Amazing. She's only ten miles down the road from me. All she had to do was get in her Merc and she could have been thrilled as often as she liked.'

India said it sounded like there'd still be a lot of chemistry between us.

I said, 'Yes. Like an unexploded dirty bomb.'

'Great,' she said. 'That'll be really great.'

I was an hour on the phone with Louie discussing what to wear.

'Okay,' he said. 'First let's visualize how the other two will dress. Kim will go for glamour. Think Joan Collins daywear.

Tobin, well, I only ever saw her in her gym kit. If she's living in Dorking I think she'll go for the quietly elegant look. Jaeger, Burberry, little pearl earrings.'

'Where does that leave me?'

'I think you need to look edgy. After all, you're the one all this hinges on. You were the one who lit the blue touchpaper. You were the one who threw the first punch.'

'And how am I supposed to achieve edgy?'

'Bring the phone up to your wardrobe and we'll go through it.'

'I don't have a lot in my wardrobe. Wire coat hangers, mainly. I have a chair piled with regrettable impulse buys.'

'I think you should wear black. I'm visualizing a long, drape-collar coat, white T-shirt, cigarette pants, statement earrings, don't-fuck-with-me shoes.'

'What are cigarette pants?'

'Straight cut, narrow.'

I said, 'Louie, in case you hadn't noticed, I have a considerable backside.'

'Trust me,' he said. 'You can wear cigarettes. Also, get your hair cut. And not at the little place on the corner with all the pensioners sitting in a row under hairdryers. Get a proper cut. In town. Edgy.'

'Stop saying "edgy". Do you know how much hairdressers cost?'

'I'll pay,' he said. 'Call it your belated Christmas present. Call it casting bread upon the water. When you ace this meeting and get a TV slot you'll find a way to repay me. Do you have a black coat?'

'Yes. I think it has a moth hole.'

'That might not matter. You don't want to look like you're trying hard. You need to exude cool confidence.'

'I also have a white T-shirt.'

'I'll bet you don't. I'll bet you have an off-white T-shirt. Buy a new one.'

'Wouldn't that be trying too hard?'

'No. You'll look like a woman who throws white Ts away after one wearing. So you don't have any sharp black trousers?'

'I have brown. Wide leg. I never wear them.'

'Elasticated waist?'

'Yes.'

'Ach! Lizzie, leave this with me.'

'But you're in Whitley Bay.'

'O ye, of little faith.'

An hour later Ellie phoned me.

She said, 'It'll have to be Saturday afternoon. I'll pick you up at one.'

I said, 'Lovely. What are you talking about?'

'We're going shopping. I got a call from your mate Louie. He's worried you're going to an important meeting looking like a middle-aged housewife.'

'I am a middle-aged housewife.'

'One o'clock, Saturday.'

I don't think Ellie and I had been shopping together since she was invited to her dad's wedding on condition that she wore a floaty dress. I found myself looking forward to Saturday. Ellie would be in charge, possibly with copious notes from Louie, and I'd just be along for the ride, the dummy to be dressed. Edgily.

I spent the evening sifting through my jewellery box. The only statement my earrings seemed to make was, 'Don't stare at me. I'm small and insignificant, nothing to see here, move along.' Kim and Turtle Face, after all those years. What on earth would we find to say to each other?

So great to see you!

You broke my teeth, you anorexic bitch.

I had a terrible dream that night. I was walking round and round Leicester Square trying to find the place where we were meeting and all I had on was a pair of brown trousers with a perished elastic waistband, so I had to hold them up. It was probably the pickled onions.

Ellie is super-punctual, these days. At 12.55 there she was, reverse parking into Deep and Pari's space. She and Nat have his and hers combat vehicles, to ferry Noah around in perfect safety. She was alone.

'Where's my grandson?'

'With Nat. We're shopping for clothes, Mum. You can't do that with a three-year-old. Anyway, he's been at Reggio all morning so he'll need a nap.'

'He's been where?'

'Reggio. It's child-led pre-kindergarten. They do painting and nature walks.'

'You used to do painting on the kitchen floor.'

'I wasn't being prepared for the Beechfield House entrance interview.'

'He's going to Beechfield House?'

'If he gets in. It's really competitive.'

'How? Do they speed-test them on bead-threading? And those places cost a fortune.'

'Nat's mum and dad are going to chip in. You're getting your hair cut at 2.30 by the way, so that gives us time to do a preliminary recce for clothes.'

'What kind of friends will he make at Beechfield?'

'Friends from good families. Nice children who eat proper food.'

'I thought you were a Labour voter?'

'So?'

It being January, the shops didn't have an awful lot in the way of coats but I did find an animal print I liked.

Ellie said, 'My brief is to get black.'

I said, 'Says who? I'm paying, so I'm choosing.'

'No,' she said. 'Louie's paying. And I am. It's a joint thing. Louie thinks keep it monochrome.'

'Have you ever seen how he dresses?'

'I'm not sure I've even met him. Did he come to the house one time in a striped blazer? Pink?'

'That was him. Like a stick of Brighton rock. He also owns a mustard check suit, so I don't know why he's so insistent on me wearing black.'

'It's slimming.'

'Not good on camera, though. Navy looks better.'

'You won't be on camera. This is a meeting, right?'

Ellie told the hairdresser to give me a choppy bob. The girl looked about fourteen. She was wearing denim shorts with thick, black holey tights. It's a trend.

She asked me if I was going somewhere special.

I said, 'No. My daughter and my best friend have ganged up on me. I'm supposed to get a new look.'

'Aw,' she said, 'that's nice.'

A choppy bob is what I'd call an un-hairdo. You look like you just got out of bed. I liked it. Ellie liked it.

'Yes,' she said. 'You look mean. In a good way.'

'Edgy?'

'Definitely.'

The guy working the next chair said I looked sexy.

Ellie said, 'Please! This is my mother.'

I said, 'It's all right. He's gay.'

'Mum,' she hissed. 'For goodness' sake.'

I wanted to go for tea and cake but she wouldn't allow it until we'd settled at least half of my outfit. So we bought an absolutely plain, boring white shirt and the ocelot print coat, because with a choppy bob you can get away with anything, and then we went to Dauber's, for old times' sake, except it's not called Dauber's any more. It's called Wired, but they still do a commendable Bakewell slice.

Ellie said there was no point looking at shoes till we'd bought trousers and I said that would entail crossing the threshold of Evans. They used to call it Evans Outsize, but they dropped the O-word to make their customers feel better.

'Absolutely not,' she said. 'Anyway, you're not that big. You're just pear-shaped.'

'Generously pear-shaped.'

'That's one strand of the Clarke DNA I managed to duck.'

Ellie takes after Alec, long torso, long fingers, no bum. Quite boyish, really.

'I don't see much of Noah these days. Is he avoiding me?'

'He's busy.'

'Do you think you'll have another one?'

'You're not supposed to ask that.'

'It'd be nice for Noah. A little brother or sister. A little Methuselah or Hepzibah. Another opportunity to perplex your nan.'

'We probably won't. Children are very expensive.'

'They don't have to be. You were quite cheap to run. Breastfed. Then lots of free veggies from Granddad's allotment. Dressed in hand-me-downs and Nana-knits. Until you were sixteen you hardly cost me anything. Although you did make up for it after that. Antibiotics for septic piercings. Plane tickets to America.'

'Ticket. I only did it once. Daddy paid the other times. M&S have big sizes. Let's go.'

I bought black boot-cut trousers and black suede oxfords. I was quite getting into it. Ellie took a picture of me with her phone and sent it to Louie. I thought he'd be performing but he called back immediately.

'Fabulous,' he said. 'Your hair is fabulous.'

'Thank you. No matinee today?'

'Yes. Just finished. Now I have to lie down with slices of cucumber over my eyelids. What about earrings? You must have earrings and they must be conversation pieces.'

Ellie said the best place to go was the Custard Factory. It's one of those regenerated inner-city places, used to be a grim part of town. You only went there if you needed to catch a long-distance coach. Now it's all galleries and cutting-edge fashion and salesgirls who stare straight through you. I prefer places like TK Maxx. You can bimble around in there all day and no one will bother you. You could probably move in, bivouac among the discounted handbags.

It was getting on for six o'clock by the time Ellie drove me home.

I said, 'I've really enjoyed this afternoon.'

'Me too,' she said. 'We never did anything like that before. This show you might be doing, what's it called?'

'I don't know. *Grouchy Old Bats. Round the Cauldron.*'

'Sounds like a real winner.'

'It won't be called anything like that. For one thing Kim won't be associated with anything that has "old" in the title. And it's probably not going to happen anyway. TV people are like that. They're really, really keen on an idea, then they lose interest and drop it. Like dogs, really. On to the next lamppost.'

'Are you nervous?'

'No. Yes. It's just a meeting.'

'You're out of practice. You used to be great in front of the camera. Remember that.'

'You never saw me. You were at school. Or still in bed.'

'I saw you a few times. Anyway, try these. Start tomorrow, half a tab. They reduce anxiety.'

Xanax. She said she'd used them a bit when she first started working in Crown Courts.

'What are the side effects?'

'Nothing. It stops the jitters.'

I hadn't really got the jitters. More the what-do-they-expect-of-me abdabs. 'I don't want to feel drowsy. I don't want to fall asleep on the Tube.'

192

'You won't. It's a very low dose. What do you mean, on the Tube? Get a taxi, for crying out loud.'

'Okay.'

'Promise?'

'Promise.'

Another white whopper.

'Mum,' she called to me through the car window, 'knock 'em dead.'

Sunday morning before church I tried everything on. I loved it. I looked the business. I wished the raccoon could see me. I almost phoned him. Then I remembered it was my Sunday for seeing my mother. On the third Sunday of the month Philip and Wendy like to go to a car boot sale. Philip buys things that need just a bit of work. His garage is stacked with gadgets you can't get the parts for.

I called Mum, asked her where she fancied for lunch.

'Philip usually takes me to the John of Gaunt,' she said. 'But they don't give you enough gravy.'

We settled on the Three Tuns. Deep, from next door, very kindly gave me a jump-start. He said I looked different. I felt different too. Invincible. Even the Paradise Circus gyratory didn't faze me. I got to Mum's around twelve.

'Oh dear,' she said. 'Whatever have they done to your hair?'

20

I started a list of topics that would make good talking points for *Grouchy Old Bats*.

1. People who completely assume you know what an app is or that you care.
2. Adverts where they say the stuff about Terms and Conditions really fast, as though that bit doesn't matter.
3. Shops playing shit music.
4. People eating on the bus.
5. Girls doing their makeup on the bus.
6. Clingfilm management.
7. Sellotape control.
6. People cold-calling you to try to sell you a different gas contract and then asking you to answer security questions.

I caught the 7.30 to Euston. It appeared to go via Land's End but it was a quarter the price of the fast service. I spilled a bit of coffee on my new white shirt, but when you take Xanax little things like that don't bother you.

I got the Northern Line to Leicester Square. Dead easy. I was early so I went for a coffee and a pee. Just as well because I discovered I had a flake of *pain au chocolat* stuck to my front teeth. My phone said I had a message. Louie. *Don't forget to blend your sockets. Big kiss.*

When I came out of the coffee place I kind of lost my bearings and set off in the wrong direction, which made me late getting to the meeting. I'd been up since 4 frigging 30 a.m. and I ended up being late. But it was okay. I popped another half-Xanax and I felt very okay indeed.

They were in the hotel lobby. A young guy in plimsolls and a leather jacket, two old ladies and India.

'Hey, Lizzie,' she said. 'You look terrific. Super earrings.'

They were big matt silver discs with black squiggles. I said, 'I got them at a little shop in the Custard Factory. You don't think the squiggles say anything rude do you? In Cambodian or Armenian or something?'

'Love it, love it,' said Plimsoll Boy, and pumped my hand. 'I'm Tark. Great to meet you.'

One of the old ladies gave me a nervous smile. Big blonde hair, long, skinny neck. Like a bouffant lolly on a stick. Valerie Tobin. The other woman rose on such a cloud of Shalimar I almost gagged. Shiny sausage-skin tights, figurehugging dress, sparkly belt. Louie got that dead right.

'Lizzie Partridge,' she said. 'It's been far, far too long.'

I said, 'Has it, Kim? It seems like only yesterday to me.'

Tark, as in Tarquin, was a project development manager for Vertical Hold. He and India had put together an idea for a weekly daytime show, five women discussing current trends, celebrity gossip, pet peeves. Two of the five would be guests, the other three would be me, Kim and Valerie. Possibly.

'For instance,' said Tark, 'we might have a show that started off discussing full Brazilians, and then it'd go wherever the conversation took you.'

I said, 'Like to anal bleaching, for instance. That would be a logical detour, anatomically. We could discuss, is a person who gets their anus bleached certifiably out of their mind?'

'Yep,' said Tark. 'I'm loving that.'

Valerie said, 'I think that was Lizzie's idea of a joke.'

It wasn't. I'd read about it in a magazine at the hairdresser's. People who look up their own fundament, don't like what they see then get it spruced up with a dab of hydrogen peroxide.

Kim said, 'I should say right up front that I wouldn't want to be involved with anything too frivolous. I'm better known for tackling more serious topics. Inner-city poverty, GM crops, that kind of thing.'

I said, 'I heard you've been flogging pineapple peelers on the Home Appliances channel.'

She looked down her nose at me. Which brought to my attention that it wasn't quite the nose I remembered.

'At least the public haven't forgotten my face, Lizzie. At least I won't have viewers saying, "Who's she?"'

I complimented her, told her she didn't look a day older. That threw her. I said, 'But, Kim, take care. If you tighten up any more you won't be able to close your eyes.'

Valerie remarked that I hadn't changed a bit either. 'Still overweight,' she said, 'and still over-opinionated.'

I said, 'Yes, guilty as charged. But the thing about carrying a bit of fat, Valerie, is it smoothes out the wrinkles, stops me looking like an old paper bag. And having opinions is the whole point of coming to this meeting. This isn't a bloody reunion. We're trying to create a TV show.'

Tark was following the conversation avidly, head swivelling like he was watching a singles final at Wimbledon.

Kim said, 'Are those men's shoes you're wearing, Lizzie?'

I said, 'Could be. They're unisex. Do you like them?'

'I do not. They're the kind of shoes lesbians wear.'

'Not necessarily. Times have changed. A lot of lesbians wear lipstick, these days.'

'So are you a lesbian now?'

I said, 'No, I still like men. Are you still with Bastard Bob?'

That stopped her short. See, I may sometimes omit to plug the computer in or lose phone numbers but I do remember things about people. Kim had no idea how much I knew about her. No recollection of that Christmas when Bastard Bob had left her and she begged me to drive over to Solihull and keep her company. I could even recall the names of her sad collection of cuddly toys. Mugglewump. Teddy Fat Tum. Marylou.

India asked Valerie how it felt meeting up with me again, given the circumstances under which we'd parted.

'Oh, that!' she said. 'Well, of course it was all staged. We thought it'd be a bit of fun, as it was Lizzie's final show. And it was. The greatest fun.'

Kim said, 'Although it did get a bit out of hand, Valerie. Lizzie went off script and bit my hand. I had to get a tetanus injection.'

I said, 'You're such a pair of liars. It wasn't staged at all. But if you can't live with the facts, never mind. I've moved on. I don't hold it against Valerie that she cost me two porcelain crowns and more dental appointments than she's had square meals. I had the great satisfaction of smacking her and no one can take that away from me. Tark, if this show happens, who would the guests be?'

He said it would be a funky mix. Women who are in the news, show business names, sportswomen.

'For instance?'

'For instance, for the pilot we might get Cass Truman.'

'Who's she?'

'Olympic trampolining bronze. And maybe somebody like Abi Cooper. She was great on *Supermarket Trolley Dash*.'

'There was a show called *Supermarket Trolley Dash*?'

'They only made one series. But Abi was great. Never lost for words.'

Valerie said, 'Kim Wilde's very nice. She and I belong to the same gardening club.'

I said, 'Valerie, we don't want "nice". We don't want five people sitting around agreeing about everything.'

India said, 'Lizzie's right. We're looking for sparks.'

I suggested transvestite toilets for another topic but Tark didn't like that idea. He said we had to be very careful about anything potentially hate-crimey.

I said, 'So you want sparks but no actual fire. You don't want too much chemistry. Just a bit of effervescence. Like Eno's Fruit Salts.'

'Got it,' he said. 'We'd probably record the pilot in Norwich.'

We all howled. He said it'd keep costs down.

I said, 'Not if Kim's going to expect a car service, it won't. Or a five-star hotel. Do they even have a five-star hotel in Norwich?'

'No need for hotels,' he said. 'We can tape two sample shows back to back and then we can all go home.'

Kim said she had to be guaranteed first-class rail travel because people tended to recognize her and expect her to chat to them. Valerie wondered if she'd be able to fly to Norwich from Gatwick.

I said, 'Almost certainly. By pig.'

'So,' Tark kept saying. 'So.' He was trying to bring the meeting to an end.

India said they'd be sounding out the networks, talking to potential guests. They'd get back to us. She said it might take a while.

I was roaring hungry but nobody else was interested in going on somewhere to eat. Valerie's driver was circling, waiting to pick her up. She offered Kim a lift to the station. Tark and India had more meetings to get to.

India whispered, 'That was great, Lizzie. Really super. Just one thing. About the trans toilets? At this stage best to avoid LGBT issues. Tark lives in Brighton. So, you know?'

I'd walked as far as Piccadilly before I fathomed what she meant by LGBT. I knew it wasn't a sandwich although it was very similar. It could have been an LBT with added goat cheese. It could have been a trade union.

LGBT MEMBERS THREATEN MORE COM-MUTER CHAOS.

It was too late for breakfast and a bit early for lunch. I went into a pub and had a large red while I reviewed the day so far. I had risen painfully early and endured a very slow train ride, sharing a table with a salesman who only stopped snacking when he was on the phone. I had attended a meeting with a teenager in plimsolls who held my career future in his young hands. The upshot of the meeting was that I might be asked to travel to Norwich to tape a pilot with two has-beens, an unknown athlete and a failed game-show host. Perhaps.

I had another large red with my steak and chips, which was probably why I fell asleep on the Tube and when I woke up we weren't even underground any more. Not only was I travelling in the wrong direction, I was at Baron's Court. But I didn't panic. I just popped another half-Xanax and felt so fantastically carefree that when I got to Euston I upgraded to first class and phoned Rodney Pooley.

I said, 'I'll be getting into New Street about 6 o'clock. Do you fancy doing something?'

'Yes,' he said. 'I do. We could see *Trainwreck*. I think it's still on. We could go for a balti. Or . . .'

I said, 'Or sounds good.'

'I think so too. I'll meet you off the train. Where are you coming from?'

'London.'

'I'll be the good-looking guy.'

Somewhere between Milton Keynes and Coventry I started to feel jittery. I'd have taken another pill but the blister pack was empty.

Louie called. 'And?' he said. 'Did they offer you sacks of money?'

'There is no money. It's just one of those maybe projects. If you ask me it's been a wasted day.'

'Don't say that. You never know. Did Kimmykins turn up?'

'She did. And Valerie Tobin. Who, get this, swears our meringue fight was staged and she enjoyed every minute of it. Kim's got a new nose, you'll be interested to hear. And the boy from the production company was wearing plimmies.'

'I bet he wasn't. I bet he was at least thirty and wearing the latest Nikes. You need to get out more, Lizzie.'

'And now I've done something really stupid.'

'What?'

'You'll be cross.'

'Tell Uncle Louie.'

'I called the raccoon and he's meeting me at the station.'

'For drinks, dinner?'

'I've already had two merlots and an 8 oz sirloin.'

'So, for something beginning with S?'

'Yes.'

'That's all right. You've held out longer than I thought you would. And today's a good time because you're probably looking fabulous.'

'Yes, I think I may be. Although Kim said I was wearing lesbian shoes.'

'That woman knows nothing. You're talking to an almost free man, by the way. Two more shows and I'm out of here.'

We went into a tunnel and I lost him.

The station was really crowded. People piling off trains, people gazing up at the departure boards, people just waiting. I did a quick scan, couldn't see the raccoon, wasn't even sure I'd recognize him. It had been a while. He might be wearing a beanie. He might have grown a beard. I strode away from the barrier like a woman who knew where she was going and what she was doing. It was the shoes.

I stopped outside a baguette bar and looked back. The crowd was thinning. There was a tall man waiting but he seemed to be holding up a card, like he was one of those meet 'n' greet drivers. I circled back round. It was him, no beard, no beanie. Just a very nice full-length overcoat and a card that said GODOT.

I'd been so worried about not recognizing him it hadn't occurred to me that he might not recognize me.

'*Sacre*-blummin'-*bleu*.' Those were his first words. 'You look . . . hot.'

'I'm not. I'm freezing. No heat on the train.'

'I mean you look great. Your hair's different.'

'It's called a choppy bob.'

'I like it. You look like you just got out of bed. In a nice way. On which topic, I was thinking. My place is out. Min's at home with a sore throat. And going back to your place probably isn't a great idea.'

'Why?'

'Well, this is all a bit impromptu. Or did you prepare the love shack before you left home?'

'Totally impromptu.'

'So if we go back to yours you'll start fussing and apologizing about the state of the house and all that.'

'How little you know me.'

'And you probably don't have a split of champagne in the fridge. So how about we go to a hotel?'

'I'm a bit skint.'

'Don't worry about it.'

'And I don't have a toothbrush.'

He steered me towards Boots. You can get anything on stations, these days. I remember when you were lucky if you could get a cup of tea.

We bought two toothbrushes and a tube of Colgate and checked into the De Montfort.

The girl said, 'Would you like luggage brought up?'

He said, 'It's gone missing. Probably still sitting in Riga. I'm waiting for a call from the airport.'

Her face lit up. 'I am from Riga,' she said. 'Did you like?'

'I was just kidding,' he said. 'We were actually in Bruges. I have no idea where our bags ended up.'

He carried it off very well.

He said, 'What were the chances, eh? Bloody Riga. What were the chances?'

He was investigating the mini-bar when my phone rang.

'Answer it,' he said. 'If it's the telly people giving you the thumbs-up we'll order a nice bottle.'

I didn't recognize the number.

'Lizzie,' she said. 'It's Kimberley. So lovely to see you today, but you and I need to talk. If this show is to have the slightest chance of going ahead we have to cut that dreadful Tobin woman out of the picture.'

21

Rodney, that is to say RJ, was going to another furry get-together. Something Fur the Weekend. In Clacton. He wanted me to go with him but I wasn't smitten with the idea of three nights in an off-season holiday camp. We'd stayed in one when I was about eight and our Philip was still a toddler. It was on Morecambe Bay. Even Dad was miserable there and he wasn't a man who expected much from life. He didn't even get placed in the Knobbly Knees contest. Draughty chalets, canteen dining.

Rodney said holiday camps weren't like that now. He said they had dining options and Wi-Fi. It made no difference. I couldn't see the point of being a plain clothes groupie while he spent the weekend in his raccoon suit. When we parted, the next morning, we agreed that we'd keep things casual between us. Casual, spontaneous, full of surprises. The first surprise was the tab for our room-service extras. It wasn't really his fault. He'd had to leave early to take delivery of a roll of latex foam at his daughter's workshop.

He called me. He said, 'You're absolutely sure you don't want to come to Clacton? We'd need to book pretty soon.'

I was quite sure.

I said, 'That was an expensive bottle of wine you ordered last night.'

'You were worth it,' he said.

'I'm glad you think so. You owe me for it.'

'Sure. Remind me next time I see you. So what are your plans for the week?'

'To meet Kim. She wants to plot the elimination of Valerie Tobin.'

'From what you've told me about this Kim, you'd better wear a stab vest. Also, for your consideration, I'm thinking seriously about doing the Los Angeles convention in October. Cali-Fur-nia. I know a few people who're going and I'm sure there'll be some other halves.'

'I'm not your other half.'

'No. Right. Anyway, think about it. It'll be a great trip.'

Kim was still living in the same very nice house. Kimbert. Kim and Robert. Kim and Bastard Bob. She was in full afternoon-tea assassination-planning war paint.

I said, 'I thought you might have moved. Weren't you and Bob getting divorced?'

'Absolutely not,' she said. 'Look, they'll be putting him out to grass one of these days and he's got a very nice pension pot. If I divorced him he'd hook up with some gormless teenager and probably marry her. He's such a fool over girls. No, no. That pension's as much mine as it is his. The years I've put in, and the work. You don't look like this at fifty-one without a lot of effort, let me tell you.'

SHOPPING CHANNEL KIM REVERSES TIME:
SCIENTISTS BAFFLED.

She said her relationship with Bob was amicable. One of those A-words that's only ever used for marriage bust-ups. It's either acrimonious or it's amicable.

'He's based in Bahrain mainly. It works very well for us. He just keeps a capsule wardrobe here.'

Funny word, capsule. I had this image of Bob zipped inside a suit bag whenever he visits the marital home, hanging in one of the closets, like a giant sweating insect chrysalis. 'Let me out, Kimmy. I promise not to diddle any more air stewardesses.'

I never met Bastard Bob but I've seen photos of him. Bob with Nigel Mansell. Bob with Jasper Carrott. Bob with some victorious boxer. He has mysterious hair that never looks longer or shorter or greyer.

Kim said, 'He still has his gym here. Well, he spent enough on it.' She showed me.

I said, 'This used to be his snooker room.'

She looked at me. 'I was here before, Kim. A long time ago.'

'I don't remember that. Did you come to one of our parties?'

'No. I came to keep you company. It was Christmas. You'd had a bust-up with Bob and you were nervous about being on your own.'

'Nervous?' she said. 'That doesn't sound like me. You must be thinking of someone else. I've got top-of-the-range security here. Motion-detector cameras, 24/7 monitoring. I've got LiveChat too.'

'What's that?'

'Well, say somebody was to break in, the people at the call centre can speak to them. Challenge them.'

'You mean like, "Oy, what do you think you're up to?"'

'Exactly. To stop them in their tracks. Scare them off.'

'What if it doesn't?'

CHEEKY BURGLAR MOONS AT TV STAR'S SECURITY CAMERA.

'Then they call the police. You're interested in kitchens. Do you like my new worktops? They're polished quartz.'

'Very nice. Although actually, Kim, I was never very interested in kitchens. Not as house features, you know. I just liked playing in them. And now not even that. I don't cook much. Straight from the pickle jar into the mouth, that's me, these days. So what's going on with you and Valerie? You two were great buddies.'

'I don't know why you think that.'

'You went off with her after the meeting.'

'It was just a lift. To the station. She was going my way.'

'She was going my way too.'

'Yes, I suppose she was. It probably didn't occur to her. She's quite dizzy, you know. Her mind flits from one thing to another.'

'Perfect for television, then.'

'And she's totally self-obsessed. You know she has a driver? And an S-class Merc. Can you believe the money that woman's made? Come and see my pizza oven.'

'And you went along with her bullshit story about the fight being staged.'

'Not really. I was just playing along, just lulling her into a false sense of security.'

We went out onto the patio to admire the pizza oven. I was expecting one of those domed clay things you see in Italy but Kim's was like a small spacecraft. I said, 'That looks very scary. Do you have to gather twigs and kindling?'

'Oh, no,' she said. 'It's artisan. Propane-fired artisan.'

'Are the pizzas any good?'

'I wouldn't know. I don't like pizza. The thing is, Lizzie, we have to cut Valerie out of the project. She's so boring. Zero personality. It's one thing to hop around a bit in a leotard and flog liquid meals, but you and I know there's more to television than that. We know how to engage with viewers. We know how to think on our feet. Now, you're the one with the contact. The girl?'

'India.'

'India. What did she say about the meeting?'

'Nothing. I haven't heard from her.'

'You mean you haven't called her? You should. We have to keep this on the boil. I'd speak to her myself but you're the one who knows her.'

'Hardly. She's dating my nephew, that's all.'

'So she's practically family. You have to call her and say something about Valerie.'

'Whatever we say I'm sure they're going to want her for the pilot. The whole premise is to bring the three of us back together.'

'Then we have to make them think again.'

★

Kim made tea. Well, Kim boiled some water while I found tea-bags. She didn't seem very familiar with her own kitchen. It was immaculate. Wiped and buffed to a state of magazine-readiness, as they say. Not a stained tea towel in sight.

She said, 'What we need is some dirt on Valerie.'

I felt that (a) there wasn't any, and (b) if there was, it wouldn't necessarily go against her. I said, 'Be careful, Kim. A bit of scandal can boost a career, not ruin it. I got lots of offers after my incident.'

'Did you? So how come you disappeared?'

'I didn't capitalize on them. I'd just met Tom and we were really happy. I kind of let things go. Didn't keep my eye on the ball.'

'Always a mistake. I never allowed marriage to distract me from my career.'

Yes, I thought. And look at you now. You're in the same boat as me. Living alone and scrabbling around for work. You have polished quartz worktops but I have Ellie and Noah, and the raccoon.

She said, 'Are you still with him? Your new man?'

'No. We were together for quite a while but things didn't work out.'

'Irreconcilable differences. Like Kate Winslet and Sam Mendes.'

'And also, Kim, on the topic of meddling with people's careers, remember what happened when you got Louie fired?'

'Who?'

'Louie Doyle. He used to do the horoscopes. Until you found out he made it all up and got him sacked.'

'Did I? Was he the gay boy?'

'Tortoiseshell glasses.'

'I remember him. He was quite good. But he wasn't fired because of me. Wasn't there some terrible scandal? Something in a public toilet?'

'He survived that, Kim. No, it was you. When you found out he didn't know how to do astrological charts you told on him. But look at him now.'

'Where is he?'

'Everybody knows Louie. He's just finished pantomime in Whitley Bay.'

'Not exactly riding high, then, is he?'

'He did a game show after *Midlands This Morning*. He's done all right. Voice-over work, ribbon-cutting, new shopping centres. I'm just saying. Don't make a fuss about Valerie. Let her self-destruct. You know, she probably couldn't care less about this project. Why would she bother schlepping up to Norwich to tape a little tin-pot show when she can sit at home and read her bank statements?'

'She won't be schlepping. She has that gorgeous car, and a driver.'

'Right. So she's not hungry for work like we are.'

'Well,' she said, 'I wouldn't describe myself as hungry for it, but the money might be good. This house doesn't run on fresh air.'

'I can imagine.'

'I just spent £200 on light bulbs.'

'I hadn't realized you were responsible for Blackpool Illuminations as well as this place.'

'It's not funny.'

'No. And I'll bet Bastard Bob's never around when a bulb goes. Since Tom moved out I don't bother any more. When a bulb goes it stays gone. A few more months and I'll be down to candles and the night light I got for when my grandson stays over. Except he doesn't.'

'You're a granny now?'

'It happens.'

'You don't look like a granny.'

'Thank you. Actually, I think this is what grannies look like, these days.'

'Bob and I never went in for children. It wouldn't have fitted our lifestyle.'

'No, I remember your white carpets.'

'Valerie Tobin's a worry though. This could be a lucrative project. It'd be a shame if she ruined it. If only there was some unforgivable little smudge on her character, to make them drop her.'

'You mean like voting Conservative?'

She put her cup down, gave me her Skewer Eyes.

I said, 'I was kidding, Kim.'

'I sincerely hope so,' she said, 'because I . . .'

'Me too. But I won't tell on you if you don't tell on me. Anyway, don't worry. They're not trying to sell this show to the BBC.'

As I was leaving she said, 'By the way, Lizzie, please try to remember to call me Kimberley. I haven't been Kim for a very long time.'

My phone rang while I was trying to park between Deep's in-laws' very nice Peugeot and Mrs Allen's niece's SUV.

A tentative voice: 'Is that Lizzie Partridge?'

I asked her to hold while I gave the Peugeot bumper a gentle nudge.

'Lizzie,' she said, 'this is Valerie. Tobin. I'm so glad to catch you. I think you and I need to talk about Kimberley.'

22

So Kim was plotting against Valerie and Valerie was scheming against Kim. As Louie said, they were probably arranging to meet and sharpen their knives together before nobbling me.

'Trust no one in this business,' he said. 'Not even the guy who mops out the studio bog.'

'So what do I say if Valerie calls me again?'

'The same as you said to Kimmykins. Beware what you wish for. Keep your enemies close. Why don't you screen your calls, you silly girl? Screen those calls and watch your back.'

Valerie didn't call me again and neither did Kim. Maybe Louie was right and they'd decided to gang up on me instead. I didn't care. Even without Xanax I found I absolutely didn't care. I was relaxed. Unlike my brother who was building up a fretful head of steam about Mum's approaching birthday.

He said, 'It's a landmark, ninety. We have to do something special.'

I sort of agreed but it was a tricky one. If asked, our mother would say she didn't want any fuss, but if there wasn't any fuss she'd be deeply offended. Philip proposed that we spring a surprise party at his house. Chicken dippers and strawberry gateau from

Iceland. Another flawed idea from the bulky portfolio of Philip Clarke. As I pointed out to him, if it was kept a complete surprise she'd be in the granddaddy of all huffs about her birthday being forgotten, and then, when she got there and everybody jumped out and yelled, 'Surprise!' she'd probably have a heart attack.

'Okay,' he said. 'You're so clever. What do you suggest?'

'You know what she really enjoys?'

'Garden centres. I take her all the time. That wouldn't be anything special.'

'She likes going to cemeteries.'

'No, Lizzie.'

'She does. She loves it. It's her victory fly-past over all the people she's outlived.'

'I'm not doing it.'

'I will. Happy to. An afternoon stroll round Handsworth Cemetery. Mum must know a dozen people there.'

'A lot of them go to Lodge Hill these days. Cremations.'

'That's okay I can take in Lodge Hill too. We can play Spot the Memorial Plaque. Then I'll bring her to your place for the "surprise surprise" and a heart attack. Did you plan on inviting the extended mob?'

'Kayleigh and the boys'll come. I don't know about Scott. He might be working. It'd be nice if your Ellie made an effort. It'll be a Saturday so no excuse for her not putting in an appearance.'

Of course, Philip had no idea how my grandson's hectic schedule tied up his parents' weekends. Reggio, Toddler Mandarin, Quantum Theory for Pre-Schoolers.

Later he called me back. 'Wendy's had a good idea. How about afternoon tea at a nice hotel?'

'Yes. And even better if preceded by the cemetery tour. But no surprises. She'll prefer to be told about it so she can book a shampoo and set.'

So that was agreed.

'Just one thing,' I said. 'If we're going out for tea do not, under any circumstances, allow Mum to see the menu prices. Her idea of a fair price for a chocolate éclair is years out of date.'

I picked her up after lunch, took her some freesias and a five-pack of those big knickers she likes. I'm sure she didn't need them. I only bought them for the joy of hearing her say, 'Well, you can never have too many undies.'

Philip had booked the Silk Road Lounge at the De Montfort for three o'clock: the Traditional Tea deal, which was finger sandwiches, and a selection of cakes but no champagne. There'd be six of us plus Noah. Kayleigh was coming on her own because Kev was taking the boys to the football. West Brom were at home to Chelsea.

'You shouldn't have,' said Mum, right on script. 'But you can never have too many undies.'

I said, 'I've got some more flowers in the car, for Dad's grave.'

'It's a very nice thought, Elizabeth,' she said, 'but you know they'll only get stolen. The last time I went I took him an artificial begonia.'

We went to Handsworth Cemetery first and worked our way back from the recent arrivals to the long-term residents. Beryl Barker, broken hip, pneumonia. No headstone yet but we identified her from the rain-sodden tags on the wreaths.

'What happened to Beryl? Did she fall at home?'

'No. Right outside her house. There's a paving stone sticking up and nobody does anything about it. You can complain till you're blue in the face. And if you phone the council they say it's because of the cut-backs.'

Kathleen Hazzard, beloved wife of Harry, mother of Pamela and Richard.

I said, 'Why are we visiting her? As I recall, you didn't like her.'

'Well, seeing as we're passing. I wouldn't have come specially. She was all right.'

'You say that now she's six foot under.'

'It was just that she could be a bit bay window.'

Ouch. A bit bay window. A picture card from my mother's deck of put-downs. 'Could she? How so?'

'Well, she was always bringing up foreign travel. "When I was on the Algarve". "When my Pamela took me to Lake Garda". Then you'd have to show an interest in her holiday snaps. Lording it over you. Not that I cared. Travel's never appealed to me.'

'Well, her travelling days are done now.'

'Yes.'

Albert Collier, aged eighty-seven. 'Sadly missed'.

'That's a bit bleak. I wonder who's sadly missing him. Didn't he have any family?'

'No. He never married. Your dad knew him from the allotment.'

We went to find Dad. Up and down the rows we went. I said we must be in the wrong section but she wouldn't have it.

216

'Look for his begonia,' she said.

We retraced our steps. Mum was flagging a bit so we sat on a bench.

I said, 'You know what I think? I reckon he's sub-let his plot and done a runner.'

'Elizabeth!' she said, but she was laughing. What a golden moment that was. My mum, amused by something I'd said.

'What about Aunt Edie and Uncle Cyril? Were they any-where near Dad?'

'I can't remember exactly. Somewhere near – 1986 Edie died. The same day as Cary Grant.'

'I didn't know that. I wonder if she saw him?'

'Who?'

'Cary Grant. When she was waiting to get in.'

I always picture long tailbacks for the Pearly Gates. Like the M25 but with celestial music, or maybe just birdsong. People getting out of their cars – well, out of their bodies I suppose it'd be. Tut-tutting and starting to chat.

'Cancer?'

'Car smash. Black ice. How about you?'

We found Auntie Edie and Uncle Cyril. 'Edith Mary and Cyril Bertram Clarke. Safe in the arms of Jesus.'

'Who chose that?'

'Must have been their Leslie. Edie never set foot in church.'

My cousin Leslie lives in New Zealand. He'd only just got back from burying his dad when his mum died and he had to turn round and fly over again. Still, I suppose it bumped up his air miles.

'What was it with you and Edie? You always seemed annoyed with each other.'

'I don't know what you mean.'

There was a rumour in the family that Mum had had a thing for Cyril but Edie beat her to it so she settled for Dad instead. Uncle Cyril was my dad's brother. He rose to great heights in office stationery. Dad didn't.

WAR BRIDE WINS SECOND PRIZE IN MARRIAGE STAKES.

'I remember Aunty Phyllis saying you'd have been a better match for Cyril than Edie was.'

'Phyllis! What did she know?'

We sat again.

I said, 'Well, I'm glad you chose Dad. He could be funny. Remember how he used to say, "How long till tea's ready, Mu? I could eat the dates off a calendar."'

'It was just a silly expression.'

'"To hell with the expense, woman. Throw the cat another kipper." That was another one. Remember that?'

'We never had a cat. Philip was allergic.'

HOPES DASHED FOR PEDANTRY SUFFERERS: SCIENTISTS NO NEARER TO CURE.

'And if Cyril had been our dad I wouldn't be me and Philip wouldn't be Philip.'

'Oh, look,' she said. 'There's Ivy Curtis. I didn't realize she was in here – 1994. "Gone but not forgotten." Well, I'd forgotten her.'

'Shall we drop by Lodge Hill before we go for tea?'

'I don't think so.'

'We could leave the flowers for Yvonne, seeing as Dad seems to have relocated and left no forwarding address.'

'I suppose so. But it's just a plaque, you know. Yvonne's isn't a proper grave.'

'Does it matter? We all end up as dust anyway. Cremation's just like the Express Delivery option. What about your friend Thelma? She was cremated. Isn't she in Lodge Hill?'

'No, they chucked her in the sea.'

'I think "scattered" is the word. In the sea is nice. I wouldn't mind that. Where did they do it?'

'Weston.'

'Weston-super-Mare? Are you sure? I went there once and I couldn't even see the sea.'

'The tide must have been out.'

'I'll say. Out all the way to Nova Scotia.'

We were about to leave when I spotted Dad. Wilfred John Clarke, dearly beloved husband of Muriel, father of Elizabeth and Philip. We left the freesias for him.

I said, 'Is this where you'll be going? Is it a two-berth?'

'Yes,' she said. 'But not till I've had my birthday tea.'

Dad was between Gladys Woodcock and Edgar Langley. I wrote it down, for future reference.

I said, 'He was a lovely dad.'

Not a tiger of a man, more a Flopsy Bunny. He always looked a bit nervous, always waiting for directions from Mum. 'Try to walk on the sides of the stair carpet, Wilf, to even out the wear'; 'If you're going to eat beetroot take that good shirt off.'

She linked her arm through mine and we walked back to the car park.

'Anyway,' she said, 'I'll tell you something about your Aunt Edie. She had a nasty streak. A terrible temper. She used to throw things.'

'Really? That's surprising. She always seemed a bit of a cold fish.'

'She'd bottle it up and then *bang*! The dinner plates that woman got through. I think she was maniac-depressive.'

When we got to the hotel Philip was having one of his red-faced blusters. The Silk Road Lounge was closed for redecorating and they were serving afternoon tea in the lobby instead.

'You people,' he was saying. He kept jabbing his finger at the hapless girl who'd delivered the news. Only air-jabbing, mind. Philip wouldn't dare make physical contact for fear of legal repercussions.

TEA RAGE MAN FACES HOTEL BAN.

'This lady,' he said, pointing to Mum, 'this lady is celebrating her ninetieth birthday. She served her country in World War Two. And you're telling me she can't have her tea in the Silk Road Lounge?'

Wendy walked away, pretended to study the 'In the Event of Fire' notice.

Kayleigh said, 'Dad, calm down. It'll be the same cakes. They might even give you a discount, for the upset.'

The girl said they'd certainly look into that possibility. She looked close to tears. My brother always picks on little people.

Mum said, 'Or we could go to John Lewis. They do quite a nice scone.'

When Philip is angry he seems to inflate. He said, 'We are not going to John flipping Lewis's. This is a special occasion.'

I said, 'But let's not make it a day to remember by you having a stroke.'

Ellie arrived, with Noah and a glitter-and-macaroni birthday card he'd made at crèche.

She said, 'What's up? Uncle Philip looks like a pink airbed. Have they run out of teabags?'

A girl came, a different one. I think the jab-ee had retired, upset. She probably needed counselling. The new girl started laying out cutlery and napkins. She said, 'The assistant manager will be with you shortly to apologize for the mix-up.'

'There hasn't been a mix-up,' Philip growled. 'There's been incompetence and inefficiency. I booked for the lounge.' He never knows when to let a thing go.

The assistant manager appeared. You have to feel sorry for hotel staff. Their uniforms only come in two sizes: Tight Squeeze and Utterly Swamped.

She said, 'I am very sorry of your upset and I will like to offer you discount on bottle of sparkling wine.'

Philip said, 'We're not having sparkling wine.'

'But,' said Wendy, in perfect unison with me, 'we could.'

'Oh, hello,' said the assistant manager, looking square at me. 'Did you get luggage okay?'

It threw me for a moment.

She said, 'Luggage not from Riga?'

Then I recognized her.

Ellie said, 'I didn't know you'd been to Riga.'

'Bruges,' I said. 'Yes, all sorted. And we'll take up your offer on the sparkling wine, thank you.'

Ellie said, 'When were you in Bruges?'

'I wasn't. Nor Riga. It's a long story and I'm never going to tell you anyway.'

Tea was nice. Noah sat between me and Mum. Ellie had brought supplies with her because we can't have Noah getting a taste for chocolate cake. Hummus, breadsticks and a carrot muffin.

I said, 'Muffins? Have you started baking?'

'Baking?' she said. 'I hardly have time to get my eyebrows done. It's the au pair. She makes all kinds of stuff. She's brilliant. How was the cemetery?'

'Quiet as the grave.'

'Very funny.'

Kayleigh's phone rang. It was Scott. She put him on speakerphone.

'Happy birthday, Nan,' he said. 'Are you having a knees-up?'

She said, 'I'm having a lovely day. There was a bit of a to-do about our booking but your dad soon sorted it out and now we're getting free champagne. Are you still seeing that nice Paki girl?'

Kayleigh said, 'Nana! You can't say that.'

'Why not?'

'It's a hate crime. And, anyway, she's English.'

Scott said, 'Yes, I'm still with India. She sends her best wishes.'

Mum said, 'We went to the cemetery, took some flowers for Granddad Wilf. Your Aunt Elizabeth drove me.'

'That's nice. See anybody you knew?'

'Oh, yes. Beryl Barker, Albert Collier, Cyril and Edie. Who else, Elizabeth?'

'Peter Gurney, Peter Davy, Dan'l Whiddon, Harry Hawke, Old Uncle Tom Cobley and all, old Uncle Tom Cobley and all.'

'Your Aunt Elizabeth is trying to be clever.'

'Hello, Aunt Elizabeth,' he said. 'I hear you had a great meeting with India and Tark.'

I said, 'Did I? I haven't heard anything from them.'

'Takes time,' he said. 'But India's quite optimistic.'

After he'd gone Mum kept saying, 'What I don't understand is, why can't I say "Paki girl?"'

Every time she said it Ellie tried diversionary tactics with Noah. Educational ones, of course.

'Do you see what's in that picture over there? It's a dromedary.'

'Gammul,' said Noah.

'No,' said my daughter, 'because a camel has two humps and that animal only has one. It's a dromedary. Can you say that?'

'Gammul.'

Philip proposed a toast. 'To the best mum in the world. Best nan. Best great-nan.'

He was quite choked, and so was I, to my very great surprise. Mum fights off all displays of affection but I think she knows I love her. Best mum in the world? Well, steady on. But she's what we had, what we've got. Of course Philip's childhood memories aren't the same as mine. 'Let him have it, Elizabeth. He's only little'; 'You're lucky to have a brother, young lady. We nearly lost him.'

We didn't, not really. It was just that whenever he got any of the childhood illnesses he'd have one of the optional add-ons as well. Complications. Bronchitis, pneumonia. They even lit a fire for him in the bedroom when he had whooping cough. Nobody ever lit a bedroom fire for me.

When the bill came he broke out his reading glasses and studied it like it was some million-pound contract he was being asked to sign. He called the waiter over. He said, 'We were supposed to get a discount on the wine. For inconvenience caused.'

'Yes, sir,' said the waiter. 'The list price is £35.'

I said, 'Wendy, will you please murmur in your husband's ear, if he makes another fuss I'll personally strangle him.'

'No need,' she said. 'I'm at the ready myself.'

Mum said, 'That girl. Scott's friend? Did I upset her when I called her that word?'

I said, 'No, you didn't. Because for one thing she's not what you said and for another she has a sense of humour. She's a nice girl.'

Mum said, 'Because I wouldn't have wanted to offend her.'

I said, 'Anyway, you're ninety years old. You have a Get Out of Jail Free card for the rest of your life.'

'What does that mean?'

'It means you're allowed to say whatever you like. Even "Paki".'

'Paki,' said Noah. 'Paki, Paki, Paki.'

Ellie said, 'Thanks, Mum. Brilliant.'

And my mother said, 'He's a bonny little chap, isn't he? Such a pity they couldn't have given him a normal name.'

23

I'd just reached that depressing stage of home decorating when you realize why sensible people pay a little man to come in. But there was no turning back. I was trying to smarten up my bedroom because I couldn't afford to keep trysting with the raccoon in hotels, and his place was a no-go because of his daughter. Time that girl moved out. I mean, seriously, what kind of twenty-seven-year-old wants to live with their dad?

I'd applied a quick coat of Mellow Melon. I lay on the bed, closed my eyes, opened them again and thought, Eww. Pus.

The phone rang. Rushing to answer it I put my foot in the paint tray.

But it was India!

'Exciting news, Lizzie,' she said. 'We have real interest from a couple of networks so we're going ahead with the pilot. The studio's booked for the 17th but we'll need you in Norwich the night before, ready for an early start. I hope you're still available.'

I said, 'Let me check my diary.' You can't let these people think you're sitting by the phone, desperate for work.

She said, 'We have a great line-up. Kimberley and Valerie, of course, and then we have Melanie Pope and Abi Cooper for one session, Tamara Hunt and Ronnie Lincoln for the second.'

'I thought it was going to be all women?'

'It is. Ronnie's short for Veronica. Although we're thinking that occasional male guests would bring added interest. Down the line. If the project takes off.'

'And who are these people you just mentioned?'

'Okay. Melanie played Cassandra in *Cloverfields*. Cassandra just died after taking a legal high, so Melanie's exploring new career opportunities. And Abi was in the girl band Awesome but she's been doing quite a lot of TV since they split up. Like *Chill Time*, for instance. It's a teen show so you might not have seen it.'

It didn't seem quite the moment to tell India that I hadn't seen anything since 4 June 1994 when my old telly burst into flames and I never replaced it. Tom used to go back to his own house to watch the cricket.

'So they're both young.'

'We need to balance the demographic. With you and Valerie and Kimberley being at the more mature end of the spectrum.'

'And what about Ronnie and the other one?'

'Tamara used to be a weather girl and then she presented an afternoon game show. Ronnie writes a very popular column in the *Sunday Herald*. Plus she's had cancer, which always makes for a popular talking point.'

'What's the show going to be called?'

'Working title is *Real Women*, although I quite like *Girl Talk*. It sounds lighter. Tamara's in her thirties, Ronnie's in her late forties. Abi and Melanie are younger but they're very professional. And the main thing is they're all great fun. Completely zany.'

Zany. Did I want to be associated with 'zany'? Perhaps. I'd managed to overcome my first reaction to 'edgy'.

'Maybe you should call the show *Mad Cows*. What do I have to wear?'

'Don't worry about that. We'll have a selection of outfits for you to choose from.'

'Are you sure? Will you have anything in my size?'

I could just picture Kimmykins and old Turtle Face rifling through the size tens and gloating.

'Absolutely. What is your size?'

'Sixteen. Sixteen generous. And I can't wear yellow.'

'I'll make a note.'

'Or orange. We haven't talked about money.'

'Ah,' she said. 'Well, as it's speculative we can only offer expenses for the pilot. But going forward, obviously we'd talk to your agent. Remind me, who is your agent?'

This, Lizzie Partridge, I thought is why you're sitting here, one slipper covered with pus-coloured paint, out of work, heart racing at the vague prospect of a perch on a daytime TV panel with four other nonentities. You no longer have an agent. Hegarty died years ago. He had one liquid lunch too many and toppled under the wheels of a bus on Corporation Street. And because you were feeling cosy and unambitious, because you were busy playing Mr and Mrs with Tom Sullivan, you neglected to find a replacement. You let things slide, you idiot woman.

I said, 'Charles Lacey.'

Because I had to say something.

'Charles Lacey?' she said. 'Don't think I know him. But by all means give him my number.'

Louie said, 'You told them Chas was your WHAT?'

I said, 'He was the only person I could think of who'd know anything about contracts. Anyway, why not? He handles you.'

'What goes on behind closed bedroom doors stays behind closed bedroom doors.'

'This'll probably never take off. You know what it's like. I'll go to Norwich, record the pilot. A day's work, two nights in a hotel, get my train fare. I don't need a proper agent for that.'

'Yes you do. You need somebody out here hustling for you, making sure you don't get fucked over. Anyway, sweet, Chas doesn't represent me any longer. I'm with JMK these days. I could put in a word there.'

'But just for now, if asked, do you think Chas'd say he represents me? Like a holding position? Would you ask him?'

'I won't ask him. I'll tell him. But we're going to Amalfi straight after Easter so he'll be incommunicado for ten days. Which might not be a bad thing. Now, how long do we have before these pilot shows?'

'Two weeks.'

'You need to lose 5lbs.'

'How do you know?'

'Everybody needs to. As a matter of fact, if you're doing TV you need to lose 10lbs but we have to be realistic here. Berries and natural yogurt for breakfast. Cabbage soup for lunch. Salmon and a big salad for dinner. No booze. Shall I write it down and send it to you?'

He phoned me three more times with words of advice.

'Make sure you claim for subsistence as well as travel. You can't function properly on Green Room carbs.'

'Take your own clothes with you. You could get there and find all they have in your size is a tarpaulin with neck frills. Cast your mind back to some of the abominations Kimmy used to wear.'

'And remember, nothing black, nothing white, nothing zig-zaggy. And no dangly earrings.'

I drew up a list.

1. Follow Louie's diet plan.
2. Get hairdresser to sharpen up choppy bob.
3. Do something about horrible paint-splodged hands and stubby nails.

I called Wendy, told her I had a cuticle emergency. She said to come round and she'd see what she could do. Such a relief to keep that kind of thing in the family.

Philip was trying to fit a new belt to Mum's spin-drier.

I said, 'Wouldn't it be simpler to buy her a new one? Can you still get them?'

'You can,' he said, 'if you know where to look. But why spend good money when I can fix this one?'

'We could get her a tumble-drier. I'd go halves.'

'She wouldn't want one. She likes her spin-drier.'

He was right. God knows, it had taken years enough to persuade her to part with her mangle.

Wendy looked at my hands and shook her head. 'Marigolds, Lizzie,' she said. 'Haven't you ever heard of Marigolds?'

She got the paint off my hands and did a nice thing with warm oil. She said, 'Are you going on a date?'

I told her about the TV thing. She said she'd need to see me at least once a week, to get my hands looking okay. 'Good thing I like a challenge,' she said. 'I mean we're looking at years of neglect here. Anyway, are you seeing anybody?'

I said, 'I'll tell you if you promise not to say how perfect Tom was.'

'Well, he was, but I won't. So who are you seeing?'

'He's an old school friend.'

'Did you find him on that Classmates site?'

'No, it was what you might call a chance encounter. And we're not really dating. All that wine-bar-or-the-Omniplex carry-on. We just meet for dynamite sex when the fancy takes us.'

'Hear that, Phil?' she said. 'Lizzie's getting dynamite sex.'

'Oh, yes?' he said. 'Wendy, have you moved my screwdriver again?'

I called Rodney to tell him about *Mad Cows*. He said he'd always known it would happen. 'We should celebrate,' he said. 'I've got to come into town later in the week. I'm picking up some new glasses. Where shall we meet?'

'Not the De Montfort. That receptionist you lied to about lost luggage? She never forgets a face. I had to explain to my whole family that I hadn't actually been to Bruges or Riga.'

'Plenty of other hotels.'

'Why don't you come here?'

He hesitated. He said, 'Have you got framed family photos everywhere?'

'A few. Not *everywhere*.'

'And I'll bet you've got a loo that doesn't always flush. And a saggy mattress.'

'If you don't think my house will come up to your high standards, why don't you tell your Minnie to make herself scarce and I'll come to you?'

'A hotel's sexier.'

'A hundred quid a night sexier. Minimum.'

'It'll be my treat. How about the Chamberlain Metro? Thursday, one o'clock? We can get a bite of lunch, launch your new career with a glass of bubbles, then check in.'

I didn't put up much of a fight. My mattress is slightly saggy and there is a knack to the toilet flush. You have to take it unawares. Also the whole house still smelt of paint. So my Louie crash diet was postponed till Friday but at least my nails were looking a lot nicer than usual.

24

I can't really remember what Rodney Pooley looked like at school. If he showed any potential, it passed me by. He was just a name used to mock me.

'You're going to marry somebody like Rodney Pooley.'

I suppose it meant he wasn't your run-of-the-mill lout. Perhaps he held doors open. Maybe he didn't practise fake belching.

The boys were years behind us girls, hormone-wise. They were still making balsawood model planes while we were in Woolworth's on a Saturday, trying out the eye-shadow testers. Then some of those boys just evolved into bigger, bristlier versions of themselves, our Philip being a case in point, and some turned into unrecognizable good-looking men.

He was in the hotel bar with a bottle of champagne in an ice bucket. The real thing.

I said, 'It's only a pilot, you know? A Spanish cava would be more fitting.'

'Never mind. We're celebrating being alive, not having to go to work this afternoon. Champagne because there's an R in the month. And it's Neville Chamberlain's birthday.'

'Is it?'

'No idea.'

'Where are your new specs?

They were like joke Groucho Marx glasses.

'They're for RJ to wear,' he said. 'It's been tricky getting frames big enough.' He had RJ's head in his bag.

'Did you put that on in the optician's?'

'Had to.'

'What did the optician say?'

'Not a word, and neither did I. It takes more than a raccoon head for two Englishmen to discuss personal matters.'

He went to book us a room while we were waiting for lunch. He was soon back.

'Now this is embarrassing,' he said. 'There's a problem with my card. It's probably the magnetic strip. Can you put the room on yours and I'll give you a cheque? I've got enough cash to pay for lunch.'

I did it, of course. I was two glasses of Lanson Brut beyond prudence. Also he was wearing English Leather aftershave. Funny how that still pushes my buttons. It's what Alec used to wear, when we were happy. Then he became a conniving, phil-andering Paco Rabanne stud. Until he met Nikki. After that he changed to Aramis. That's how I knew something more serious than an office quickie was occurring. So he might have been a lying, double-crossing rat but at least he didn't sully my happy memories of English Leather.

I'd brought an overnight bag with me but at about 4.30 I suddenly felt out of sorts. Rodney was asleep, I had a cham-pagne headache and I was ninety-five quid out of pocket for a hotel room I didn't really need any more. I wanted to go home, use my own toilet, make a chip butty, read my Val McDermid. Holding in your midriff bulge can get very tiring.

I got dressed. I could have slipped away unnoticed if I hadn't dropped my hairbrush on the bathroom floor and woken him.

He said, 'Don't go.'

'Tell me one good reason.'

He looked under the bed covers and grinned.

'Give me an hour or two,' he said, and closed his eyes.

I said, 'I'm going. I have stuff to do. Don't forget to send me a cheque.'

'Mm,' he said. 'And have a think about California. We should book it soon.'

'I can't afford California.'

'You will do when you get this telly series. After the furries convention we could drive up to the wine country. Napa Valley. Nice little hotels. It'd be great.'

'I didn't get the TV yet. I'm not counting my chickens.'

'You'll get it. Think positive.'

He hauled the covers up to his ears and settled back down to sleep. I closed the door behind me very quietly.

I don't know if he stayed overnight and had his money's worth — my money's worth. My mind was on other things for the next couple of days. Ellie was in a fix. She had a trial starting at the Crown Court in Hereford, Nat was away at a conference in Bratislava, and the brilliant, muffin-baking au pair had scarpered.

I said, 'Not gone to Bratislava with your husband, I pray.'

'Don't be ridiculous,' she said. 'She's eighteen.'

You'd think a criminal lawyer would have a more jaded view of human nature.

'So could you possibly mind Noah? It'll just be for one day. Nat's back on Monday night.'

I said I'd be happy to help. 'What's the big case?'

She was defending a man accused of breaking into a farm shed with intent to steal tractor diesel.

'And his defence is?'

'He was lost. He took a wrong turn up the farm track and stopped his van because he needed to pee.'

'In somebody's shed? Couldn't he go in a hedgerow? Men can pee anywhere. What time of day was this?'

'Early morning.'

'How early?'

'Three.'

'And you're defending this chancer?'

'It's what I do, Mum. He's entitled to a defence. If anybody should be on trial it's the farmer. He shot at him.'

'I don't blame him. It's a pity he missed.'

'He didn't. My client nearly lost a toe.'

'Nearly? Sounds like that farmer needs shooting practice.'

'You can't go round shooting people just because they're inadvertently on your property.'

'Really? Something wrong with that picture. What was the farmer supposed to do? Go down in his jimjams, offer him the use of his facilities? Take the thieving scumbag a flashlight and a funnel?'

'You don't understand.'

She was dead right. But I put it on my list of things the Mad Cows could talk about.

I didn't really have a plan for my day looking after Noah. It was around midnight on Sunday when it occurred to me that I had no toys in the house. I needn't have worried. When Ellie dropped him off early on Monday morning he came fully equipped: two bags of educational activities, several changes of clothing, a pushchair that converted to a cherry-picker, a Zimmer frame or a combine harvester. Also a musical talking potty.

I said, 'What does it play, Handel's *Water Music*?'

'I think it's "Frère Jacques".'

'Isn't he big enough to use the toilet?'

'Why must you complicate everything? He'll graduate to the toilet when he's ready. He likes it when the potty says, "Wow!" And, please, don't give him sugar.'

Noah had brought his own food.

'Anything else?'

'It'd be great if you did a bit of work with numbers and letters. There's a magnetic board in one of the bags. And scissor skills. Give him half an hour of cutting out. There's an old *Guardian Weekend* magazine in the bag. Did I tell you he's been diagnosed as left-handed?'

'Diagnosed? Ellie, it's not a disease.'

'You know what I mean.'

'Are we done?'

'No swearing.'

Off she went. She hoped to be home by six. I'll bet she hadn't even made it to the motorway before we went off-script. I made us eggy bread, white sliced with maple syrup. Noah's had a smiley face made from blueberries, which he picked off and arranged very carefully on the side of the plate.

Next up, geography. He had this magnetic map of the world with landmark pieces to put in the right location. Taj Mahal, Statue of Liberty, that kind of thing. Where does the Eiffel Tower go? Up your nostril, of course.

The postman came. There was no cheque from the raccoon.

Noah explored the house while I cleaned up. He came down-stairs with my alarm clock, a sink plunger and a gadget I'd wasted money on to try and tone my bingo wings.

I said, 'Shall we get your letters out and make some words?'

'No,' he said. 'What dis?'

'An exerciser.'

'Why?'

'To give me strong arms.'

'Why?'

'So I can hug you.'

He ran to the other side of the kitchen table and glowered. 'Where Landa?'

Iolanda was the au pair.

'She's gone on holiday. Granny's looking after you today.'

'Want Landa.'

'Well, tough, little buddy. You're stuck with me.'

'Don't like this house,' he said. But he'd figured out that his options were limited. 'Where your choglit?'

I told him the chocolate didn't arrive till after lunch. Chocolate was my reserve weapon. I couldn't deploy it too early in the day.

★

He played for an hour with the plunger, the exercise doofer and my rotary whisk. Well, why not? My meringue-making days are over.

It was only 9 a.m. Time had slowed to an imperceptible crawl. Einstein could probably have explained it.

I thought we'd go to the supermarket. That'd while away an hour. But then I remembered I didn't have a car seat for him, and to tie him in with a scarf, the way I used to do with Ellie, was now strictly forbidden. It'd be just my luck to get pulled over by the police.

The only thing for it was to go on foot. But that was a good idea. The sun was shining. We might even stop by the park. That would eat up a couple of hours, plus the time it took me to work out how to unfold the pushchair. Ellie seems able to do it with one hand.

I managed it eventually but it was a hollow victory because I broke one of my Wendy-ed nails and Noah refused to sit in the damned thing anyway. We set off at the pace a three-year-old can manage when he's carrying a sink plunger.

Noah, I must say, had top playground-detection sonar. As we neared the park gates he picked up speed without me saying a word.

The climbing frame and the playhouse were his favourites, for which I was thankful. I've had a dislike of swings since the age of nine when I accidentally knocked my brother flying. It was hardly my fault if he was stupid enough to waddle into the path of an occupied swing. Hardly my fault if Mum wasn't watching him. But I got smacked on both legs anyway, for 'nearly killing him'. I should have that out with her some time. Excessive and unfair use of corporal punishment.

238

We were able to pick up the pace after the park because Noah was knackered and agreed to ride the rest of the way to the supermarket in his princely chariot.

I said, 'What shall we buy for lunch?'

'Choglit.'

'What else? Do you like little sausages? Or fish fingers?'

'Choglit.'

Ellie phoned. 'How is he?'

'How's who?'

'Very funny.'

'He's fine. Stop fussing. We've been to the park.'

'That's nice. Did you use the sanitizer on his hands afterwards?'

'He didn't get dirty.'

'Mum! Haven't you ever heard of toxoplasmosis? Or Weil's disease? Disinfect his hands now, please! The stuff's in the green bag.'

'Does he like grapes?'

'Yes, but you must sit with him while he eats them. They're a big choking risk.'

'How's the case going?'

'We're waiting to be called on. He likes strawberries too. Got to go.'

Noah and I turned down the fruit and vegetable aisle and ran smack into Tom and a female. Geraldine.

He introduced us. I was 'an old friend, Lizzie. And this must be Noah,' he said. 'I haven't seen this little fellow since he was a baby.'

Geraldine wasn't a baby person. You can always tell. They

try to put on a friendly face but the strain is all too evident. I don't say that by way of condemnation. I'm not really a baby person myself.

She said, 'Is that a sink plunger he's holding?'

Tom said, 'Seems like you could have a future plumber in the family, Lizzie.'

They were looking for salad spinach. I'd heard there was a shortage. Watercress can be nice, raw or wilted in a little butter. Such are the things you talk about when you meet an old lover and his new woman in the supermarket.

'Well, Thomas,' she said, 'we'd better get a move on.'

I'm pushed to tell you much about Geraldine. Salt-and-pepper hair, rimless glasses, beige anorak. Nothing distinctive except possibly the thinness of her lips. Tom used to say he fell in love with my lips before he'd even met me, when I used to lick my fingers on *Midlands This Morning*. They talk about Nigella doing it but I was years ahead of her.

I said, 'Nice to see you . . . Thomas.'

The rims of his ears turned red.

As we got to the house Deep and Pari were having a new fridge-freezer delivered. I asked Deep if I could have the cardboard box. He brought it round just as Noah was emerging, scowling and cranky, from a deep sleep. Even the potty saying, 'Wow!' didn't delight him.

Lunch was strawberries, choglit and breadsticks. Then we played table football for a while with drinking straws and popcorn. The second half of the match was something of a washout because Noah kept eating the ball, but it got us to 2 o'clock.

Only four hours to go and I still had the fridge carton up my sleeve.

I opened it out very carefully and made it into a slide – positioned it on the stairs, taped it to the skirting board and the banisters. It was pretty brilliant, though I do say so myself.

When Ellie arrived, just after 5.30, I'd fallen asleep on the sofa and Noah had taken all his magnetic numbers and letters and arranged them in a line that reached from the kitchen to the foot of the stairs. He had also forgotten to ask for the musical potty.

Ellie said, 'What a clever boy. Have you made a word?'

He had. It said CPQ6EENL8TSSAAAY9. Or something similar. He showed her the slide. 'Mine,' he said.

'That was very creative of you, Mother,' she said.

'But?'

I can always tell when there's a 'but' coming from my daughter. She calls me 'Mother'.

'We like him to wear a helmet for all active play.'

I said, 'Eleanor, he was sliding down ten steps onto pillows.'

'Yes. Well. Just for future reference. And did you do any cutting and sticking?'

'No, we did cutting and throwing the pieces on the floor. What happened at court?'

'Acquitted. We'll probably go for compensation now.'

'For what?'

'Loss of earnings. My client was on crutches for weeks.'

'And what's his profession?'

'He deals in second-hand goods.'

'Such as somebody else's diesel? Acquitted! If I were that farmer I'd be ready to turn a gun on myself.'

241

'He's not out of the woods yet. He could be charged. He should be. Wounding with intent.'

'With the intent of not having his diesel nicked. Would you defend him?'

'Obviously not. But somebody will. Thanks for stepping in at short notice. I'm really grateful.'

'Has Iolanda turned up?'

'No, she's definitely gone. I thought she'd left some of her stuff in her room but it was just empty shopping bags. The agency's sending a couple of possibles tomorrow. Nat can interview them.'

I was exhausted. I could have stretched out on the sofa and stayed there till morning but I rallied enough to go down the slide a few times before I dismantled it. Afterwards it occurred to me that if it wasn't secured on both sides I could have kept it there. Just lift it out of the way when I needed to walk upstairs, flip it back into position if I fancied sliding down. It was a consideration.

I found the Great Wall of China and several squashed blueberries under the kitchen table. The sink plunger had disappeared without trace. Noah must have stashed it in his bag of educational toys. I do hope so.

It was quite late when my phone rang. I didn't recognize the number. It wasn't Kim and it wasn't Valerie Tobin.

A husky voice said, 'Is that Lizzie? This is Janet. Coleman. Pooley.'

25

Janet Coleman! My insides did a Mexican wave.

The first thing I said was, 'Has Rod had an accident?'

Not cool. If I ever murdered someone, which is not completely beyond the realms of possibility, I just know I'd blurt out something incriminating in about ten seconds.

She laughed. 'No,' she said. 'He's fine. I just wanted a word. How are you? It's been a long time.'

My voice, when I found it again, came out squeaky.

She said, 'Sorry to put the wind up you. I've been dithering about whether to phone. It's about Rod.'

I said, 'You are divorced?'

'Oh yes,' she said. 'Years ago. Don't worry. I don't want him back.'

'And you're in Spain?'

'I am.'

'How did you get my number?'

'From our Minnie. She knows Rod's been seeing you.'

So his daughter wanted to put a crimp in things for us.

'And?'

Janet said, 'Listen. Keep your hair on. Minnie knows what

243

he's like. She's seen how things can end up with him. To be honest, Lizzie, she's fed up with desperate women turning up on her doorstep looking for him.'

'Her doorstep?'

'Well, it is her house. Just answer me one thing. Has he borrowed money from you?'

I said he hadn't. It was true. Half true. He just owed me a few quid, that was all.

'Okay,' she said. 'That's good.'

'Janet, I don't have anything to lend. And, anyway, he doesn't seem to have any money worries.'

Another half-truth.

She said, 'Yeah, that's the problem. When he hasn't got it he just gets somebody else to pay. Did he give you the retired-businessman story? Did he give you the old import−export baloney?'

'Are you saying he didn't have a business?'

'He's had several. They just don't last. Upholstery-cleaning, juice bars. Cake Face, that was one of his. Edible photos.'

'But not import−export.'

'No. Well, I suppose you could say. Importing other people's money into the Bank of Rod. Look, I don't want to cause trouble. I just thought you ought to be warned.'

'Okay.'

'Funny, really, you two hooking up after all these years.'

'Yes.'

'I used to see you on the telly sometimes, when you were doing your cooking.'

'And you're settled in Spain?'

244

'Oh, yes. I've got a business here. Holiday lets. All upmarket, all premier properties with heated pools. If you ever want a nice place to stay just email me. We're called Jandro Rentals. You'll find us on the web.'

'Jandro as in "Janet"? What's the "Dro" short for?'

'Alejandro. My partner.'

I didn't write it down. I had no intention of looking her up. There's probably some way people can tell if you've been looking at their website and I wouldn't give her the satisfaction. She'd already ruined my evening.

She asked me if I was in touch with any of the old gang. But I was never in the old gang. That was the whole point. I was Swanky Clarke. Outsider. Gang of One.

She said Pauline Ogden was in Australia. And Gillian Glover had had a win on the lottery, not millions but a nice amount and she hadn't let it change her.

Behold, Janet Coleman brings you tidings of great joy. Pauline Ogden is unlikely ever to cross your path again, Gillian Glover has not been corrupted by new-found wealth, and your lover, though he has a history of financial misconduct, might just, let us keep our fingers crossed, have turned over a new leaf.

She said it had been nice talking to me. I agreed. What else could I say? Fuck off, you crowing, sun-kissed dog in the manger?

She said, 'Probably best if you don't tell Rodney I phoned you?'

'That would be an awkward conversation.'

'Right. Just be careful, that's all I'm saying. Be warned by a survivor. Don't re-mortgage your house or anything crazy.'

We laughed.

I said, 'Is that what he did?'

'And the rest,' she said. 'Like father, like son. That's why the Pooleys were always on the move when they were kids. Only in his dad's case it was card games. Rodney's not a gambler. He just likes spending. Nice suits, champagne, fancy hotels.'

I called Louie.

He said, 'The bounder!'

I said, 'But what if it's not true? Janet Coleman could just be trying to ruin things between us. She never liked me.'

'She called you all the way from Spain.'

'So she said. It didn't sound like she was in Spain.'

'You mean there was no background noise of castanets and men shouting "*Olé!*"?'

'She and the daughter could be in cahoots. Kids always want their parents to get back together.'

'Do they? I don't recall Ellie interfering in your love-life.'

'Because she refused to acknowledge that I had one. Until Tom came along she thought I was just a sad, unfuckable relic of a bygone age. And even after he moved in. Tom was very discreet. He never got frisky if Ellie was around. I saw him today, funnily enough. In the supermarket with his new woman. She goes on cycling holidays and she has no discernible lips. Or hips. Geraldine. Hipless, lipless Geraldine.'

'Can we just concentrate on the raccoon? Let's look at the evidence. His ex says he taps women for money. By the way, didn't he tell you she was a hopeless drunk? She says she runs a business. Well, that's worth looking into. But the main thing is, he hasn't borrowed from you.'

'Not really.'

'Lizzie?'

'The magnetic strip on his credit card was damaged. I paid for our hotel room last week. He's going to pay me back.'

'So that's all right, then. As long as he does. Point of information. Why do you keep meeting in hotels? Why not his place, or yours?'

'He says hotels are sexier.'

'Not some of the ones I've stayed in.'

'There's also the possibility that his house isn't actually his. I think it might be his daughter's.'

'But there's still your house. So we have here a man who'd rather pay for a hotel room than go home with a proven sexpot who also happens to be a renowned and accomplished cook. And how much was the corkage on the champagne? You could've gone to Lidl and bought three bottles for that kind of money.'

'I've kind of gone off champagne too. It gives me a headache.'

'Stick to the subject. I don't want to drizzle on your parade, darling girl, but I am starting to wonder about this Rodney. Describe his clothes. Does he dress expensively?'

'He dresses smartly. Wool trousers, not jeans. He was wearing a suit last week.'

'What brand? Paul Smith? Hugo Boss?'

'How should I know? When you first got together with Chas, did you check his labels?'

'Damned right I did. Although, clothes-wise, Chas is an open book. If you analysed his DNA it'd have Gieves & Hawkes woven all the way through it. Single vent or double?'

'I beg your pardon?'

'His suit jacket. One vent or two?'

'Does it matter?'

'It can say a lot about a man.'

'What do you wear?'

'Single, always. You hadn't noticed?'

'No. And that says what?'

'That I'm conscious of having a bit of a Londonderry and I know that a single vent makes it appear smaller. Chas can wear two flaps. He has a negligible bum. What about his watch? Patek Philippe, Vacheron Constantin, Ticka-ticka-Timex? Or underwear? You must have noticed that. Calvin Kleins are very distinctive.'

'He has a nice overcoat. I think it's what they call a Crombie.'

'Is it, by gosh, by gum? Well, then, I think it's time to sum up before the jury retires. On the one hand, he seems to enjoy the finer things in life and may well have had a genuinely dodgy strip on his card. On the other, much of what his ex said does sound a faint alarm bell. Muffled, and a couple of streets away, but I hear it. Do you hear it, Lizzie?'

I had to confess I did. 'Why can't I meet a nice straight-forward man?'

'You did. You got on each other's nerves and now he's with the Lipless One. Don't interrupt my train of reasoning. And on another hand . . .'

'That's three hands.'

'On another hand, you really, really like Rodney, you're long overdue for some moonlight and roses, and this Janet Coleman used to be your arch-enemy. Albeit in a different century. Right?'

'Right.'

'So next time you see him, which you surely will, just keep your purse tightly closed. If he insists on a hotel again, leave your plastic at home.'

'Unless he sends me a cheque this coming week.'

'In which case yah boo sucks to you, Janet Coleman, we never liked you anyway. What are you going to wear for *Mad Cows*?'

'I haven't decided.'

'Will it take place on sofas or behind desky things, like *University Challenge*?'

'I don't know.'

'Then find out. No sense worrying about bottom halves if all they're going to see is your top. How's the diet going?'

'I looked after Noah today. We had chocolate.'

'But burned off a million calories playing on the see-saw, I'll bet.'

'I had quite a lot of chocolate. And now this. How can I diet when I'm in emotional turmoil?'

'Sometimes emotional turmoil is a weight-loss programme in and of itself. Remember when what's-his-name dumped me? I lost pounds.'

'And your silver teapot.'

'No, it was a sugar-caster. Georgian. And a snuffbox and a nice silver photo frame. What a beast he was. He could at least have left me Mother's photograph. But if Janet Coleman has robbed you of your appetite, think of it as a favour. By the time you face the cameras you'll have cheekbones.'

I didn't sleep. Why would Janet Coleman call me? Would I have warned any of Alec's little conquests that he was just a randy mongrel disguised as middle management? No, because once he'd broken my heart I didn't care what he did to anyone else's and, anyway, none of them lasted more than a few fumbles. For Alec it was all about the chase. Until he met Nikki. I did hate her for a while, mainly because she was young and had long swishy hair, but I wouldn't have called her, wouldn't have told her it was only a matter of time until something else in a skirt caught his eye. And then when she had the twins I just felt sorry for her because Alec's idea of helping around the house was putting his CDs in alphabetical order. Of course, he was earning more money by the time he was married to Nikki. Living in America they probably used a laundry service for all those damned shirts of his.

Janet had said Rodney had a history. Let's suppose her intentions were honourable. Let's suppose she wasn't a scheming, envious loser who'd waited forty-five years for an opportunity to sabotage my love-life. I thought I could maybe hire a private detective, get the facts, nothing but the facts. Then I gave myself a talking-to.

'You *cannot* hire a private detective. You are waiting for a cheque that may never arrive and you need to buy two stunning but TV-compatible blouses and a return ticket to Norwich.'

Louie called me every morning that week to see if the raccoon had paid his dues. I was beginning to wish I hadn't told him anything. Friday, a cheque arrived.

He said, 'Is it signed?'

It was.

'And it's not drawn on the Bank of Never Never Land? Good. I secretly wanted a happy ending. What colour tops are you taking for Monday?'

'Blue and a different shade of blue.'

'I always say you can't go wrong with blue. Where did you get them?'

'From the back of my wardrobe. Right at the back.'

'Lizzie! Are they stained? Do they have shoulder pads?'

'They're not that old. And hardly ever worn.'

'No stone-washed denim?'

'Have you ever seen me in denim?'

'We've all done things we regret. But I still think you should have bought something new. I ought to have come up there and been your personal shopper. Should I come today? I could. We can shop tomorrow.'

I told him no, much as I'd have loved to see him. I needed time to think about the show, time alone in front of a mirror practising photogenic looks.

He said, 'Well, if you're sure. But if you don't get this gig because of blouse-failure I shall never ever forgive myself.'

The boy at the bank said, 'I'm sorry, Mrs Partridge, but have you had this cheque for some time? Only the date on it is last year.'

I said, 'It's a mistake. Does it matter? It's not like it's dated for next year.'

He said unfortunately it was the bank's policy to reject cheques written more than six months ago. And as there was a queue of people tut-tutting behind me the only course open to me was to step outside, phone Rodney Pooley and ask him what the fuck he was playing at.

'Oh, Lizzie,' he said. 'Our first quarrel.'

I said, 'I need that money.'

'Of course you do,' he said. 'It was bloody careless of me.'

His voice kept coming and going. He was driving.

He said, 'Look, I'm on my way to Clacton now, to the furries' weekend. As soon as I get home on Monday . . .'

Then we got cut off. About an hour later he sent me a text message: *SOOOOOOrrrrreeeeee. Sad face.*

26

It appeared I was the first to arrive at the hotel but I couldn't be sure. When I mentioned the names Kendrick and Tobin to the boy on the desk his eyes glazed over. I don't think he was a receptionist in the usual sense of the word. I think he was only there to make sure people didn't walk off with TV sets or the exquisite artwork.

I suddenly had a raging desire for crap food, which was why, when Kim phoned me, I was sitting under a flickering neon light in a deserted burger bar. That American guy Hopper could have painted me. Kim was at a hotel, but not my hotel.

'Lizzie,' she said, 'there's budget and there's "budget". I refuse to stay in a place where they don't even give you a wafer of soap. I mean, I travel with my own Molton Brown, but it's the principle of the thing. Call your agent. Tell him to get you a room here.'

I said I might. It wasn't a lie. More a misleading impression of my true intentions.

She said, 'We need to talk. The Tobin creature's here too.'

All the more reason for me to stay put. Otherwise I could be up half the night with Kim lobbying me about Valerie and Valerie lobbying me about Kim.

I said, 'Kim, there's nothing we can do about Valerie. We have to tape the pilot and let the chips fall where they may.'

'Ha!' she said. 'No wonder your career is in the doldrums. The band girl. Abi something. She's here.'

'What's she like?'

'Not really a girl. Late twenties, I'd say. And not very bright. She thought the town was called Norfolk. She has no idea where we are.'

'It could be an act. You know? Silly old me! Audiences like that kind of thing.'

'As long as they don't like her too much. This is *our* show. She's just a guest. By the way, she's Abi with one *b*, in case you're interested. Shall I ask about a room for you?'

I said not to bother. It was only for one night and it was a short walk to the studio.

'Walk?' she said. 'Are you out of your mind? Tell them they have to send a car for you.'

When I got back to my hotel Tark was just checking in.

I said, 'So I'm not the only one who's slumming.'

He blushed. 'Ah,' he said. 'I imagine you've spoken to Kimberley. I'm afraid she drives a very hard bargain.'

'And where she leads others follow. Valerie and Abi with one *b* have upgraded too.'

'I suppose you're horribly cross.'

'No. It means I'm spared having to spend the evening with them.'

'Super,' he said. 'Great.'

I got to the studio just after eight. Kim was running round the clothes rails like a madwoman at the January sales. Anything she fancied she tucked under her arm so no one else could get their hands on it. I went to Makeup. Ronnie Lincoln was in the chair. Forties, spiky red hair, big green sweater.

I said, 'I hope you weren't hoping for anything glittery from Wardrobe. Kim's going through the cocktail wear like a one-woman plague of locusts.'

'Aha,' she said, 'you must be Lizzie Partridge. Your reputation for sneering precedes you. Let's have some fun.'

'Have you met Abi with one *b*?'

'Yes. She's generously endowed in two departments. Breasts and stupidity.'

'I wonder why they chose her.'

'Same as the rest of us probably. Availability. Desperation. But also, of course, everybody's following her love-life with bated breath.'

'Are they? Why?'

'With NB Killah? The rapper? Is it on or is it off?'

'And? Which is it?'

'The latest is that he wants to get back with her but she's taking time out to concentrate on her new career.'

'By appearing on *Mad Cows*? That is desperation.'

'Have they changed it to *Mad Cows*? Brilliant.'

'No, they wouldn't use anything that might offend. I think ignorance of this Abi story will give me a certain novelty value.'

'You really don't know about her and Killah? You're winding me up.'

'I swear.'

'Do you live on some remote island that doesn't have broadband?'

'Birmingham. Without a telly.'

'Crikey. Is that because you belong to a religious sect?'

'Yes, the Church of Total Abstainers. What's the set like?'

'It's a curved desk, kind of translucent white. I think they've recycled it from some prior doomed panel show.'

'I thought they might have gone for something more informal. Pine chairs and a kitchen table. Coffee mugs.'

'Or a wine-bar theme. That'd work. Girls' night out. High stools, drinks with parasols.'

'You wouldn't catch me trying to climb onto a bar stool with an audience watching me. They'd have to winch me into position before they let them in.'

NB Killah's moll arrived with her hair in rollers the size of beer cans. Her eyelashes entered the room before she did and her bosom entered before the eyelashes. The makeup girl suggested I go and change while she combed out Abi with one *b*.

I said, 'Actually, I already changed. This is it.'

'Oh,' she said. 'Sorry. I just thought . . . But you know what'd look great with that blue? A chunky necklace, red or gold. Or a scarf? Dress it up a bit.'

Ronnie said, 'You've been bumped, Lizzie. You've been put on standby for the makeup chair. Never mind. Come and get a coffee.'

The coffee was feeble. The pastries were pretty good.

Ronnie said, 'So how did you get this gig? I know you did a cooking thing but that's a while back.'

'India, from Vertical Hold? She's my nephew's girlfriend.'

'Wow,' she said. 'No offence, Lizzie, but that is top networking.'

Ronnie had a newspaper column but she hadn't done much television. The networks were wary of her flog-'em-and-hang-'em opinions. She said, 'They're taking a risk with me but they can always tape another pilot if I get out of control. But I'm also the Cancer Interest so you can see how I might be useful. Wheel me out occasionally. Big sad eyes. "How's it going, Ronnie? Not dead yet?" It'd be great for the ratings.'

She'd had breast cancer, has breast cancer. She said, 'It appears to be on Pause at the moment but you never know. Anyway, I'm not very interested in talking about it. I'm only doing this because I enjoy arguing with dimwits and TV pays silly money. You'd better go and see if Big Hair has vacated the chair. They'll be letting the punters in any minute.'

Our starter topics for the first session were:

1. Is it ever acceptable to smack a child?
2. Would you have cosmetic surgery?
3. Opening up about cancer.

Ronnie said, 'We'll see about that.'

The studio was packed. It's a hobby for some people, getting free tickets to watch a show being recorded. No weirder than driving to Aberystwyth to dress up as a raccoon, I suppose.

Kim was on first, Kimberley, our chosen leader, wearer of the sacred earpiece. She introduced us one by one and we had to walk onto the set and sit in our designated seats. That was when I slightly regretted wearing a skirt instead of trousers. What passes for a merely sturdy ankle in the flesh can look like something out of Sherwood Forest through a camera lens.

She referred to me as 'my dear, dear friend and survivor of many a 6 a.m. makeup call, TV cook *extraordinaire*, Lizzie Partridge!'

The floor manager makes sure you get applause even if the audience don't know you from Adam's cat.

We started. Angela from Thetford wanted to know, should parents be free to smack a child? I was determined to get off the mark quickly because as soon as you've spoken your nerves disappear.

I said, 'Who's going to stop them?'

'The police,' said Abi. 'Don't you know the law?'

Ronnie said, 'Well, for a start, it's not against the law so get your facts straight, Abi. Reasonable chastisement is perfectly legal. And Lizzie and I have years and years of hands-on experience of bringing up kids.'

'Or hands off, as is now advised.'

That got me my first twitch on the mirth-o-meter.

Had I ever smacked my daughter?

'Yes, until she became a seething cauldron of teenage hormones. After that I was slightly afraid of her so I used heavy sarcasm instead.'

Kim said, 'I may not have been blessed with a family but that doesn't stop me having an opinion and quite honestly I'd like to be able to smack other people's children.'

I said, 'Go, Kimberley! And their parents too, if they give you any grief.'

'You go to a restaurant and they're screaming and dropping food underfoot and creating havoc. You book a nice hotel and you can't enjoy the swimming pool because they're running around with inflatable crocodiles and piddling in the water.'

Abi shook her big hair in sorrow. She said, 'That's a terrible attitude. I will never, ever smack my children. Violence leads to violence. Everybody knows that.'

Ronnie said, 'And yet here's an interesting statistic, Abi. How about the 40 per cent increase in primary-school classroom violence over the past four years? All those little darlings who've never felt a tap on the leg. I tell you what, you come back to me a few years from now when one of your kids has done a Jackson Pollock with his spag bol and we can discuss this again.'

Back and forth we went. The audience was middle-aged. They'd put in time at the coal-face. They were with us. Abi was outnumbered and Valerie Tobin hadn't even opened her mouth.

It was Kim's job to manage the conversation, if necessary, but she seemed oblivious to Valerie's silence.

I said, 'Valerie? What do you think? A quick smack or a lengthy discussion with a misbehaving child?'

'I can see both points of view,' she whispered, and grabbed her glass of water. She was in a funk. Brain flat-lining, dry mouth. She'd become a piece of furniture. Ronnie noticed it too. She changed the subject, threw Valerie a lifebelt.

'So, sistahs, what do we think of this lovely set they created for us?'

I said, 'I don't like the slight violet glow when it's all lit up. It's how I imagine one of those cryogenic facilities. Anybody here fancy getting frozen, to await future medical break-throughs? Hoping and praying there aren't any major power cuts.'

It was time to take a breather and change topics. Vertical Hold were taping the show with commercial breaks in mind.

Kim hissed at me, 'You shouldn't have said that, Lizzie. About medical breakthroughs.'

'Why?'

'Because we're going to be talking about cancer in the final segment.' She didn't say the word 'cancer'. She mouthed it.

I said, 'I never mentioned cancer.'

'I'm in charge, Lizzie,' she whispered. 'I'm the most experienced presenter here and I'm leading the discussions so please don't mess with the running order.'

I said, 'Then be in charge. Do something about Valerie. She's got camera-freeze.'

'Good,' she said. 'Strip her of her merchandise and she's nothing. We'll soon be rid of her.'

Our second topic was cosmetic surgery. Would any of us try it? I plunged right in.

I said, 'I'm not sure that's the right question. Let's start with "Have any of us already been there?" Kimberley?'

I knew for a fact she had. The first year I was *In the Kitchen* she'd had her eyelids lifted over the Christmas holidays, and I was pretty sure she'd had something major done one summer when she and Stuart took a three-week break from the couch. And then there was her nose. That had definitely had a bump shaved off.

She said, 'No, I haven't. I'm not saying I wouldn't, down the line, but I don't think I need it yet. How about you, Lizzie? You've got a few years on me. Do you have any plans to go under the knife?'

'Not unless my life depends on it.'

Abi said she'd definitely have cosmetic surgery because when you're an icon you owe it to your fans always to look your best. There was no point in asking Valerie because she'd lost the power of speech and, anyway, it was obvious she hadn't had anything done. Valerie wore her wrinkles like campaign medals. Awarded for seventy years of successful breathing. And why the hell not?

Ronnie said, 'Abi, tell us about becoming an icon. How did that come about?'

Abi shrugged her shoulders. 'It just happened, really, after Awesome broke up and I went solo.'

'So you woke up one morning and your agent called you and said, "Abi, you're an icon."'

'Kind of.'

'Amazing. And how does that feel?'

'It's quite a responsibility.'

'Must be. I can't begin to imagine, can you, Lizzie?'

There was a little ripple from the audience. Uncomfortable laughter. Ronnie was on dangerous ground. They liked Abi.

Kim said, 'Well, fascinating as this is, we're not here to interview Abi.'

I said, 'Quite right. Let's talk about liposuction. I love the idea of it but I'd never do it. I'd be frightened of it going horribly wrong. Very appealing, though. Getting hoovered down a few dress sizes.'

A cracked voice said, 'Why don't you just eat less?'

Valerie Tobin.

I said, 'Great heavens, it must be the seventh day after a new moon.'

Abi and Kim looked at me.

Ronnie said, 'She means "The Oracle has spoken." Rare event. Classical reference. Lizzie just raised the educational bar.'

The audience was silent. Big mistake, Partridge. Nobody likes a clever clogs. Claw your way back. Eat a little low-cal humble pie.

I said, 'Valerie, you're quite right. I do eat too much. Excess could be my middle name. But that's my pleasure, that's my choice, and seeing that I don't want to live for ever, you know? Would you have work done? For the sake of your career? As a TV person?'

I thought she'd recovered. I thought she was ready to join the discussion and take me on but no. She just shook her tortoise head and went back under her shell. I pressed on.

I said, 'Kimberley, I'm sorry to be a bore but don't I remember you having a bit of hoover-work done? When you were on daytime? You can tell us. It won't go any further than these four walls.'

Big swing on the Laff-o-Graph.

'That,' she said, 'was colonic irrigation, which is an entirely different matter. It was for health reasons and it's hardly a topic for a tea party.'

'Oh, I don't know,' said Ronnie. 'Some of us have already talked a fair amount of crap this morning. And you and Lizzie go back a long way. As the therapist said to the irrigation hose.'

Boom-boom. Cheap laughs. Ronnie and I made a good team. Keep the show rolling. Clinch this, Lizzie, I thought, and you'll be able to afford a new front door.

Kim put on her solemn face for the third segment. I'd seen her do it a thousand times, that seamless transformation from Amused by a Dog That Can Open a Fridge, Camera Two, to empathetic eyebrows for People Facing a Bleak Christmas, Camera One.

'Sooner or later cancer touches all of our lives,' she started, 'and it can be hard to know what to say to the sufferer. Ronnie here can speak from personal experience. She won't mind me sharing with you that she's been battling cancer.'

There was a lot of concerned murmuring from the audience but not enough to drown Ronnie's groan. She said, 'Well, for a kick-off, I haven't exactly been battling cancer. Cancer picked on me, I don't know why. I never took its name in vain. It got me in a corner and knocked me about. I let it rob me of five weeks while I was getting radiation treatment and a year of planning my life around chemo cycles. To be honest, there were several occasions when I felt like saying, "Okay, you win, I'll just fuck off and die." '

'Mm, mm,' says Kim. 'Gosh. Absolutely.'

Abi said, 'My nan . . .' But her lip wobbled and she couldn't carry on. I put my arm around her shoulders, which gave me a bird's-eye view down her Grand Canyon. Those breasts are definitely not God's gift. Her hair smelled of Elnett.

Kim said, 'Like I said, cancer touches us all. So how should we talk about it? What can we do to support the afflicted?'

Ronnie said, 'Don't call us "the afflicted". That'd be a good start. And don't put on a funeral face when you see us coming. We're feeling bad enough without having to cheer you up.'

Applause.

'Don't say, "Let me know if there's anything I can do to help." Just do something. Make dinner for my kids because I can't get my head out of the toilet bowl. You think I'm going to phone and ask you? I'm not. And do not bring me scented candles. No. Scented. Candles. Bring me a bottle. Help me drink it.'

More applause.

'This is such a bummer of a discussion. Cancer is hands down the least fun I have ever had. I've probably offended half my friends saying what I've said, and Abi's ruined her eye makeup. Let's talk about something else. We're all girls together. Let's talk about blowjobs.'

The audience howled with joy, Kim knocked over her water glass and the floor manager touched his earpiece. We were going to get cut off.

I said, 'Better make it a quick one, Ronnie.'

Ripple of laughter.

'My thoughts exactly,' she said. 'Get it over with fast and pop in a Tic-Tac. Why do men think we enjoy it? Are they insane? You, grinning male camera-person, don't you know the difference between a moan of ecstasy and the sound of gagging? Seriously.'

Wild applause.

Tark appeared. 'Thank you, everyone,' he said. 'Thank you very much. That'll do nicely.'

27

Melanie Pope and Tamara Hunt had arrived for Round Two. They were just in time to witness the post-mortem on Round One. It wasn't pretty. Guts were spilled. India looked tense. Tark was pacing up and down.

'What the hell?' he kept saying. 'What in the name of Jesus?'

Ronnie said she'd only been trying to liven things up.

I said, 'The audience loved it.'

He said, 'I'm not talking about the blowjobs. I'm talking about dead wood. Okay, here's what's going to happen. Ronnie, you'll have to stay for the second tape. Take Valerie's seat.'

Valerie said, 'What about me?'

'Oh,' he said, 'so you can speak.'

There was the merest ghost of a smirk on Kim's face but Tark soon wiped that off.

'Tamara,' he said, 'you sit in the driving seat for this session.'

Kim said, 'But I have earpiece experience.'

'So do I,' said Tamara. 'I've hosted three seasons of *Fingers on Buzzers*.'

Valerie said, 'Tarquin, where do you want me?'

'On the A11,' he said. 'Heading south. Go home, Valerie. This is not your thing.'

Kim said she certainly hadn't slogged 150 miles to appear with a nervous amateur.

Ronnie said, 'I didn't realize you actually drove the train here, Kimberley. I thought you just sat in First Class.'

Valerie said she'd travelled just as far as Kim and was being treated very shabbily.

Kim said, 'You brought it on yourself. How can you be on a panel if you never open your mouth? I knew you weren't up to it. I said so from the very start. Stick to the exercise videos, that's my advice. Leave this kind of thing to the professionals.' She flounced off, went to freshen up her lipstick and squeeze herself into a different glamour garment.

India said, 'And, Tamara, just a light touch on the tiller, okay? We'll only give you directions if it's absolutely necessary. Try just to let the conversation happen.'

Our starters for the second session were:

1. Have you got/would you get a tattoo?
2. Are self-service tills a blessing or a curse?
3. Will Camilla ever be Queen?

Melanie Pope had a lot of people outside wanting to tell her how devastated they'd been by her death and to get her autograph.

Ronnie said, 'A clear indicator of the mentality we're dealing with. They don't know the difference between a soap character and the actress who played her and is now out of work. Lizzie, I need you to be my lookout. I'm going to have a quick rummage through Kimberley's bag, see if there's anything of interest. If she comes back, have a loud coughing fit.'

I wanted no part of it.

'Spoilsport,' she said. 'Well, I'm going to sprinkle a little itching powder under this lot otherwise the project'll be dead by nightfall. I mean, Melanie Pope? There's not much going on between those pretty little ears. And Tamara Hunt? She should stick to weather forecasts. Just keep watch. I'll be quick.'

I didn't. I went to change my blouse. Melanie was in Wardrobe considering a red jumpsuit. I thought it looked like prison-wear. I said, 'Just make sure you empty your bladder before you put it on.'

She looked at me.

I said, 'I wore one of those in the Seventies. If you need a pee the sleeves dangle. It can be tricky. So you were in *Cloverfields*? You must have known Craig Eden.'

'Who? Don't think so. Oh, did he play Dave Pickering?'

'I don't know. I never saw it. But I know he got written out around the end of last year.'

'Yeah, that was Dave Pickering. I wouldn't say he got written out. He didn't really have many lines. He more, like, faded. He wasn't, like, a *name*.'

SOAP IN THE EYE FOR AXED STAR CRAIG.

'How come you never saw *Cloverfields*? Do you live somewhere foreign?'

'No. I haven't got a telly. How did you feel when they decided to kill off your character?'

'It was my idea, actually. I felt ready for a change. You know? I want to stretch myself.'

'Such as by trying out for this show?'

'Trying out? I'm not trying out. If it goes ahead it'll just be a sideline for me. Depending on my availability. No. I'm getting a lot of interest for films.'

'Good for you.'

'Yeah, the dying story let me really show what I can do.'

'It was a drugs death, right?'

'Yeah. Miaow Miaow. So it was, like, educational as well. About legal highs? I did a lot of interviews about it. I was on *The Full English* and *The Early Show* and *Woman's Hour*, but that's just radio. What did Abi Cooper wear this morning?'

'A peach-coloured thing with ruffles.'

'Low-cut, yeah? Flashing her tits? Fuck it, I'm going to wear this jumpsuit with the zip pulled right down.'

'Why not? Show what you've got as well as what you can do. How long did it take you to die?'

'Three episodes. I was on life support. I got loads of letters. People didn't want it switched off but we had to because we'd already taped the funeral. How come you got asked to do a TV then?'

'I was on a daytime show, cooking. It was years ago. You were probably watching *Playdays*.'

'Yeah? Awesome. Kimberley Kendrick started out on daytime.'

'I know.'

'My mum loved her when she did *Gems Direct*. She bought a ring off of her. It was for her wedding anniversary but she had to buy it herself because my dad couldn't be arsed. She's really, really glamorous, Kimberley. Like from the olden days.'

'Do you think so?'

'Yeah. When I'm old I'd like to channel her. She's an icon, really.'

'Funny. Abi Cooper used that word too. Icon. Not about Kim. About herself.'

'No way! Abi Cooper? She's nothing. Can't even sing. She lip-synched at the Brits.'

'So you don't rate her?'

'Fuck, no. She's just Killah's babymother.'

Ronnie explained it to me. Abi was quite big when she was part of Awesome but her solo career hasn't happened so her stock has fallen, except that she was with NB Killah for long enough to beget a child, who is probably still in nappies but has a diamond ear stud.

'Name?'

'Can't remember. Something idiotic. I'll look it up.'

Ronnie had one of those phones that does everything. Internet, photos, tells you how far you've walked or how many calories in a white chocolate frappuccino.

'Susan? Mary? Jane?'

'Ah. The counter-intuitive approach. You're ignoring the trend for rappers to shake up the bag of Scrabble tiles in search of a baby name. It's a boy, actually, Abi's kid.'

'Okay. So not Peter or Michael. Or Archie. That's made a comeback. My grandson goes to Tumble Tots with an Archie.'

'You're a granny? Respect. Here it is. Abi and Killah's child is called U'neeq. With an apostrophe between the U and the N.'

'That shows some originality, throwing in a random apostrophe.'

'You could say. You seem to have a charitable streak in you, Lizzie. I thought you were a fellow sneerer. I'm not sure you belong on this show.'

'I think it's quite encouraging. Using an apostrophe. They've created a kind of secondary market in a disappearing form of punctuation. If they get back together and have another child maybe they'll use a semicolon. Set a trend.'

'That's probably already been done. They're highly competitive, those rappers. Kids' names, bling display, vehicle pimpery. Hey, look what I found.'

She had Kim's driving licence.

'You opened her bag?'

'It was already open. It was just sitting there. I'm not *stealing* it. I'm just borrowing it. Want to take a guess?'

'Her age?'

'Of course her age. The world's closest-guarded secret, after the recipe for KFC.'

'Fifty-nine.'

'Fifty-nine! Are you an incurable flatterer or do you need an eye test? Ooh, Tamara's getting in position. I think we're on.'

First up, tattoos. I was the only panel member who didn't have one.

I said, 'Kim? You shock me.'

She said hers was just a small one, a dragonfly, on her hip but she wouldn't show us, not even when I offered to reveal my stretchmarks as a quid pro quo.

She said, 'I don't know why you're looking at me like that, Lizzie. Helen Mirren's got one.'

Ronnie had a kind of clematis-with-tendrils design along

the edge of her foot. She said it hurt like a son-of-a-bitch while they were doing it and she had to wear flip-flops for a week afterwards because her foot was so swollen. Did she regret it?

'Oh, no. It's quite pretty. I mean, I didn't enjoy childbirth, but I don't regret my kids.'

Tamara had 'Nirvana' down the back of her neck in Sanskrit.

Melanie said, 'I love Sanskrit. I've got "Om" on my back.'

I said, 'Why?'

'It brings me peace. Om's really powerful. I'm getting "Hope" next. On my shoulder.'

Ronnie said, 'Okay, Lizzie, you've had your eye-roll. But if somebody held a gun to your head, what tattoo would you get?'

'"An armed moron made me do this."'

'Good one. And where would you have it?'

'Hidden inside my big knickers. It'd be a secret between me and the undertaker. And, by the way, does anybody get these Sanskrit scribbles checked for spelling mistakes?'

HINDUS DEMAND APOLOGY AFTER TATT SHOP BLUNDER.

On the topic of tattoos I was outvoted by the audience. Only the real greyheads agreed with me, which confirmed my suspicion that we're not only living longer, we're staying stupid for longer too. However, they were with me all the way on self-service tills, and so were Ronnie and Kim. It was Melanie's turn to be outvoted.

She said, 'But it's quicker.'

I said, 'Not if there's an unexpected item in your bagging

area, it's not. And what about old people? It freaks them out having to deal with a talking machine.'

She said, 'Well, my mum manages all right.'

Ronnie said, 'Melanie, your mum's not old. What is she? Forty-five? Lizzie's talking about real oldies. The girl on the checkout might be the only person they get to speak to all week. A little chat at the till, could be something they look forward to.'

Tamara said, 'And what about if there's a problem? Like you notice the yogurt's past its sell-by date or the milk carton's leaking?'

Melanie said she didn't do dairy. She might have played a blinder on that life-support machine but reasoned argument evidently wasn't her strong suit. She said, 'But think of the people who have to work on those tills. I wouldn't do it.'

Oh, dear girl, I thought. Don't tempt the Fates.

MEL CHECKS OUT: SOAP EX SPOTTED WORKING IN ASDA.

Tamara said her biggest beef with supermarkets was all the unnecessary packaging, but Tark or India must have said something in her earpiece because then she said, 'As you know, I'm very eco. But we can talk about green issues another day.'

And Kim murmured, 'Don't bank on it.'

That second session moved along well. We had more energy without the Valerie Tobin drag-chute, and Camilla clinched the throne by three votes to two, although Tamara thought the whole Royal Family would be facing redundancy sooner rather than later, so I suppose you could say it was a tie.

Melanie said her mum still cries about the way they treated Princess Diana so they definitely wouldn't be putting any bunting out for Charles and Camilla. It was as good a reason as any. Mine was more frivolous. Queen Camilla doesn't sound right. But, then, neither did Queen Diana. They're not queenly names.

Ronnie said, 'She can change it. Victoria's first name wasn't Victoria.'

'What was it?'

'I can't remember. Winifred. Olive. Kylie.'

Melanie said, 'The other thing is, Camilla's dead old. So's Prince Charles. If you ask me, they're past it. They ought to retire. My granddad had to when he was sixty-five. It was compulsory.'

Kim said, 'There isn't a compulsory retirement age for royals. Anyway, they're not old, they're mature. I think they'll be great. Pensioning people off just because they've reached a certain stage in their life is a ridiculous waste of talent and experience.'

'I totally agree,' said Ronnie. 'Take television, for instance. If you're a woman, once you get a few crow's feet or a bit of jaw sag you're history. That's what's great about this show. We've got the voices of youth but we've also got fabulous mature women, like Kimberley and Lizzie.'

'Hear, hear,' said Kimmykins, going like a clapped-out old ewe to the slaughter.

Ronnie said, 'I'm forty-seven and proud of it. What about you, Tamara? Did you hit thirty yet?'

Tamara owned to thirty-two.

'Lizzie?'

I said, 'If I was looking for a man, which I'm not, I might use fifty-nine as a dating age because, sad but true, it doesn't sound quite so desiccated. But I'm sixty-four.'

'Same as Camilla, then. Kimberley, what about you?'

'Fifty-eight,' she said. 'But may I say, Lizzie, you have very good skin for your age. And you, Ronnie. I wouldn't have put you at a day over forty.'

Ronnie winked at me. She said, 'Flattery will get you nowhere, Kimberley. Fifty-eight? Any advance on fifty-eight?'

Kim twiddled with her rings.

'Do I hear fifty-nine, do I hear sixty, sixty-one?'

Melanie said, 'What? What's she on about?'

Tamara said, 'But just to get back to Camilla for a minute . . .'

I said, 'Yes. Camilla. Do we think she's tried the crown on yet? Just to see how it feels.'

Tamara played ball. 'She could do it when the Queen's up at Balmoral. Have a practice with the wand too.'

'It's called a sceptre. And I think only Charles gets one of those. He gets a sceptre and an orb. Not sure about Camilla. She'll have her hands full anyway, with her cigs and a Coronation zip lighter.'

I did my best to rescue Kim but Ronnie was determined. She said, 'Come on, Kimberley. You can't hymn the praises of the older woman and then tell porkies about your own age. Look what I've got.'

She held up the driving licence.

There was a howl from the audience, then everything went very quiet.

Kim said, 'You've been in my bag? How dare you?'

Ronnie said, 'Lighten up, Kimberley. I'm just having a bit of fun.'

'See what so-called journalists will stoop to?' said Kim. 'Going through people's dustbins. Hacking into their phone messages. Gutter press is dead right.'

Tamara touched her earpiece and nodded. The audience were loving it. I shouldn't have been surprised. People used to stand for hours to watch a hanging.

Ronnie pressed on: 'So where had we got to in the bidding? Was it sixty-one? Sixty-two? Sixty-three, anyone? Lady over there, looking a bit cross in the jade cowl-neck? Do I hear sixty-nine?'

Tamara said, 'Well, I'm told we're out of time. Kimberley can take her secret home with her, and Camilla can sleep a bit easier tonight.'

Kim was first off the set. I grabbed the licence from Ronnie and ran after her.

She said, 'I'll kill the bitch. Were you in on it?'

I swore I wasn't. Ellie once explained the law of criminal conspiracy to me and I might have been on shaky ground but, as far as I was concerned, Ronnie had acted alone.

I said, 'Kim, it was a joke. The audience loved it, Tark's smiling and, anyway, you look amazing.' I felt that pretty much covered it.

Ronnie said, 'No hard feelings, Kimberley. You're a trouper.'

'Piss off,' said Kim.

'Get over yourself,' said Tamara. 'Like anybody gives a fuck how old you are.'

'What?' said Melanie, late to the party again. 'What happened? What's going on?'

India said they were very happy with how the second session had gone. That she and Tark would tidy it up a bit when they got back to London and then they'd be pitching it to the networks.

Ronnie said, 'I hope you won't tidy it up too much.'

Kim said, 'I've got a cab coming, Lizzie. I don't know about you but I don't enjoy infantile behaviour. There's a train in half an hour, if we get a move on.'

I told her to go ahead without me. My ticket was for steerage so I wouldn't have been able to sit with her even if I'd wanted to. I said, 'I thought I'd go to Evensong at the cathedral. Get a later train.'

'Oh, yes,' she said. 'I remember that now. You always were a bit holy.'

Ronnie and I went for a drink.

She said, 'You're annoyed with me. You think I went too far.'

'You did. But that's probably what it takes.'

'It is. And Kimberley's okay. She's sitting on that train right now, plotting her revenge. And that's good. Fireworks. It's a selling point. Nobody's going to buy a show that's just *Question Time* with vaginas. And how come she travels First Class but you don't?'

'She insists on it. I can't be bothered.'

'You should. In this business, the more you demand the more they respect you. Same again?'

'Aren't you driving?'

'Car service. That's what I'm saying, Lizzie. Ask, and it will be given.'

Ronnie lives near Cambridge. Husband who works in the City, two girls, nine and seven, and a live-in nanny.

'Isn't it awkward having somebody living with you who's not family?'

'You get used to it. My husband grew up with staff so he taught me how to handle it. You just think of them as wallpaper and you don't converse with them any more than you have to. Ours is Polish. The girls have learned a few words from her. Not the most useful language in the world, but there we are.'

'My daughter's thinking about getting a nanny. She had an au pair but that didn't work out.'

'Au pairs are useless. I should know. I was one. All I was interested in was tunnelling out and getting laid. Tell your daughter to get a plain-looking nanny. It's a tough ask because a lot of those Eastern European girls are drop-dead, but it's worth the search, for peace of mind. The husband factor, you know. You don't want some Nina Dobrev looky-likey bending down to unload your dishwasher.'

I'd never heard of Nina Dobrev but I got the picture.

I said, 'My son-in-law's the earnest egghead type. He wouldn't be interested in a nanny.'

'My husband comes home, falls asleep on the sofa, then he's

up and gazing at the screen as soon as the Hong Kong markets open. Nevertheless, there's no sense in tempting a man. You married?'

'Divorced.'

'Seeing someone?'

I'd have liked to talk. I'd have liked to tell another female about the raccoon and the duff cheque and the phone call from Janet Coleman but I decided you needed to be very careful around Ronnie Lincoln.

I said, 'I'm carefree and single.'

'And are you really going to church or did you say that just to shake off Kimberley?'

'I like Evensong. It's beautiful.'

'But you believe in God and all that stuff?'

'Most of the time.'

'Wild. You don't seem the type.'

I'd heard that before. It's true, sneering isn't a very Christian activity. But justified snarling? That's different. Jesus was known to snarl. O generation of vipers.

I said, 'So what do you reckon? Did we give value? Tamara was okay, sharper than I'd expected.'

'Yes. I'd keep her. And Kimberley's a treasure. She's the deluded gift that keeps on giving. What about Melanie and the other one? Killah's chick.'

'I'd have them on occasionally. They could be the token dimwits.'

'My thinking exactly. And there are plenty of others out there. It's a rich seam, Lizzie. I might suggest a few names to Tarquin.'

I was sitting in the cathedral when my phone buzzed. A message from Rodney. I'd have liked it to say, *How'd it go, sexpot? Meet you off train? Advise ETA.* What it actually said was *Car transmission fucked. Visa card fucked. Stuck in Clacton. Need help. Pls call.*

I turned my phone off. The choir sang Geoffrey Burgon's Nunc Dimittis. For that alone I'd have travelled to Norwich.

28

Louie said, 'Under no circumstances are you to phone that man. Let him moulder in Clacton with his clapped-out vehicle. Tell me about Kimmykins. I want to hear every gruesome detail.'

He did a wonderment whistle when I told him about the driving-licence incident.

'That was a very mean trick. So she's sixty-nine?'

'At least. Ronnie's not saying. She's keeping the information for possible future use.'

'And do we like this Ronnie?'

'The audience did. Vertical Hold did. I quite liked her. I could work with her. She was the best of the bunch.'

'Watch your back, though, Lizzie. She'll obviously stop at nothing.'

'I just wonder if I really want to do this anyway. It wiped me out. Two forty-minute sessions and I was exhausted.'

'It's the adrenalin, darling. You're just out of practice. But you do want to do it, because from little acorns big fat contracts may grow. I'm speaking as your career adviser now, Partridge.

As the significant other of your agent, I'm hungry for my fifty per cent of his fifteen per cent. I want to go on lots and lots of expensive holidays.'

Louie recommended continuing the cold-shoulder treatment with Rodney. Which was why I ignored my phone when it rang four, five times in quick succession and then I answered it because it was getting on my nerves. I was just going to tell him to get lost.

But it wasn't Rod. It was Wendy.

'Lizzie!' she screamed. 'You've got to come. You've got to help me. Please.'

I said, 'Let me speak to Philip.'

All I got was a whimper. Then I realized. It was Tuesday. They'd be visiting Mum. They must have found her dead and Philip was too poleaxed to speak.

'Please come, Lizzie,' she sobbed. 'I don't know what to do.'

Then she was gone. I tried calling her back but all I got was the engaged tone. I grabbed my bag and coat and prayed to St Jude that the car would start. So it had finally happened. It was a moment I'd sometimes imagined but there had been so many false alarms, so many twinges and wuzzy turns and mysterious wandering aches that part of me believed my mother would live for ever.

When Dad died we'd known it was coming. We only had a few weeks to prepare ourselves because there'd been a delay in getting a diagnosis. Every time I said, 'Dad, get yourself down to the doctor's,' Mum would dream up another reason why there was really no need.

'That cough,' I remember her saying. 'I think it's something in Albert Collier's potting shed that's causing it. I'll bet he's got all sorts of chemicals in there.'

Dad did spend a lot of time down the allotment in Albert's shed but I think the only chemical he came into contact with there was Teacher's C_2H_6O.

She said he was tired all the time because he had nocturnal leg twitch. 'Of course he's exhausted,' she said. '*I'm* exhausted. He keeps me awake for hours with his feet jiggling around.'

She said he'd lost weight because he'd disobeyed her and eaten a Scotch egg after its Best Before, which had given him the runs, 'And he's never been the same since.'

And the pain between his shoulder blades was the result of helping Pearl Minchin lift her shopping trolley up the steps to her maisonette, an unnecessary act of kindness, according to Mum, because Mrs Minchin had two sons who ought to do the heavy lifting for her. The fact that one of them lived in London and the other in Peterborough cut no ice with my mother. Pearl was acting the helpless maiden and Dad was enabling her.

'And do you know why her trolley was so heavy? Cat food! She feeds every blummin' cat in the neighbourhood. We'll be overrun with them.'

In this way Dr Muriel delayed Dad's diagnosis of lung cancer until the only thing to do was prop him up on lots of pillows and have the district nurse come in twice a day. I used to give him smashed-up ice cubes to suck. We had a couple of weeks. We had time to say the things you need to say.

'Best dad in the world.'

'My Lizzie.'

'Remember Llandudno?'

'Rain.'

'All week. Great chips, though.'

I wasn't actually with him when he died. I'd gone home to iron a few shirts for Alec but it didn't matter. There weren't any loose ends. And perhaps it's easier to go if people aren't hovering, listening to your breathing. I think that's why he asked for a cup of tea, to get Mum out of the room. He was cannier than people gave him credit for, my dad.

But Mum was different. I had unfinished business with her. I wanted to hear her say it, just once. If she'd gone and died without waiting for me I was going to be furious. If she'd had a stroke and lost the power of speech she could bloody well go to therapy until she was able to spit it out or scrawl it on a piece of paper. Love. Proud. Very.

I kept trying Wendy all the way up the Bristol Road. Engaged, engaged. And Philip's mobile just rang and rang. Tuesday. Mum's morning for ironing. A ninety-year-old living alone doesn't have much in the way of laundry but she even ironed her towels and her dusters, so that filled an hour until Philip visited. There were Go/Stop signals on the Pershore Road. Resurfacing. I like the smell of tar but not when I'm in a very big hurry. There were tailbacks to get onto the ring road. A stretch of Walsall Road was reduced to single lane because of broken glass. Then everything pulled over to let an ambulance go through.

It was just one bloody thing after another, a conspiracy to prevent me reaching my mother in time to hear her dying words. Glenville Road, Glenville Avenue, next up, Glenville

Close, no through road. I pulled up just before the corner of Glenville Drive, to prepare myself. There'd probably be an ambulance, and neighbours gawping. I turned into the Close. There was no ambulance, no gawpers. No Wendy's car, no Philip's car. Had they left without me? Had she been rushed to hospital, her life hanging by a thread? Was that the ambulance I'd just pulled over for, blue lights flashing?

I was about to hammer on the front door, then realized there'd be no point. I found my key. The radio was still on. I heard the twelve o'clock pips. Jeremy Vine's programme was starting. I called out, 'Mum!" I don't know why. And there she was, in the kitchen doorway, alive and breathing, with a can of Mr Sheen in her hand.

'Elizabeth!' she said. 'You gave me such a fright. I thought I was being raided.'

I said, 'Raided?'

'The police make mistakes,' she said. 'That lot who're living in Hilda Sanderson's old house, I think they're druggies. Those bedroom curtains have never been opened since the day they moved in. And when the window-cleaner knocked, to see if they wanted their windows done, they pretended not to be in.'

Hearing my mother using the word 'druggies' made me want to laugh but, strangely enough, I burst into tears instead.

'Oh dear,' said Mum. 'You're upset about something. Come and sit down and I'll make you a cup of Bournvita.'

Muriel Clarke's pharmacopoeia: Germolene for grazed knees, Syrup of Figs for constipation, Vicks for chesty wheezes, Sloane's Liniment for pulled muscles, and Bournvita for sadness, disappointment or grief.

I said, 'I thought you were dead. I really thought you were.'

She said, 'You must have had a bad dream. Have you been eating cheese before bedtime?'

'But Wendy called me. Has she been over this morning?'

'No. Philip comes on Wednesdays now. Mondays, Wednesdays and Saturdays. Tuesdays never really suited me because I go to Mothers' Union in the afternoon. And Wendy hardly ever comes with him. I suppose she's got her reasons. Not that I mind.'

So then I started wondering. Was I losing my mind? Was it a dream? I hadn't got home from Norwich till nearly midnight and I had eaten cheese. Also toast and Marmite and a Magnum. I looked at Mum. She was just her usual self. 'So you've not spoken to Wendy? And you've not had a funny turn?'

'I never speak to Wendy. Are you going through the Change?'

'The Change? About ten years ago. More. What the hell is that to do with anything?'

'Well, I have to say, you don't seem right, Elizabeth. Imagining things. Getting yourself all het up. And I don't like what you've done with your hair just lately. It's too jazzified for your age. You know that was when your Auntie Edie went peculiar? After the Change.'

It was an oft-recited chapter of family history. After the menopause Auntie Edie had become even more difficult. She'd stopped cooking hot dinners and she'd forced Uncle Cyril to take her to Dubrovnik, to name but two warning signs of escalating oddness.

'Have you spoken to Philip this morning?'

'No. I think you've got low blood. I'll make you a sandwich. It'll have to be ham because I haven't got much in.'

'I'm not hungry. Wendy called me. She said, "Please come," so I thought you must have had a fall.'

'Well, I haven't. Ring her up. Find out what she wanted. Perhaps she's had a fall. I wouldn't be surprised. Those silly shoes she wears. I'll get the key.'

There was a lock on my mother's phone. She said Philip had put it on.

'Why?'

'To stop people taking advantage and running up big bills.'

'What people? There's nobody else here.'

'I'm just telling you what Philip said.'

'So every time you use the phone you unlock it and then lock it again?'

'It's a bit of a palaver but you know what he's like. He's only trying to be helpful.'

'He's barmy. Take the bloody thing off and put it away. I'll try Wendy again on my mobile.'

In my big hurry I'd left my phone in the car. Three missed calls. It rang again just as I picked it up from the foot well but I didn't recognize the number.

A man's voice said, 'Is that Lizzie? This is Kev. Kayleigh's Kev. Only there's been a bit of a mishap. It's your Philip. He's met with an accident.'

All the time he was talking I stood looking across at Mrs Sanderson's old house. Mum was right about the curtains. They had 'Drug Den' written all over them.

Kev said, 'He was trying to mend a microwave for his mum.'

'She doesn't want a microwave. She's afraid of them.'

'Wendy said he got it at a car boot. If I'd known I'd have told him not to mess with it.'

'What happened?'

'He got a shock off it. People don't realize.'

'Is he burned?'

'Not exactly. The thing is, his heart stopped.'

'Bloody hell, Kev. And did they get it started again?'

'No.'

'What do you mean? He's dead?'

'Yes. I'm sorry.'

'Philip got an electric shock and he's dead?'

'Yes. So Kayleigh wondered if you could break the news to her nana. To Mrs Clarke. Muriel.'

'Did a doctor see him?'

'Ambulance. They came pretty quick apparently.'

'But they couldn't do anything?'

'No.'

'And is he still at the house?'

'I think they've took him to the hospital. Kayleigh's gone with Wendy. And I've got to phone Scott next, soon as I've finished talking to you.'

'Okay. Struth, Kev, I don't know what to say. And he's definitely dead?'

'Yes.'

'Have you seen him?'

'I'm at work. Kayleigh seen him.'

'Right.'

'I'm very sorry for, you know . . . Everything. So, if you could let Mrs . . . Nana . . . Clarke, know?'

Mum had come to the door. She said, 'Don't stand there with your phone to your ear. The druggies'll think you're reporting them. They'll send somebody to drive by and shoot you.'

My mother watches too much television.

I went in. She'd made me a ham sandwich and cut it diagonally because she thinks I have some pretty fancy notions about food presentation.

How to break the news to her? Before she sat down? While I toyed with the sandwich?

She said, 'You can run me to Mothers' Union seeing as you're here. It's at two o'clock. We're having a talk from a lady who's worked in Africa for donkey's years teaching the little black children. You can stay for it, if you like. They won't mind that you're divorced. Well, he's dead now anyway so you could say you're a widow.'

'Why would I do that?'

'To stop people talking. And it's not as though you're still living over the brush with that Tom. Not that I told anybody about that. Eat your sandwich. Do you want some mustard?'

I was trying to think what to say. The main thing was not to let her find out that the stupid microwave had been intended for her. I wished Tom was there. He was good at situations.

I said, 'Mum, that was Kayleigh's husband on the phone.'

'Tea or squash?'

'Neither. He called me because there's been an accident.'

She put the mustard jar down. 'Oh, no. Is it Kayleigh? She does drive fast.'

'Kayleigh's fine. It's Philip.'

She banged her hand down on the table. 'I knew it! I broke

288

the handle off the milk jug last night, and Rene Holderness has got a blood clot. I've been waiting all morning for one more thing to go wrong.'

Mum's Rule of Three.

'What's he gone and done now?'

'He got an electric shock.'

'Silly boy. How did he do that?'

'He was trying to mend something. I'm not exactly sure.'

'That'll teach him. Is he all right?'

'Not really.'

'Is he in hospital?'

'It's pretty bad.'

Muffed it, Partridge. That was your cue. Is he in hospital? No, Mum, he's dead.

She said, 'We'd better get over there quick. I'll just change my cardigan.'

Deep breath.

I said, 'Mum, sit down.'

Then she knew. Her face turned the same colour as her hair. 'That can't be right,' she said.

No, I thought, it can't. You don't do that kind of thing to your old mum.

She said, 'Are you sure?'

'Kev said it would have been a very big electric shock. It stopped his heart.'

'We're going to the garden centre tomorrow. We get a cup of coffee there.'

We went and sat together on the sofa. I held her freckly old hand and she kept looking at me, searching my face for a different end to the story. She seemed to shrink. I swear, in the bat of an eye, she was shorter and thinner and much, much older. It was like watching someone go down a plug hole.

She said, 'He never was strong. When he was born Nurse Smith said . . .'

You'll be lucky to keep him.

'Whatever was going around, measles, chicken pox, anything, he'd have it worse than anybody. He'd always get . . .'

Complications.

'And then when he lost Yvonne. I thought that'd . . .'

Finish him.

'Whatever shall I do without him?'

I said, 'You've got me, Mum.'

'Well, I know that,' she said.

I made her a cup of tea.

She said, 'I shall have to go and see him. There could have been a mix-up. Sometimes they do the wrong operation. Cut off the wrong leg. I read it in the papers. It's all foreign doctors, these days. Finish your sandwich and then we'll go to the hospital.'

'Let me talk to Wendy first.'

'It's nothing to do with her. What's it to do with her?'

'She's his wife, Mum.'

'A boy needs his mother at a time like this.'

I got through to Kayleigh. She said, 'I don't know as you should bring her to the hospital, Aunty Lizzie.'

'Is he badly burned?'

'Just his hands and his arms. He don't look a mess but, still, seeing him, you know, lying there? It could kill her.'

'What if it does? She's ninety. It might be what she wants. How's Wendy?'

'In pieces. She can't go home on her own. I'll bring her to ours. Reece'll have to double up with Brandon. I'm halfway through shampooing my carpets, but it'll have to wait. The doctor here said she might need to be put under sedimentation.'

Sedimentation. Pure Yvonne. Kayleigh is her mother's daughter. Am I mine? I think I might be. A glass-half-empty kind of person with a sour view of the human race. I didn't want my little life disturbed. I didn't want to have to keep an eye on poor widowed Wendy, or move into Mum's back bedroom and have to listen to her crying about my silly kid brother.

29

We drove to the hospital in silence. Philip wasn't in A and E, of course. You can't lie around there occupying a cubicle once they've certified you dead. We walked a country mile along corridors. A young nurse took us, plonked us on chairs, told someone we were there to view the deceased. Bring out your dead.

Mum said, 'They'll be wondering where I've got to at Mothers' Union.'

'Is there somebody you'd like me to phone? One of your friends? To let them know what's happened?'

'No, thank you.'

Come to think of it, her friends are all dead. It'll be seventy-year-old whippersnappers at Mothers' Union, these days. Just acquaintances. Women too young to have had a war.

The door opened and Kayleigh and Wendy came out. They looked dazed, puzzled, like everything was out of focus. Little wonder. They'd been whacked round the head with a sudden and ridiculous death on a perfect sunny morning. Wendy sat down.

Mum said, 'How is he?'

Kayleigh looked at me.

Wendy said, 'He's dead, Muriel. You do know that?'

'Of course I do,' said Mum. 'Elizabeth told me. I'm not soft in the head. But why ever didn't you stop him?'

I put my hand on hers to try to hush her but Mum's override button isn't located on her hand. I'm not even sure she has one.

Wendy said, 'Stop him? How was I supposed to do that? Anyway, it was your bloody microwave he was fiddling with.'

'Hm,' says Mum. 'I'll ignore that remark.' She didn't, though. She kept on: 'Because I haven't got a microwave. But you've forgotten that. You're probably not thinking straight, with everything that's happened. So I won't take offence.'

Kayleigh leaned against the wall. I gave her my seat.

She whispered, 'I'd never seen a dead body before.'

When Yvonne died Scott and Kayleigh weren't allowed to see her. I thought they should. She looked lovely once they'd given her a bit of cheek padding and blusher. I thought it'd help them to see her looking peaceful, but I was shouted down. Everybody said it'd give them nightmares. So they were left to imagine things for themselves and have a different kind of nightmare.

She rummaged for her lip balm. 'Right,' she said. 'We'd better get off. Brandon'll be home from school in half an hour. I'll take Wendy to ours for tonight. Kev'll go round to Dad's, make sure everything's locked up.'

'Did you speak to Scott?'

'Kev did. He's on his way. What will you do about Nana? Will you take her to your house?'

Mum said, 'She will not. I'll stay in my own home, thank

you very much. And you can stop that whispering. I can hear every word you're saying.'

The door opened again. A young man popped his head out, very solemn. Were we there for Philip Clarke? We were.

I said, 'Mum, are you sure about this? We don't have to do it now. We can come back tomorrow.'

'Of course I'm sure,' she said.

She went ahead of me.

'I'm his mother,' she said. And the young man gave her a little bow.

Philip didn't look like a man who'd had an electric shock. I was afraid it might have left him with a grimace, or that his hair would be standing on end, but no. He looked like he was sleeping, only with a bit of the air let out of him. Slow Puncture Man.

Mum told him he was a silly lad. Fifty-eight years old but in her mind he never quite made it to manhood. I don't know how he fared in the playground because I moved up to Peakirk Secondary just as he started infant school but I fear he was a marked boy. His mum lingering at the gate to make sure he crossed the playground safely, bunny-rabbit mittens on a string and a bull's-eye on his chest that said 'BULLY ME'.

Neither of us cried when we saw him. Perhaps it was too soon for that.

I felt absolutely nothing, except exhausted. Mum told the empty shell of her son to take care.

We drove to my house afterwards so I could pick up a few overnight things.

She kept saying, 'There's no need to stay with me. I'll be all right.'

In the end I put it to her that it'd be for my benefit. I said, 'If I stay at home I won't sleep. It'd be nice to have someone to talk to.'

'If you say so,' she said. 'But the bed will need airing.'

I swung by Tesco's, bought a couple of cottage pies, frozen peas, two bottles of red and a sweet sherry for Mum.

She said, 'I only have a drink at Christmas, to be sociable.'

Still, somebody made a dent in the sherry that evening, between the many phone calls.

'You answer,' she said. 'Whoever it is, tell them I'm not available.'

First up was Joyce from Mothers' Union, calling to see if Mum was ill because it wasn't like her to miss a meeting. She said, 'Poor Mrs Clarke. Tell her we'll all be praying for her. Have you let the Reverend know?'

That hadn't occurred to me. Mum considered herself a paid-up Anglican but she rarely went to church. It was since they started using a guitar on Sunday mornings instead of the organ. She's kind of Anglican-lite, but she has her limits.

I asked her if I should call the vicar, ask him to drop by with a few words of comfort.

She said, 'No, thank you. He wears jeans.'

After Joyce had spread the word, the calls came in thick and fast. Carol, Jean, Margery. I lost track and Mum didn't want to be bothered. Then Scott. He said, 'Change of plan at this end. Wendy doesn't want to stay at Kayleigh's. You can't blame her. They're packed in like sardines and Reece's room's a shrine to

West Brom so I'm taking her home and I'll stay with her. Kayleigh's talking to the undertaker about dates. How's Nana doing?'

'Stoic. Barricading herself against condolences and offers of help. You okay?'

'Yeah. What a day, though. I can't get my head round it.'

'Me neither. It's the suddenness of it.'

'And the stupidity.'

Ellie said to let her know as soon as the funeral was arranged because she couldn't just drop everything at short notice.

I said, 'Surely even lawyers have to bury their dead.'

She said, 'It's not like we were close.'

True enough, Philip had never featured strongly in her childhood. He wasn't the kind of uncle who conjured coins from behind your ear.

I said, 'However, there are your nana's feelings to consider. She'd appreciate having her family around her.'

She sighed. She said, 'Then give me Kayleigh's number. I'll tell her which slots work best for me.'

'Ellie,' I said, 'listen to yourself. Your uncle's funeral will not be arranged at your convenience.'

Mum said she wasn't hungry but she managed a bit of toast. I lit the gas fire.

She said, '*Coronation Street*'s on in a minute.'

'I thought you'd stopped watching it.'

'It's not like it used to be. They've brought Asians into it.'

'Because that's what Salford's like, these days. Same as Sparkbrook and Bordesley Green. Times change.'

'Well, I don't care for it. It's gone right off since Mike Baldwin had his heart attack. But Philip still liked it so I'll watch it for him.'

Kayleigh phoned with the latest. She sounded knackered.

'A week on Thursday, 1 o'clock at the crematorium. I couldn't get anything sooner. They've got a backlog. I've booked two cars. Me and Kev and the boys'll go in one, and you and Scott can bring Wendy and Nana in the other. Then afterwards there's a pub just down the road. They do sandwiches and biscuits, tea and coffee. If anybody wants anything stronger they can pay for it themselves at the bar.'

'What about a priest? Your nana's vicar could probably do it.'

'No, Wendy don't want anything like that. The undertaker's gave me a list of whassisnames. Not celebrities.'

'Celebrants?'

'That's it. I'll get one of them. And you can pick your own music.'

'Somebody should say something.'

'How do you mean?'

'A few words, about your dad. Scott could do it.'

'Yeah? Well, I'm not. You could, though, seeing as you know about these things.'

What could I say about Philip? A simple, honest man who bumbled through life, trying at all times to do the right thing and frequently failing. A devoted son, a grateful husband, a quietly chuffed father and grandfather. A tetchy brother, though. He never forgave me for being older and quicker, and maybe for managing to slip the old apron strings too. No, better, really, if Scott said the words of tribute.

'Cheers, Aunt Lizzie,' said Scott. 'Nice work, delegating. Do you have any suggestions how I can avoid using the word "plonker"?'

I called Louie after Mum had gone to bed.

I said, 'She's not cried once. I thought she'd keel over when I broke the news to her but she's plodding on, same as usual. She even insisted on doing the washing-up.'

He said, 'She's probably thinking it won't be long till she sees him again.'

I hadn't thought of that. Louie might be right. Perhaps she was picturing him waiting for her, like at airport Arrivals. He'd be there at the barrier, ready to whisk her off and show her the ropes, and they'd be together for all eternity. Who'll be waiting for me? Nobody, probably. Or just some driver holding up a card that says 'LIZA PEWTRIDGE'.

30

We spent the next day looking at old photos. Philip aged one month, Philip aged three months, me and Philip burying Dad in the sand at Colwyn Bay, Philip and Yvonne on their wedding day, Philip with his leg in plaster. That was the result of a domestic mishap too.

He'd been at home with the flu, felt bored, decided to defrost the freezer compartment of the fridge. He'd taken a screwdriver or a chisel or some other ill-advised implement to hack off a stubborn chunk of ice, punctured the fridge lining, run to get his toolbox in a hopeless bid to stop the gas hissing out, slipped on the wet floor, busted his tibia. Yes, my brother had previous for ridiculous accidents.

I said, 'What would you like to do about funeral flowers?'

'I don't know. Nothing silly.'

'Such as?'

'Somebody at Nora Schofield's sent a corgi made out of chrysanths.'

'Did she like corgis?'

'I suppose she must have. It looked more like a pig to me but they said it was meant to be a corgi.'

'We could ask your neighbour for some sprigs of apple blossom.'

'How do you mean?'

'Instead of a wreath.'

'You do come up with some notions, Elizabeth.'

'It was just a thought. I hate wreaths.'

'Anyway, I don't really know them next door.'

'Why? They must have been in that house two years at least.'

'I keep myself to myself.'

When they came home from work, I went round and asked. They were a nice young couple.

'Blossom?' he said.

'The pale pink stuff on the tree at the bottom of your garden.'

'I hadn't noticed it,' he said. 'Help yourself. Take as much as you like.'

Eight days when nothing much happened, except that Kayleigh's Kev bought a black tie and Wendy discovered that the bills still kept dropping through your letterbox even when you'd had a sad loss. It looked like rain around lunchtime on the Wednesday so I climbed over the fence with a pair of secateurs and cut a couple of branches. I ripped a hole in my tights but it was worth it. There hadn't been a lot of simple, unembellished beauty in Philip's life. He wasn't even allowed a bird-feeder because Yvonne hadn't wanted the mess. It seemed only right to give him a few fallen petals for his final journey.

We assembled at Wendy's. The hearse pulled up at 12.45 on the dot.

There was a football shirt wreath from Kayleigh and Kev and

the boys. Red and white. Scott said they were West Brom's away colours. Their home strip was navy which would have been a bit of a challenge for the florist. Yellow roses from Wendy. I gave the apple blossom to the undertaker, who placed it on the coffin.

Mum said, 'That was Elizabeth's idea so blame her if you don't like it.'

Wendy said, 'No, it's nice. Makes a change.'

I asked her if she'd decided what to do with the ashes. She shook her head.

Mum said, 'He could go in with Yvonne.'

'He could not,' says Wendy. 'He was *my* husband and I don't want to hear any more Yvonne stories. I'm sorry, Scott, I know she was your mum, but anybody'd think she was Mother bloody Teresa.'

Scott gave me a weak little smile.

I whispered, 'Let it pass. Wendy's feeling raw and your nan shouldn't have suggested it anyway.'

There were a lot of people waiting outside the chapel when we pulled up. I thought they might be lingerers from the previous ceremony but Wendy said the girls from her salon were there so it was definitely our crowd. Then I spotted Big Rita and Little Maureen.

Here's what happens. They carry the coffin in, family members follow, then everybody else piles in behind them. Wendy had chosen a Beatles' song, 'The Long and Winding Road'. The celebrant's suit jacket was too big for him. The sleeves reached his knuckles. He also had trouble pronouncing his Cs and his Ss. He called Philip 'the detheathed'. Perhaps such details wouldn't matter to you.

Ellie came in late. She had to sit near the back. Scott described his dad as a contented family man and a hard-working provider. A collector of Dinky toys, a long-time member of the Cactus and Succulent Club, a West Bromwich Albion supporter. They were thin pickings but he did a good job with what was available. He spoke of how Wendy had given him a new lease on life. Of how fondly he'd be remembered by his children and grandchildren.

Kayleigh howled. Wendy sobbed. Ryan and Reece and Brandon fidgeted in their suits. I looked at Mum. She was perfectly composed. Dusty Springfield sang 'Goin' Back' while the coffin moved away and the curtains closed. I did feel sad, but for Mum mainly. He should have been more careful. Great heavens, he fussed enough about everybody else. He might have shown some consideration and kept himself alive and well until Mum was gone. Now I was all she had and she didn't seem to want me. I had a horrible feeling that the few tears I did shed were for myself, not for Philip.

They played some kind of jokey, jolly march as we left the chapel. Scott said it was the theme music for *Match of the Day*. Kayleigh's boys had chosen it. I grabbed Ellie.

I said, 'When I die I want a full requiem mass. And when I slip behind the curtains I'd like Fauré's In Paradisum.'

'Noted,' she said. 'Sorry I can't stay for the tea. I've got a client to see in Winson Green. Will you give Wendy my apologies?'

As we came out into the sunshine the first face I saw was Louie's. Then I really cried.

'Whoah!' he said. 'I came to cheer you up, not for you to get snot on my new linen jacket.'

'You drove all the way from Cornwall?'

'Chas drove. And we stayed at a rather spiffy boutique hotel last night. I'm willing to suffer for you, darling, but only between 600-thread sheets. What a lot of people. I thought your brother was Philip No Friends.'

'So did I. I don't know who any of them are.'

'A contingent from Cactuses and Succulents, presumably. Is the raccoon here?'

'We haven't spoken so he won't know about it.'

'Correct answer. But how nice of Tom Sullivan to come. You do manage your exes very well, Lizzie.'

'Tom's here? I didn't see him.'

'Then go and find him. I'm not dashing off. We can talk over the funeral meats.'

Tom was just getting into his car. He said he'd read the death notice in the *Evening Mail*. 'It was very sudden,' he said. 'Was it a coronary?'

'Electrocuted himself. The stupidest waste of life. He was trying to mend a second-hand microwave my mother didn't even want. Are you coming to the pub?'

'I can't stay. We're off to Kenya tomorrow and there's still a lot to do.'

'Kenya? Blimey, you get about these days.'

'We're doing a cycling challenge. Well, it's Geraldine, really, but I'm going to have a crack at it. You can sponsor me if you like. It's in aid of osteoporosis.'

He and the Lipless One were flying to Nairobi, then across into Tanzania to climb Kilimanjaro.

I said, 'You'll need a holiday after that.'

He said, 'And I'll be getting one. The beaches look very nice. Please tell Muriel I'm very sorry for her loss.'

Louie walked with me to the pub. He said, 'So the sweet boy with the ponytail is the dreaded Scott? The formerly dreaded.'

'Yes. Hasn't he turned out well?'

'Very. But he has a girlfriend?'

'India. On whom my television hopes are built.'

'Damn. You and I might have ended up related by marriage.'

'You've got Chas.'

'But there's no harm in window-shopping.'

Is there a sadder sight than a dry wake in a down-at-heel pub? Louie ordered a bottle of red and Little Maureen and Big Rita joined us. They claimed Louie as their long-lost celebrity friend because of the time Yvonne got up a group of us to go and see the Hunkies at the Apollo and he and Chas came with us.

The mourners settled into three clusters. The Mothers' Union ladies sat with Mum, the nail-salon girls looked after Wendy, and the unidentified men scrummed around the egg and cress sandwiches and eyed the beer pumps. Kev and the boys watched a big telly with the sound turned off and Kayleigh wandered about with a teapot. Which just left Scott.

I said, 'We should circulate.'

'Okay,' he said. 'I'll take the nail ladies and Nana's mates. You do the suits.'

It turned out only a couple of them were cactus enthusiasts. It was an interest Philip had let slide in recent years. The others were all blokes from the Leccy Board, people he'd worked with.

Philip had been well liked but efficient, they said. Fair but firm with non-payers. He knew the system inside out, was helpful to newcomers learning the job, and after his retirement had been greatly missed by the arrears team on inter-departmental quiz nights. My brother, the apotheosis of an assistant office manager.

Scott said he'd sensed an undercurrent of hostility from Wendy's group, except for one older woman with nails and lips the colour of orange sherbet. She'd given him an appreciative pat on the backside.

'Maybe they're worried about Wendy's inheritance.'

'What? Worried that I'm going to challenge her for a share of Clarke Towers?'

'Some kids would.'

'Not me. She's welcome to it.'

'How do you feel, now it's all over?'

'I don't know. A bit punch-drunk.'

'I still can't believe it.'

'Same here. I do feel sad but not like Kayleigh. It's really hit her. But he and I weren't, you know, not lately . . . It's not like when Mum died. She left a great big hole. With Dad it's more like a faint indentation.'

I knew exactly what he meant. Philip Clarke was here. Or was he?

Chas picked Louie up from the pub. He drives a Jaguar with leather seats.

'Condolences,' he said. 'But, Lizzie, you never visit us. Was it something I said?'

I promised I'd try to get down there later in the summer.

'Any time,' Chas said. 'Just come. We'll give you the room with the sea view, and in return you can cook that mustardy rabbity thing. Bring a chap if you're seeing someone.'

Louie said, 'She's not. But that nice Tom Sullivan turned up today, and if you ask me he still carries a bit of a torch for her.'

I said, 'That could be very dangerous, trying to cycle up Kilimanjaro balancing a flaming brand on his handlebars.'

Chas said they really ought to leave. Louie hugged me.

I said, 'Do you have any idea what it meant to me, seeing you today?'

'Not another word,' he said, 'or I'll get tearful and then I'll have to take out my contacts. Anyway, I have a confession to make. You know I said I was never *ever* going to do another pantomime?'

'Where is it?'

'Kettering. But I won't have to do any dancing. And it'll only be a four-week run.'

'And you will be playing?'

'The Sheriff of Snottingham. Wait, do I hear the sound of career barrels being scraped? Yes, I think I do.'

'Kettering's where? Northamptonshire?'

'Ask my driver. It's definitely not as far as Whitley Bay.'

'I'll come and see it. I might even bring Noah. If I'm allowed. Ellie might want to run the script past the PC police first.'

People were dispersing. Kev settled up with the pub. Wendy left with the nail technicians. Scott went to catch his train.

Kayleigh said, 'What are we going to do about Nan?'

I said, 'She's all right, you know. I'll stay with her again tonight but I think it's getting on her nerves a bit, having me there. I'll probably go home tomorrow.'

'Dad went over every week. Never missed.'

'I'm not your dad. We'll work it out. If she's lonely I'll go.'

'She'll never let on she's lonely. I'll try and get over on Sundays. It's what Dad'd want.'

She started to cry. Poor kid. Always expected to be the grown-up. Even diamond Kev, who knows how to fix gas boilers, even he might feel overwhelmed if he had to supply thirty pairs of clean socks a week and keep an eye on an aged relative.

I went back to Glenville Close with Mum, wondering how soon after a bereavement it wouldn't be considered cruel and unnatural to leave her on her own. She put the kettle on.

She said, 'You don't have to stay, you know.'

'Do you want me to go?'

'I didn't say that.'

I said I'd probably go home in the morning. She seemed to relax after that. She really wanted to be alone. I went to Rock 'n' Roe as soon as they opened, brought in cod and chips. The phone rang a few times.

Mum said, 'Leave it. I'm tired of people feeling sorry for me. It's worse than when your dad passed, people squeezing your hand and looking at you all gooey-eyed.'

'It's because Philip was your son. They're thinking it's the worst thing that could happen, to live longer than your own child.'

'Yes. And they're glad it's me it's happened to and not them. They're thinking, Poor Muriel Clarke. But I'm all right, Jack.'

BEREAVED PENSIONER HITS NAIL FIRMLY ON HEAD.

She got the box of photos out again, spread them on the table in some kind of order.

I said, 'Shall we get you some albums to put them in?'

'If you like,' she said. She sounded so weary.

I was looking at a picture taken when I was about six. Mum, Aunty Edie, Uncle Cyril, me, sitting on a blanket in Cannon Hill Park, 1953. Coronation year. I was wearing a pale blue dress with puffed sleeves and smocking. I loved that dress.

I said, 'You must have been expecting Philip.'

'Yes,' she said. 'Only I wasn't showing yet.'

'Who took the photo?'

'Your dad.'

It was always Dad. That's why there are so few pictures of him.

I must have looked at that photo a hundred times but it was like I was seeing it for the first time: Aunty Edie looking away into the distance, Mum with her eyes downcast and a little smile. And Uncle Cyril's hand slipped round her waist and resting on her little Philip bump.

I was looking at the pictures over her shoulder. She couldn't see that my face was burning but she knew I'd noticed. There are absolutely no flies on my mother.

I picked the photo up and went and sat opposite her.

I said, 'Uncle Cyril was very fond of you.'

'Yes, well . . .' she said.

A tear dripped off her chin.

I said, 'But it's all a long time ago.'

SHELL-SHOCKED DAUGHTER STATES THE BLEEDING OBVIOUS.

Mum looked at me and I thought for one moment she was going to shut me down, going to try to put the secret back in the box with the photos. But then she said, 'It wasn't what you think.'

I said, 'Mum, I'm not thinking anything in particular.'

Which was a downright lie. I had that sick, knotted feeling you get just before a big announcement. Do you find the defendant guilty or not guilty?

'You weren't Cyril's if that's what you're wondering.'

'Yes, it was what I was wondering.'

'You were your dad's.'

She smoothed the tablecloth. I asked her if she'd loved him.

'Who?' she said.

'Uncle Cyril. Dad. Either. Both.'

'They were different.'

I'll say. Dad was short, quiet, unremarkable, but capable of drollery and surprising little acts of rebellion. Like drawing a shaving-soap face on a freshly polished mirror. Uncle Cyril was a big man, self-important, known to deliver the occasional ponderous pronouncement.

Ye gods, how had I missed it? Philip was Uncle Cyril to a T. He was Uncle Cyril minus the salesman's blustery bonhomie.

'Did Aunty Edie know?'

'We never talked about it.'

'She looks pretty brassed off in that photo.'

'Edie always looked like that.'

'Did Dad know?'

'No.'

I'll bet he did. My dad was no fool. I'll bet he thought, I know where that great lummox sprang from.

'You always liked Cyril. Aunty Phyllis said you'd vied with Edie for him.'

'Phyllis! What did she know! She swanned off to Argentina.'

'She didn't swan off, Mum. She married an Argentinian. He wouldn't have found much scope for cattle ranching in Stirchley. So I'm definitely Dad's?'

'Of course you are. You've got his eyes. You're slapdash like he was. Anyway, Cyril wasn't properly demobbed till the end of 1946. They kept him in the Territorial Reserve. I was already expecting you by the time Cyril came home.'

'Dad was a good man.'

'I'm not saying he wasn't. He just didn't have a lot of get-up-and-go. You see, he was never the same after Burma.'

Coming home from the Far East, settling down in grey old post-war Brum, that must have taken some getting used to. Standing eight hours a day at a turret lathe, waiting in all weathers for buses must have been pretty draining too. Not like Uncle Cyril who landed very nicely on his size twelves. He drove around in a company car, with a boot full of paper clips and desk diaries. Suddenly 'I'll bring you some free samples, Muriel,' took on a whole new meaning.

I decided to play along, keep her talking. It might be my last chance as well as my first. I topped up her glass. 'I realize now where Philip got his height and his big feet.'

'Oh, yes. Cyril was a big man. He was in the Coldstream Guards, you know.'

Was it the sherry or did I hear a faint swell of pride in her voice? Cyril was in the Guards. My dad was in some bog-standard infantry division. 'So when he and Edie adopted Leslie, it obviously wasn't because Cyril was firing blanks.'

'There's no call to be vulgar, Elizabeth. Edie couldn't have children. She had women's troubles.'

And husband troubles it now transpires.

'It must have been weird for Cyril, raising an adopted ginger when he knew his natural son was growing up with you and Dad.'

'Leslie wasn't ginger. He was auburn. Cyril had lovely wavy hair.'

And, yes, so did Philip. All the tortures I'd endured as a child, the Twink home perms, the sleepless nights in curlers, the plastic rain hoods, all to coax my hair into waves like my brother's. All failed.

'Your nancy-boy friend's got nice hair. He said, "You won't remember me, Mrs Clarke." Well, I did remember him, because I saw his picture in a magazine when I was at the hairdresser's. He was in a pantomime somewhere.'

'It was so nice of him to come to the funeral.'

'It was. It's a pity he's that way. He'd have suited you.'

'But, Mum, did you love Cyril? Or was it just a fling?'

'What kind of question is that?'

When they came to Sunday tea Uncle Cyril used to give Philip half a crown and me two shillings. I thought I was on a lower tariff because I was a girl.

Mum said, 'He told me he'd leave Edie, if I was to say the word.'

'Why didn't you?'

'Because you didn't do that in those days. You stuck with what you'd got. And I mean, if he'd told Edie he was leaving her, she'd have had one of her episodes and he'd have given in to her. Then where would that have left me?'

Up Shit Creek with a wavy-haired cuckoo in the nest, that's where.

I said, 'After Dad died, did you and Cyril ever think of getting together?'

'Gracious, no,' she said. 'He'd gone thin on top and he was waiting for a new knee. Anyway, I couldn't be bothered with all that. He'd come round, of course, if I needed a washer changed on a tap.'

I'd never heard it called that before.

She said, 'He used to bring me Meltis New Berry Fruits. He knew I liked them.'

It had been a long and difficult day and I'd definitely had too much booze.

I said, 'Now I understand a lot of things.'

And out it all tumbled. Sixty-odd years of waiting to be told I was the loveliest, cleverest, best daughter in the world. I said she'd always preferred Philip. She said I was upset about him passing away, as was only to be expected. I said I'd always had to take a back seat. She said Philip wasn't like me. He'd needed more care and attention, that's all. I was getting nowhere, spinning my wheels.

I said, 'Well, I'm glad Dad was my dad.'

I sounded like a mardy child. My doll's pram's nicer than your doll's pram.

She was still smoothing the tablecloth. It's what she does when she's thinking.

Then she said, 'You know, your father was very proud of you.'

I looked at her. I said, 'Is there anything you'd like to add to that? On a personal note?'

She said, 'We're not a family that goes in for a lot of hugging and kissing.'

'That's true.'

'It doesn't mean we don't care about one another.'

'No.'

'But you're a very good daughter to me.'

'I hope so.'

'I always say to people, "I couldn't ask for a better daughter than my Elizabeth."'

'Do you?'

She drained her glass. 'And I love you very dearly.'

I believe she may have found childbirth easier than coughing up those words.

I said, 'I love you too, Mum.'

It was a precious moment, worth waiting for. And then what I thought but didn't say was how relieved I was to have a reason at long last for never having liked my brother. Spawn of Cyril Bertram Clarke. Reproach of Aunt Edie's barren, prolapsed womb. Coddled and cosseted nincompoop bastard of a manila envelope salesman.

31

Louie said, 'The little minx! But, you know, I always thought your mum had a twinkle in her eye.'

'Not a twinkle. It was an ominous glint.'

'So that's where you get it from.'

'Thank you so much for coming yesterday. But I feel terrible. You drove all that way and now it turns out he wasn't even my brother.'

'He was your half-brother, Lizzie. You knew him from the day he was born. That counts. And I enjoyed it. No, wrong word, but you must admit you do get some fabulous mismatches at funerals. The Hush-Puppy men breaking custard creams with the nail-istas. I mean, where else would such people ever meet? And Muriel's vestal virgins. What must they have thought of the music? And nary a mention of God.'

'It was Kayleigh's choice. I think Wendy just let her get on with it.'

'I rather took to Wendy. She seemed mellower than his first wife.'

'Yes, as long as there's gin to put in her tonic she's not too fussed about the state of the skirting boards.'

'Was I right in sensing relief as much as grief?'

'There has been talk.'

'Men?'

'Going out a lot in the evening. She could have been meeting her friends for all I know. But if she was looking for a bit of action you couldn't blame her. Philip was happy just to sit in front of the telly chain-eating Pringles.'

'Sounds like she won't be in her widow's weeds for long. And that Scott! He is beyond cute. The terrible stories you used to tell about him. Could you possibly have been mistaken?'

'No, he was a horrible little tyke. Too much telly, too many cheezy doofers. But now . . . Arguably he's better company than Ellie.'

'Ellie's all right. I thought she looked very elegant yesterday, very business-like. She didn't stay long, though, did she? Why didn't she come to the pub?'

'Work. She had to get to Winson Green prison to talk to some lying, thieving piece of excrement she's defending.'

He said, 'I can see if they ever appoint you Lord Chancellor, Lizzie Partridge, the venerable principle of innocent until proven guilty will be straight down the WC.'

I sent Ellie an email. There's so little point in phoning her. It's easier to get through to WestGas Customer Services than it is to my daughter. I wrote: *This is your mother. Please call me as I have something VERY important to tell you.*

And she did, within the hour, so now I know the best way to make contact with the far side of the moon.

She said, 'What is it, Mum? Are you all right? You don't have cancer, do you?'

'Not as far as I know. But I just found out something totally . . . I don't know. Mind-blowing. Philip wasn't really my brother. Your nana, get this, had a thing with her brother-in-law, with my Uncle Cyril. Result: Philip.'

'Holy shit. She actually told you this?'

'Yesterday, after the funeral.'

'Out of the blue?'

'Of course not out of the blue. We were looking at old photographs and I suddenly realized something. Body language. There was this picture. Nana was expecting Philip and Cyril had his hand on her, near her belly. You could just tell.'

'So you asked her?'

'I just gave things a little push and out it all came. Lubricated by Cyprus sherry.'

'Wow. Did she seem, like, racked with guilt?'

'No. She was quite matter-of-fact about it. I got the impression Granddad Wilf didn't quite cut it in the sack.'

'Please! Let's not go there.'

'So now certain things about Philip make sense.'

'You mean why he was such a clueless windbag and absolutely nothing like you?'

'I think I've identified a compliment in there somewhere. Thank you.'

'How do you feel about it all?'

'Good. I feel okay. Happy, even. I'd been worried about not

feeling very grief-stricken. Now I'm off the hook. How's the nanny working out?'

'Not great. I gave her Noah's schedule and I told her our non-negotiable rules but she still seems to please herself.'

'Is she taking him to crack dens?'

'She took him to a playground we don't like. She has child-minder friends who go there.'

'What's wrong with it?'

'It doesn't have rubber mulch safety surfaces and, frankly, they're not the kind of children we want him mixing with.'

'I thought he was down for Beechfield. There's no telling who he'll meet there.'

'What do you mean? Beechfield's very exclusive.'

'The money they charge, half the parents must be bank robbers. Or oligarchs. Any Russian names on the PTA? You might want to check that out.'

'Was that Tom I saw at the crematorium yesterday?'

'Yes.'

'I thought you were finished.'

'We are. He's got a new woman. They go on cycling holidays.'

'I thought he looked fit.'

'You know I'm up for this TV thing?'

'Yes, Mum. I organized your haircut.'

'Well, if I don't get it, and I probably won't, I wouldn't mind helping with Noah, say two days a week. If the nanny doesn't work out. Maybe Nat's mum'd do a couple of days too.'

'I don't think so. She's a very busy woman.'

'Is she? What does she do?'

'She's on committees. She does lots of stuff.'

'What, like, folding serviettes for the Blue and White dinner dance? Shopping for new golf gloves?'

'Don't be snarky. Anyway, we need a proper nanny.'

'As opposed to a woman who raised you to be the highly successful person you are today? With perfect teeth. Independence of spirit. And a strong immune system because of your judicious exposure to normal household dirt.'

'Okay. For all that, I'm grateful. I just don't think you're nanny material. Hey, so we've both got half-brothers, only you didn't find out till yours was dead.'

'That's true, although in your case it was all above board. Your father's last effort at spreading his genes. How are his little afterthoughts?'

'No idea. I don't hear from them. Not little, that's for sure. They're probably shaving by now. Do you think Uncle Philip ever suspected who his father really was?'

'No. I mean, why would you? Even if you had a smidge of curiosity, which he didn't. He wasn't an imaginative thinker. Like, he didn't stop to imagine what the consequences of sticking his screwdriver into a microwave capacitor might be.'

'Mum,' she said. 'Thanks for the offer about Noah. But I bet you will get that TV. You should. Just, in future, if you email me to say you've something *very* important to tell me, could you please add a little codicil, something like, *PS: don't worry, I don't have cancer.*'

The doorbell rang. I didn't actually register what it was immediately because recently it's been making a very feeble noise.

Maybe the rain got into it. So there was this faint bleating sound and then the letterbox rattled. I could see someone through the glass but the door was sticking so I shouted for them to go round the back. It was Rodney Pooley. He was holding a very lavish bouquet of sweet peas, white roses and silver eucalyptus.

I was not looking great. My choppy bob had deteriorated into a haystack with structural failure, my eye bags bore witness to ten restless nights in my mother's guest bed, and I was wearing my monster claw slippers.

'Hello, Foxy,' he said. 'I thought I'd surprise you.'

I said, 'I don't like surprises. You should have phoned. What if I'd been away?'

He said he'd had a sudden compulsion to drive over and find me. He gave me the flowers. He gave me those heavy bedroom eyes. I told him about Philip. He tucked my haystack hair behind my ear and kissed the corner of my mouth. Gets me every time.

When I woke he was sitting up, surveying my half-painted bedroom.

He said, 'What do they call this colour?'

'Shades of Catarrh.'

'Do you intend keeping it like this?'

'Until I summon the will to redo it.'

'I'll help you, if you like. I'm pretty handy with a paint roller. What's for dinner?'

I don't know if it was the sex that had cleared my head or the sheer presumption of the man.

I said, 'Do you remember the last time I heard from you? Your last message to me?'

'No. Remind me.'

'You were in Clacton, the transmission had gone on your car and you wanted to borrow some money.'

'That wasn't very romantic, was it?'

'Not only that. It was cheeky, because you already owed me for the Chamberlain Metro.'

'Did I? Shit. I forgot about that. I'll go to the ATM.'

'Good. There's one on Bristol Road.'

'Actually, it might have to be later in the week. I need to watch the old cash-flow.'

'So do I. Those flowers must have been expensive.'

'You're worth it.'

'Quite possibly. But I'd rather have had my hundred quid.'

'And you shall have it, I promise. We could go out for dinner, if you don't feel like cooking.'

'No, thank you. I don't want to get into any more dodgy credit-card situations with you. I'll make us a quick pasta. Olive oil, garlic, bit of chilli. You can go and buy some wine while I have a shower.'

He came back with two bottles of Jacob's Creek and an overnight bag.

I said, 'What's this?'

He said, 'It's just for a couple of nights. Minnie needs some space.'

The spaghetti was ready, the table was set and I really wanted my dinner. I decided I'd serve the home truths later, instead of dessert.

He said I seemed distracted. 'Are you worried about your mum?'

'No. She's fine. Incredible, really, considering. Made of steel. You never talk about your parents.'

'Both long dead. They'd split up, though, years before. How's the telly project going?'

'Slowly. Where did you go after you moved from Carisbrooke Road?'

'Can't remember. We always moved a lot, with Dad's work.'

'What did he do?'

'This and that. What's with all the questions? Are you checking on the Pooley family fortunes?'

'How about your sister? What happened to her?'

'Beverley? I never hear from her. She lives in Ludlow. Married to a prick. No kids.'

'And you've got Minnie.'

'Yep.'

'Who has apparently chucked you out.'

'I didn't say that. We don't always see eye to eye, that's all. She's got a big costume order. Winged dragons. She brings work home from her studio and there's stuff everywhere. It's not a big house.'

'And she wants it to herself. Seems reasonable. A young woman like that, she doesn't want her dad lodging with her.'

He put down his glass.

I said, 'Because I'm right in thinking it is her house and not yours?'

He said, 'Has she been talking to you? Have you been snooping?'

'No. But I had a very interesting conversation with Janet.'

'Janet? You phoned Janet?'

'No. She phoned me. There's an all-points alert out for you, Rodney. The man who turns up on the doorstep with a suit-case. A man who lives beyond other people's means.'

He gave a sour little laugh. 'Janet actually phoned you? So Minnie's been sticking her oar in. What a pair of snakes. Her and her mother.'

He pushed his dish away. I didn't say anything.

'Look,' he said, 'it's true I've had a few problems. And I'm sorry I forgot about your money. I've been through a rough patch, but I'm getting back on my feet. I've got a couple of irons in the fire.'

BIRMINGHAM SUBURB HIT BY HEAVY FALL OF CLICHÉS. NO CASUALTIES.

I said, 'I hope you have because I certainly can't afford to keep you.'

He said if that was the case I'd put him in a difficult position because he couldn't go back to Minnie's that night. And I sur-prised myself by telling him to go and blag a hotel room, or drive to Ludlow and throw himself on the mercy of his sister and her lawfully wedded prick.

'Fine,' he said. 'Suit yourself. I hope you can live with your conscience, forcing a man to sleep in his car.'

And, as a matter of fact, I found that I could.

He took the second bottle of shiraz with him. Waste not, want not.

I said, 'Do you want your flowers back as well? See if you can get a refund?'

'Fuck you,' were his parting words. 'Fuck you and Janet and the whole fucking lot of you.'

★

I called Louie. I was shaking so much it took me three goes to hit his number.

He said, 'You done right, girl. My heart is bursting with pride.'

'You don't think I was too hard on him? I didn't overreact?'

'You mean to his lying, freeloading and generally reprehensible and slippery behaviour? I don't think so, darl.'

'It's such a disappointment. He was the best lay ever.'

'Let's say, "best lay to date".'

'At my age?'

'When you're on the telly every week you'll be fighting them off. Just one thing. You didn't let him take any compromising photos?'

'You mean like a close-up of the salad drawer in my fridge?'

'You know what I mean. We don't want him selling his love-rat story to the tabloids.'

'There is no story.'

'Good. And you know there was always going to be the stumbling block of his hobby. I couldn't see you trotting along to those furry conventions. Weekends spent with the odour of stale synthetics. Not your scene, Lizzie.'

I always feel better after I've talked to Louie. And I fear this has finished me with raccoons for life.

32

A week passed. I wondered whether to phone Minnie Pooley, just to make sure her dad was all right, but Louie absolutely forbade it.

He said, 'Of course he's all right. He's had prior experience. And what if he's back at home already? I'll bet he is. I'll bet he's slithered back in. What if he answers the phone? He'll think you've had a change of heart. He'll start wheedling. Do not call that number. Delete it. Come down to Cornwall and I'll do it for you.'

I promised I'd go and visit once I'd heard from Vertical Hold.

Wendy wanted to know if there was anything of Philip's I'd like to have. I couldn't imagine what. Then I remembered my dad's war medals.

'What medals?' she said. 'I thought he didn't have much of a war.'

I said, 'He got the Burma Star, the Defence medal and the Victory medal, same as they all did. They should be in an old Huntley & Palmer's biscuit tin.'

'I'll have a look,' she said. 'He kept all sorts of old junk.'

'It's not old junk, Wendy. It's important memorabilia of my dad. His dog-tags should be with his medals. I'd like those too. And his old shaving brush.'

'Why do you want that?'

'Because Dad used to let me lather his chin when he was shaving. I used to stand on a chair to reach him. It was always me, never Philip. By rights I should have been given that brush when he died.'

'Muriel probably thought you used Immac. You all right, Lizzie? I've never heard you get sentimental before.'

'Not sentimental. I'd just like to have my dad's things. So you're having a clear-out?'

'Yes.'

'Are you selling the house?'

'Yes.'

'Where will you go?'

'The flat over the salon.'

It was later that evening when the phone rang again.

'Hello, Lizzie,' said a friendly voice that I totally did not recognize. 'This is Simon.'

He must have heard the wheels of my mind creaking into motion. Simon?

'Simon Sullivan,' he said. 'Tom's son.'

Silent Simon, husband of motor-mouth Tessa. I felt slightly nauseous. I said, 'This can only be bad news.'

'Well, yes and no. Dad's had a bit of a prang. He's in a back brace.'

'I'm sorry to hear it. If he's in the Orthopaedic I'll pop in to see him.'

'He's not,' he said. 'He was abroad when it happened. He still is. In Kenya.'

'Doing his bike ride.'

'Yes. They think he must have had a dizzy turn. Altitude sickness, probably. He fell off his bike and tumbled down quite an incline.'

'So is he too injured to travel?'

'They flew him back to Nairobi and he's coming home tomorrow. He'll need surgery but not for a week or two. He's got two broken bones in his spine.'

'Poor Tom. Well, let me know how he gets on. And give him my best wishes.'

'The thing is,' says Simon, 'we're in a bit of a fix because Tessa and I are off to the Norwegian fjords tomorrow.'

'Very nice.'

'And Dad's going to need help.'

'He's got Geraldine.'

'Not exactly.'

'What does that mean?'

'Geraldine doesn't feel she can cut her trip short to travel back with him. It's understandable. She trained very hard for this cycling challenge. And the rest of her group are all having a week at the beach. So, you know?'

'No, I don't know. She won't give up her holiday? What does Tom say about that?'

'Well, of course he's not really himself at the moment. He's taking a lot of painkillers.'

'Is he mightily pissed off? He should be. Has he told her where to stick the pointy end of her helmet?'

Simon has a silly, girlish giggle for a grown man. Then I saw where this was heading.

I said, 'And I suppose you're not inclined to cancel *your* trip? To look after your old dad in his hour of need?'

'In principle,' he said, 'I would. It goes without saying. But it's rather tricky. Norway's a very special trip. It's for Tessa's fortieth.'

'So what exactly are you asking of me? You want me to drive round there every day with a casserole?'

'I think he's going to need a bit more help than that for a few days. Showering and stuff. I mean, I wouldn't ask but you did live together.'

'Is Tom party to this arrangement you've cooked up? He did leave me, you know. He voted with his feet. Do you really think he wants me soaping his back?'

I heard a little mutter-scuffle going on in the background and Tessa came on the line. 'Look, Lizzie,' she said. 'You're making this more complicated than necessary. Geraldine's not available. We're not available. He's flying into Heathrow on Thursday. I've organized an ambulance to drive him home and they have your number. They'll tell you what time to expect him. The keys are in the usual place.'

'And if this isn't convenient to me?'

'Why? You don't work.'

'You don't know what I do.'

'Well, if you won't help him he'll have to pay for a nurse. He'd probably pay you for your trouble if that's what you're angling for.'

'I don't charge for acts of friendship. But, as I recall, Tom has two sons. Where's Christopher in all this?'

'He's very busy with work. Anyway, you can't expect a man to know what to do. So are you going to do it or not?'

I said, 'I will do it, Tessa, but only for Tom's sake. I wouldn't go to the foot of the stairs for you and Simon.'

Click. Call ended.

I looked up broken backs. Never look up medical conditions just before you go to bed. You won't sleep. Two broken vertebrae. Was his spinal cord affected? Had I agreed to nurse a paraplegic ex until Lipless and Hipless deigned to come home?

I wrote a plan on the inside cover of *The Summer of Naked Swim Parties*.

1. Replenish Tom's fridge.
2. Alert his GP.
3. Get name of reputable nursing agency.

Even after I'd done that I didn't sleep well. It was daylight when my phone rang but very early.

'Your husband's flight just landed. We hope to be under way by seven. Should be with you between nine and ten, depends on traffic.'

I said, 'He's not my husband,' but the line dropped.

A defibrillator-strength coffee and day-old stir-fry chicken and I was out of the door.

Tom used to keep a spare set of keys in his rockery, two stones from the dianthus. But he got rid of the rockery, to accommodate Geraldine's vehicle, I imagine. I had no choice but to call Simon.

'Ah,' he said. 'Yes, new hiding place. They're taped under a window ledge. The little window, at the side of the house.'

You'd never catch Tom going on holiday and leaving a crumpled bed or a cup in the sink. He used to run the hoover over my floors before we went away for a weekend.

'What if something happens to us?' he used to say. 'What if there's a pile-up on the motorway? Or the plane crashes? You don't want people coming in here and saying, "Look at the state of the place."'

Fridge, immaculate and empty, except for a small carton of long-life milk. Kitchen cupboards, clean, orderly and devoid of anything you'd be tempted to snack on late at night. Chia, kale chips, green tea. What do you want when your girlfriend has dumped you at Jomo Kenyatta airport and you've flown through the night with broken vertebrae? Rice pudding.

I called the ambulance woman to see if I had time to go to the supermarket.

'Crikey, yes,' she said. 'The M40's chocker and we're taking it steady anyway because of his back.'

Tom loves his food. I'd missed cooking for him. It was my marmalade ice cream that first brought us together, and my beef cooked in stout. He'd spotted me in the coffee shop at the hospital and plucked up courage to tell me he always watched the show. I'd been visiting Yvonne, and he'd been visiting his wife. People often used to recognize me in those days.

He made me have half of his Danish pastry, said I looked starved. I told him he needed his eyes tested. I never expected to see him again but I did, months later. His wife had died and he was taking a box of chocolates for the nurses. He asked me if I'd care to go to a tea dance with him, and that was that. Until it wasn't any more.

It was chilly for June. I turned the heating on, cut some roses for the hall table, made a start on some chicken soup. I'd pictured him being carried in on a stretcher but he walked in, very slowly, an ambulance woman either side of him. He looked pinched and grey. He hadn't shaved in days.

'One hubby, safely delivered,' they said. 'There she is, Tom. The face you've been dying to see.'

'Yes,' he said. 'Thank God you're here, Lizzie.' And his bristly chin wobbled.

He went straight to bed. Dr Jindal said to give him as much paracetamol as he wanted and there'd be a letter from the hospital about getting a scan.

I said, 'This all seems a bit casual, for a broken back.'

'Not broken,' says the doctor. 'Just bit crumbled. It can happen in elderly person. Hospital will repair with cement. Very simple. He will be good as new.'

'How long will he be in hospital?'

'Four hours. Maybe five. Bring tiffin box in case.'

Tom wanted tea.

'Cake?'

He managed a smile.

'Sticky ginger or orange curd?'

'Yes,' he whispered.

There was one of those Alpine cowbells hanging above the

kitchen door, a souvenir of a holiday he and Barbara went on years ago. I unhooked it and took it up on the tea tray. I said, 'I'm absolutely beat. I've been up since six. Ring this if you need anything. I'm going for a nap on your new sofa.'

'Don't go,' he said. 'Lie down beside me.'

I said, 'All right. But no funny business.'

He said it hurt to laugh.

That was Thursday. On Friday I was summoned to Wendy's to pick up my family heirlooms. There was already an estate agent's board outside the house.

She said, 'I know what you're thinking. It's too soon.'

'None of my business. They say you shouldn't make any major decisions straight after a bereavement.'

'Yes, they do say that, don't they? Well, I'll risk it. What's the downside? Feeling a bit weepy sometimes? Missing the salmon-pink bathroom tiles? The upside is I'll be able to afford a Christmas cruise. Miami to Cozumel. I can't bloody wait.'

By Sunday Tom felt well enough to go for a little walk. I'd bought him a retractable walking stick from Argos. He took my arm. He said, 'People'll think you're out with your father.'

Geraldine was flying home the following Wednesday. I said I'd be gone straight after breakfast.

Tom said, 'There's no need. She knows the score.'

DOMESTIC SLOB TROUNCES NEAT-FREAK IN PENALTY SHOOTOUT.

I said, 'Tom, her stuff's still hanging in the wardrobe. Her *Cycling Active* magazines are piled up in your living room.'

They were piled very neatly, I might add.

'But Lizzie,' he said, 'promise me you'll come back. As soon as she's gone.'

I said, 'This vacancy that's arisen unexpectedly. Is it for a nurse, or a companion or what?'

He said, 'Silly old fool seeks similar for cake, foreign travel and occasional sex.'

Monday I took Mum to get her feet done. It used to be Philip's job.

She said, 'This is my daughter, Elizabeth. I don't know what I'd do without her.'

Which fired the starting gun on a somewhat fabulous week.

33

The first thing that happened was Ellie phoning me to tell me she was pregnant.

I said, 'That's wonderful news. You don't sound very happy.'

She said it wasn't planned. She said it had implications for their plan to educate Noah privately.

I said, 'Well, I'm thrilled. I wish I'd had more than one.'

'Why?'

'In case you're too busy to look after me in my old age.'

I told her about Tom's selfish brats. She said I shouldn't get involved.

'Unavoidable,' I said. 'What are you going to do in an old friend's hour of need?'

'Just be careful. What if the other woman wants back in?'

'That's for Tom to deal with. But my prediction is she'll run in, gather up all her beigerie and her spirulina powder and piss off.'

'And then what? Are you going to move in? Is he moving in with you?'

'No, no. I already got that T-shirt and it didn't suit me. We'll keep separate establishments. I'm not saying there won't be any sleepovers but they'll be optional extras. When's this baby due?'

'December.'

'You know I'll help? With Noah. If I'm not working.'

'You still didn't hear from them?'

'Nothing. I'm resigned. Television people are like puppies. They can be locked onto one thing, chewing your slipper or flogging a talk show, and the next thing you know they've been lured away, distracted by some new squeaky toy. Have you picked out any names yet? Please choose one with your nana in mind.'

'You mean a name she'll like?'

'I mean a name that'll *exercise* her. I reckon that low-level irritation with the world is what keeps her going. Bathsheba would work, or Ezekiel. Call your next child Ezekiel and I think your nana will power through to a hundred.'

Geraldine had told Tom she'd come at 10.00. I left his house at five minutes to and she was just getting out of her car. She was very tanned. Like a small seedless grape that had shrivelled on the vine.

I said, 'I've left the door on the latch to save Tom struggling out of his chair.'

She gave me the smallest possible head movement that would qualify as a nod. I asked her if she'd managed to finish the cycling challenge.

She said, 'We both know why I'm here. There's no need for small-talk.'

I said, 'You're quite right, Geraldine,' and I gave her the finger. Sadly she had her back to me and didn't see it.

I called Tom after lunch to see if the coast was clear. He said she'd been gone for hours.

'Come for dinner,' he said. 'It's been so nice having you around again. We can order Chinese if you're tired of cooking for me.'

I wasn't. I was tired of having to remember to put the teabags directly into the bin without dripping. Tired of having to put the newspaper back exactly as I'd found it even if nobody else was going to read it. But tired of cooking for Tom? Never.

I said, 'How about pork saltimbocca with buttered spinach?'

He said, 'How about chocolate almond ice cream to follow?'

'Strawberry.'

'And a DVD?'

'Not Harry Potter.'

'*A Serious Man.*'

'Never heard of it.'

'You've never heard of anything.'

I was at the Affordable Red end of the wine aisle when my phone rang. It was India.

She said, 'First I want to thank you so much for taking part in the pilot.'

That's what they say before they tell you you didn't get the job.

I said, 'Did the project get rejected or just me?'

'It was a question of getting the right mix,' she said. 'The right balance.'

'So it's me who's out. Who's in?'

She hesitated.

I said, 'It's okay, honestly. It wasn't quite up my street. I mean, I wouldn't have wanted it to be too cosy and sisterly, but I don't like blood on the walls either. I imagine Ronnie Lincoln's in?'

'It was a tough call. You're both great. And quite similar in many ways.'

Except Ronnie is younger and hungrier and she has the unenviable bonus of an ongoing cancer story. Will she, won't she? Television loves anything like that.

'And what about Kim?'

'We're in talks with Kimberley's agent. I wanted to give you a heads-up on that. I know you two go back a long way.'

'Further back than Kim likes to admit.'

'But what I really wanted to discuss with you is another idea that we think you'd be perfect for. The working title is *Grub*.'

'As in food?'

'Yes.'

'With an exclamation mark?'

'I don't see why not. What we're thinking is, the kind of food men love. Every week we'd have three guys with zero cooking skills. Your role would be to teach them. With loads and loads of humour, of course.'

Of course. Choppers at the ready! Grab your baps! So there it was. *Grub!* Vertical Hold's new squeaky toy. Did I want to play with it? Yes, I rather thought I did.

'How will you recruit your victims?'

'Usual way. Invite applications. We'll get a lot of girlfriends writing in, volunteering their blokes. Then we interview to weed out the no-hopers. We need guys with personality. And we're thinking we might do a Christmas Celebrity Special. Maybe Wayne Rooney, Jeremy Clarkson, Hugh Grant. You get the picture?'

'I do.'

'There's a lot of excitement about this, Lizzie, and we think we've found a co-presenter for you. His background is straight acting but we see him as the perfect foil for you. Strong woman, vulnerable guy. His name's Craig Eden.'

'No! The Joop Loop has-been?'

'Sorry?'

'The one who used to be in *Cloverfields* only nobody missed him when he left?'

'You know him? He didn't mention he knew you.'

'He doesn't. We shared a seafront bench of misery for five minutes after he got the chop from that soap. Are you sure about him? I didn't notice a sense of humour.'

'Well, nothing's fixed. Obviously we'd look at various options. It has to be someone who can pick up an innuendo and run with it. We'd want a bit of chemistry between you but nothing icky. Ideally a guy who can empathize with the kitchen virgins.'

I said, 'I can tell you exactly who you need. Louie Doyle.'

'*The* Louie Doyle? Doesn't he do pantomimes?'

'He's done lots of TV. He hosted *Spin to Win*.'

'How well do you know him?'

'Very well. We've mopped up a few of each other's messes over the years. He also gives me fashion advice. And he thought your Scott was very cute. But don't worry, I nipped that fantasy in the bud.'

'He met Clarkey?'

'At Philip's funeral.'

'He never said.'

'Let's just say he was admired from a distance.'

'Can you give me Louie's number?'

'Sure. He's with the JMK agency, if you're serious.'

I found I'd picked a £20 Barolo off the shelf while I was talking to India.

Louie answered on the second ring.

I said, 'Is that *the* Louie Doyle?'

He chuckled.

I said, 'Question. If you had something that might possibly – although nothing definite, you understand – be a reason to celebrate, would you spend £20 on a bottle of wine?'

'*Yessss!* You got the gig and Kimmykins didn't.'

'Actually, Kim did get it and I didn't. I got a much better offer. Maybe. And so did you. Maybe.'

'Put the nice bottle in the wire basket, honeychile, and tell all.'

Tom and I were already deep into the Barolo when she called me.

'Lizzie,' she said, in her droopiest, tragic-face-to-camera, sooner-you-than-me voice. 'I've just heard. What a travesty.

I mean, Ronnie Lincoln instead of you? I swear, those people wouldn't recognize talent if it ran up and bit them on the arse. I am so, so sorry.'

'Are you, Kim?' I said. 'Are you really? How very sweet of you to call.'